Windsong

By
Marylou Bugh

To my literate son with love — mom

D1319302

Table of Contents

One

I slipped down the stairs when I was supposed to be in the bathroom brushing my teeth and cornered Mother in the sun room. Mother had her coffee served there every morning and not to be bothered, but I was bursting with summer plans and grown-ups wasted too much time. I had to make my case before Nanny noticed my absence.

"Sabrina, whatever are you doing down here in your pajamas?" Mother asked when I slid open the glass door, but she didn't really expect an answer. She already turned her attention out the huge windows that gave her a view of the back lawn landscaped with flowers and trees and a path that wound down to the small pond that she never visited.

"Can we go to Windsong this week?"

"Of course not, dear. We go in the middle of July and stay through August. You know that."

"Why can't we stay there all summer?" I demanded. I wanted the six weeks to expand from the day I got out of school until the day I had to go back.

Mother sighed. "Your father established those dates, Sabrina. Nanny Bickel takes her vacation then and so will we."

"But Nanny could have the whole summer off," I argued. "Wouldn't she be glad to have the whole summer?"

My father appeared at the door, briefcase in hand, dressed in a suit and tie, even though the summer morning promised a warm day. When he saw me, his dark brows furrowed over his eyes that looked the color of blue ice. "What's this, Sabrina?" he demanded. "Why are you down here bothering your mother?"

"I-I want to go to Windsong this week," I said.

"What you want, young lady, is not how this house runs. Where is Nanny Bickel?"

"Upstairs."

"It's obvious she's not tending to her duties leaving you to run through the house in your pajamas."

I really didn't much like the nervous, over-vigilant Nanny Bickel, but I knew Father's disapproval terrified her and fair was fair. "She thinks I'm brushing my teeth."

"Then go upstairs and brush your teeth."

He turned to Mother and his eyes softened. "Sorry, darling. We can't have the children breaking the house routine just because school is out. I'll have a talk with Nanny Bickel this evening."

My mother waved her hand and her flowery dress fluttered like a garden of butterflies. "I'm sure we will be fine, dear."

I crept back upstairs trailing my hand along the silken banister that gleamed from the maid's constant polish. How different this wood from the dark trees that surrounded Windsong. No bark, no branches, no leaves to give the banister a name in its final resting place miles from the forest where it grew. Trees were alive, but this banister was dead.

Nanny's voice caught me before I reached the top of the stairs. "Where in the name of heaven did you run off to, Sabrina?"

"I tried to get you more time off this summer," I said in an attempt at putting the best light on my transgression. I didn't think it a good time to tell her of Father's threatened 'talk'.

"How many times have I told you not to go downstairs until you're properly dressed? Running around in your pajamas. It's a disgrace."

My brother, William Denham the Third, came out of his room, neat and polished. He wore shorts and a polo shirt, but looked as dressed as Father with his suit and tie. "You wanted Mother to go to Windsong today, didn't you?"

"Not today," I said defensively. "This week."

"That's never going to happen. July 15th to August 28th is written in stone and Father holds the keys to the Ark of the Covenant."

I had no idea what that meant. Two years older than me and several years past that in intelligence, I dubbed him Willy Billy, my only defense against being bested by him in every way, even in the way we looked. Willy Billy resembled Mother with his fine bone structure, blonde hair and skin that tanned to fine honey. I resembled no one, stocky, wild-haired and green-eyed with a complexion that either freckled or burned every summer.

"There's no stone that says it has to be July 15th to August 28th," I argued.

"Well, that's the way it is and if you keep pestering Mother, Father might take her to Windsong and leave us here. How would you like that?"

My argument about stone paled into insignificance against Willy Billy's new twist on my misbehavior, far worse than cornering mother still in my pajamas. I burst into tears. "There's no stone," I blubbered.

"It was a metaphor," Willy Billy said which left me more confused than ever. Nanny Bickel caught his eye. "Not to worry, little sister," he amended. "We'll be model children for the next six weeks, and by the middle of July, he won't even remember you running around in your pajamas. Isn't that so, Nanny?"

Nanny Bickel looked at me doubtfully. "I certainly hope so, Master William."

"I certainly hope so, Willy Billy," I sniffed. Willy Billy rolled his eyes. He pretended he didn't like his nickname, but he never acted really angry. Maybe he liked it better than William Denham the Third, and maybe it would bother him more if I called him by his full name, but somehow, his nickname had become our code, he big brother, me pesky sister but allied in the house of Father's rules.

I went to the bathroom and brushed my teeth and put on the clothes Nanny had laid out, but Willy Billy's words held little comfort. My well-planned argument for Windsong had failed, and now Nanny would hang over me all summer like a cloud blocking the sun. But I wondered, for the first time, the reason for all our rules. Why not talk to Mother in my pajamas? Why did our trip to Windsong always start on July 15th? Why did we stay in Nanny's care and only appear for dinner properly dressed?

Other kids in my class lived in Bloomfield Hills, but none had a live-in nanny. Most had mothers who either went to work carrying briefcases like my father or headed organizations that would make the world a better place. Betsy's mother visited our class and told us about kids in Africa that needed vaccinations and Harold's mother ran a food drive at Thanksgiving so everyone would have a holiday dinner.

Mother went to the club with Father occasionally, had the bridge club ladies over once in awhile, but she didn't seem busy enough for us to have a live-in nanny. Willy Billy said that's how Grandfather grew up and that's how Father grew up. A live-in nanny and rules about pajamas and family vacations went on for a long time in our family, and I decided when I grew up, I would live with no rules at all.

With that thought, I resigned myself to Nanny's monotonous summer regimen conducted in the schoolroom on the third floor. Even though I was going into sixth grade and Willy Billy into eighth, Nanny kept track of our progress during the school year and followed up with summer lessons every morning, ill-matched to the bursting summer outside. This year I was cursed with fixing my lagging math grades. Willy Billy didn't have any lagging grades, so he got to read whatever he wanted and give Nanny his book reports.

After lunch, we could have friends over or do what we wanted but half my friends already left on their vacations. I dragged out my scrapbook of Windsong and sat in the garden and planned what I would add this year if we had this year. Thanks to my pajama blunder, the summer had started out all wrong.

Soon enough the summer got worse. As promised, Father called Nanny Bickel to his study after dinner. "Will he fire her?" I asked Willy-Billy as we hung over the banister waiting for Nanny to reappear.

"I doubt it. What would he do with us then?" Willy Billy said. "We're already getting a little too old for a nanny, but who would make sure you didn't wear your pajamas half the day? Who would make sure you caught up your math this summer?"

I ignored Willy Billy's taunts. "If she gets fired, she'll have to go back to Alaska."

"She wouldn't have to. She could find another job in Michigan."

We knew Nanny Bickel had come from a hard-scrabble family in the land of the northern lights, as Willy Billy described it.

That made Alaska sound like a magical place although it hadn't been for Nanny Bickel. Her father drank too much and her mother shot moose to feed her kids and Nanny moved out at sixteen. We knew more about her from eavesdropping on her phone conversations than Father probably knew. She held several jobs before she landed on our doorstep and, in spite of Father's rules, the best job she had ever had.

All of a sudden. I started to cry. "If she gets fired, it'll be my fault." In that instant, I forgave her nervous over-vigilance. She couldn't end up tending bar or cooking hamburgers at a truck stop again. It wasn't fair. Nanny had somehow finished high school and got through community college so she could be a proper nanny. She even attempted to look like a proper nanny. Although I wasn't sure of her age, she couldn't be much over thirty, but she held her small figure upright as if it would make her look taller and older, bobbed her pretty brown hair into a short, severe cut and it seemed she wore the dark-rimmed glasses to conceal her eyes that looked far younger than the serious older woman she pretended to be.

Willy Billy put his arm around my shoulders. "She won't get fired. She'll have to put up with us until I get shipped off to

Exeter and you get shipped off to--" he stopped. "Some kind of girls' boarding school."

"But then Nanny will be without a job anyway," I protested.

"That would be different than getting fired," Willy Billy said. "Father would give her a recommendation and she would take care of somebody else's kids. She'll have to teach them math," he teased.

"I can do math. I just don't like it," I said.

"We just want to get to Windsong this summer, right?"

I nodded. Willy Billy had a way of making sense.

When Nanny came up the stairs, she looked red and flustered.

"Did you get fired?" I blurted.

"Your father wishes to see you," she said, ignoring my question. "Both of you."

When we went into Father's study that we seldom visited, he sat behind his big dark desk. The bookcases filled with law books, the black leather chairs and the thick maroon carpeting all fit with his job as a lawyer, although every day he went downtown to his real law office of Ahern, Denham and Sealy.

"Sit down, children," he said.

I hastily slid into one of the leather chairs in an attempt to be the model child. It whirled around and Willy Billy put a hand on the arm and brought me to a stop before he carefully took the other chair.

Father glared at me and ran his hand over his short, dark hair as if I gave him a headache, but he ignored my bad entrance and picked up a paper in front of him. The girls in my class thought Father handsome, but they had never gotten that icy stare. "I've looked into summer programs for both of you."

My heart sank. He would keep us from going to Windsong after all. "Father, I'm sorry about the pajamas," I blurted. "It will never happen again."

"I certainly hope not," Father said. "But your behavior brought it to my attention that you children need something to fill your time. William, there's a six-week tennis class at the club for youngsters 12 and up. I've enrolled you for that."

"Thank you, Father," Willy-Billy said. "I've always admired the game."

I knew he lied through his teeth. Willy Billy would rather eat glass than pit himself against a direct opponent. He only liked long-distance running, competing against himself. No surprise why Father had chosen tennis for William. He had played college tennis and won trophies and probably expected Willy Billy to excel at it as well.

"Sabrina, the only thing I could find for an eleven-year-old is"
— he looked pained—"a soccer camp at the high school."

"Soccer!" I exclaimed before I remembered to follow Willy
Billy's example and say I always admired the game. "I don't
know how to play soccer."

"The coach assured me that you will learn the game with other
new comers."

Willy Billy glared at me.

"Yes Father," I said. "I'll do my best."

"It will give your following weeks a routine and structure.
Nanny Bickel has been apprised of your schedules.   Any
questions?"

We knew better than to have any.

"Very good then." Father stood up, his signal for our dismissal.
Although no more than average height, he always seemed
twice as tall in the way he stood, erect and self-confident.

The coach had neglected to tell my father that almost every one
of his summer class had played soccer since kindergarten. Only
Rita Gavin and I were thrown into the game without a clue.

Rita only laughed at our predicament. "I've been dumped here
for a few hours of adult supervision," she told me the first day.
"I can't really see the sense of kicking a ball around."

"But I get mad when they kick the ball away from me and half the time I get kicked too."

"Yeah," Rita laughed. "But I get 'em back. The coach does not seem happy with the way I play but I got a few kicks in. I don't think I'll be on his team next fall."

"Neither will I," I said.

"Let's go to the mall afterwards," she said. Rita, a year older than me, already wore lipstick and had tried smoking. Although she was supposed to go home after practice, she seldom did and from all I knew, nobody noticed as long as she appeared at dinner.

"I can't," I said. "Nanny picks me up after practice and I'd better be here."

"A nanny!" Rita exclaimed. "Now that's a stitch."

I felt my face heat. "I want to go to Windsong," I blurted. "If I don't follow the rules, I might have to stay home the whole summer."

Instead of laughing at me, Rita said, "Bummer. So let's go have a coke before your nanny shows up. I know how to knock a couple of cans out of the machine."

After that, Rita and I became allies and sometimes managed to get on the same team. Afterwards, we shared cokes and told stories. Rita turned out to be the only thing I liked about the summer program.

When Nanny picked us up from our sessions, Willy Billy looked clean and composed, and I came home disheveled and sweaty. Nanny did her best to groom me for evening dinner, but I could tell from Father's frosty stare that I didn't measure up. If Father got any reports from my soccer coach, he didn't say, but I'm sure he noticed what Nanny Bickel's efforts couldn't conceal, especially the time my black eye stood out on my freckled face like Lone Ranger's mask.

Willy Billy had already gotten good reports from Father's country club. "The coach says you show potential, William," Father said toward the end of our summer programs. "Very good."

When Willy Billy told me he would rather have spent his time in the library, I didn't give him any sympathy. "Then you shouldn't try to be so good at it," I said.

"I just try to get the ball on the other side of the net. What else can I do?" He shrugged. "I don't try. It's just the way it is."

I didn't like Willy Billy's answer for everything being the way it is. It sounded like Father with his rules and programs to keep everything the way it was. But keeping the rules worked. We went to Windsong on July 15th.

Two

I gave Windsong its fanciful name to our rustic, sprawling cabin in the Upper Peninsula less than a mile from Lake Superior and the name stuck, perhaps because it had a certain truth. It stood on a rise and caught summer breezes off the lake, although it also caught the winter gales that tore off loose shingles and pounded unsecured shutters from their hinges.

On our trip there, Mother, strapped beside Father in the front seat, commented on the fleeting scenery and, in spite of Father's concentration on his private marathon, he always smiled and agreed with her. Willy Billy and I knew that six weeks of freedom depended on our silence unless spoken to. Willy Billy read most of the time, but I couldn't. Reading in a moving vehicle gave me a headache.

Although Father drove us to Windsong every summer, he never stayed, not even for a few days. As soon as we were deposited, he drove back to the city. I wondered why he, so careful of the order of our lives, allowed our Windsong summers at all. Why did he leave us with Mother for six weeks when the rest of the year we were in Nanny Bickel's care? Of course, Aunt Hetty and Uncle Lew moved in as soon as we arrived although they lived in Clareburn, only twelve miles away.   Uncle Basil visited as well, but Uncle Lew and Aunt Hetty kept the cabin running, not good substitutes for Nanny Bickel. Their rules were simple. Find something to do and show up at meal times.

But I didn't question six weeks of freedom too closely. If that's the way it is, according to Willy Billy, it worked for me. I waded creeks and collected bugs and frogs and flowers and pestered Uncle Lew for names to label my collection.

"Sabrina, muddy again," Mother protested helplessly.

"She wants to be a scientist," Willy Billy said.

"Willy Billy wants to be a poet writer," I retorted, since I didn't know whether his remark defended or defamed me. Although Willy Billy and I wandered the woods together, he had no interest in capturing bugs or frogs.

"His name is William," Mother chided me.

"Clean up for supper," Aunt Hetty interrupted, stirring a pot of stew on the propane-fueled range.

"Father likes Mother, but he must not like Aunt Hetty and Uncle Lew. That's why he doesn't stay at Windsong," I said to Willy Billy the next day on an excursion to my favorite spot in the woods. A creek ran down to the lake and occasionally left swampy spots where I found all sorts of wild life to add to my collection. "And he probably doesn't like Uncle Basil either."

"Good observation," Willy Billy said. "Mother grew up in the Upper Peninsula, but Father treats her like a beautiful flower, sprung from forest fungi that he plucked and transplanted in a crystal vase. If an errant shoot springs up from her fragile stem, Father cuts it away before it overtakes his blossom, the centerpiece of his carefully designed life."

"You made that up," I said.

"I did," Willy Billy agreed. He peered into his notebook. "I think it could be a poem." Willy Billy had been put into a talented gifted class at school, but I could see why he found it hard to find friends when he talked like that.

I spotted a blossom I had never seen before and carefully plucked it. Maybe Willy Billy had a point. Mother appeared at breakfast perfectly dressed as if she was still in Bloomfield Hills. Aunt Hetty wore faded jeans or shorts and tee shirts and kept a six-pack in the refrigerator to fuel her cooking, sweeping and laundry. Yet my mother and Aunt Hetty, as unlike as any two sisters could be, got along famously. While Uncle Lew chopped wood and fixed broken shutters and torn shingles, Aunt Hetty supplied stories of people they both knew, and

Mother listened as raptly as a four-year-old listening to a fairy tale.

I wondered what it would be like if I had an older sister instead of Willy Billy, but I couldn't imagine myself, a doll-like younger sister taken care of by an older sister with hair as wild as my own, although Aunt Hetty's was an indeterminate brown, laced with streaks of gray. She told me that once her hair had been as red as mine.

"Father thinks I'm one of those offshoots," I said.

Willy Billy carefully stepped around a patch of swamp. "You're probably right," Willy Billy said. "Let's follow the creek down to the lake shore."

I followed him, even though I would probably not find anything new for my collection but Willy Billy and I had the rest of the summer to ourselves and we shared each other's favorite places.

As the summer went on, Willy Billy's fanciful words about Mother plucked and transplanted into a crystal vase gnawed at me and the questions I usually asked Uncle Lew and Aunt Hetty now circled around Mother's Upper Peninsula years. I started asking Mother questions, since she often sat at the huge kitchen table for her morning coffee, but I soon learned that she could be as closed as if she sat on the sun porch at home. "All these questions, Sabrina. You're making my head ache," she said. "I grew up here, married your father and we live in Bloomfield Hills."

Then Aunt Hetty would send me out of the kitchen.

I eavesdropped when Aunt Hetty told her summer stories to Mother, but I didn't know Joe or Barb or any of the other names in Aunt Hetty's stories which were mostly reports of marriage, divorce, children or death. When I recounted them to Willy Billy, he found them much more interesting than I did. He wrote stories about Joe and Barb's divorce, Dan's adventure getting caught in an early blizzard, although he made up more than I ever told him.

"You just make stuff up," I accused him.

"I do," he agreed.

"What if I made up a name for this tree?" I protested. "It wouldn't be true."

"It's okay to make up stories that aren't true as long as you don't pass them off as true."

"But Barb and Joe are real, Dan's real. I wouldn't like it if you made up a story about me."

"I haven't written a story about you, little sister. Catching frogs and picking flowers just doesn't make a good story." Willy Billy laughed, "unless you fell in the creek and drowned."

I spied a praying mantis, motionless on a twig and forgot my argument with Willy Billy.

I turned to Uncle Lew, my fund of information about plants and frogs. He could tell me the name of every plant and insect I found but either he didn't know or didn't tell anything else. A tall, lean man, he worked for the local lumber company and did carpenter work in his spare time. "I don't know the answers to all these questions you're asking," he said. "I married your Aunt Hetty before she graduated high school. I was graduated. That was enough. I make a living for both of us."

Aunt Hetty told me Windsong's history, the home where she and Mother and Uncle Basil grew up. "Your bedroom was once mine and your mother's," she said. "We had bunk beds in there. As you can see, the damn room is too small for anything else. I slept on the top bunk and your mother always got the bottom. Uncle Basil slept in the room William has."

"It's even smaller," I said.

"Barely the size of a broom closet," Aunt Hetty agreed. "Your mother's room now was once our parents' bedroom."

"It's bigger."

"A lot bigger before the inside bathroom took up space." Aunt Hetty launched into life with an outhouse and without hot water. Windsong, for all its rustic details, had been renovated far beyond the place that Aunt Hetty and Mother had known in their growing years. The front room still had a fireplace, but the floor, once rough boards, was now carpeted and comfortable furniture replaced the lumpy couch that their father had found by the side of the road for pickup. Although the kitchen still had high cupboards with plywood doors, the kitchen wood stove had been replaced with a gas range, the hand pump replaced with a hot and cold-water faucet and the back room, once a room for traps and guns now had a washer and dryer.

On one of our excursions, this time to one of Willy Billy's favorite spots, I told him my findings. "I knew as much," he said.

"You did not," I said.

"I think Nanny Bickel should get off her math kick and fill you in on Michigan history. Most places around here were like that and a lot of them were torn down and rebuilt."

"Why Is Windsong still here?"

"It's Mother's family home," William said, "although we both know how Father feels about Mother's family. He could put Mother in much better accommodations for six weeks."

"Why doesn't he?" In spite of Aunt Hetty's description of Windsong, she had not touched on anything beyond Mother getting the lower bunk when they shared a bedroom. Aunt Hetty talked about the neighborhood school, the garden planted every spring after the last full moon in May and the difficulties of cooking with a wood burning stove. Although I learned a lot about Mother's life before Bloomfield Hills, Mother and Father's story was absent from Aunt Hetty's tales.

"We don't know." Willy Billy said. He threw a twig into the stream and we watched it twirl toward the lake. How far would the twig be carried by the lake's waters? Would it end up on the opposite shore? Or would it be caught up and cast close to where it had started? "Maybe it's okay not to know."

"It's not okay with me." Once Mother walked on the beach, filled the bird feeder and steeped tea, worked in the garden, ran to the outhouse and put up with a wood-burning stove.

"Curiosity killed the cat."

"And satisfaction brought him back," I retorted.

Willy Billy jumped up. "Your turn to lead, little sister. Find a creepy crawler that stumps Uncle Lew."

My curiosity got little satisfaction.

All too soon, August 28th arrived and so did Father. Aunt Hetty and Uncle Lew loaded our bags into the trunk and Father offered a few civil words that sounded like he talked to our cook when he liked the meal or to the maid when she worked overtime for one of the dinners he occasionally hosted for important people; the evenings Mother wore the beautiful gowns that hung in her walk-in closet, the flower in the crystal vase as Willy Billy said in his poem.

When I hugged Aunt Hetty good-bye, I thought Aunt Hetty and I were the shoots that Father would have liked to cut from the flower in the crystal vase.

Three

Willy Billy prepared me for my first day of sixth grade with stories of the new building intentionally built like a Minoan maze and teachers whose dragon reputations struck fear into their captive students by springing unexpected tests or sending them to the office for an unknown transgression of middle school rules.

"That's the way it is," he counseled me. "It's just about more rules and we know how to follow rules."

I thought of my math grades and my abysmal failure on the soccer field. Willy Billy's description filled my nightmares.

Rita met me in the hall when I came in the door. "Hey Sabrina, did you sign up for soccer?" I could hardly believe she acted as if we had known one another for years.

"I'd rather meet the Minotaur in hand-to-horn combat," I said.

Rita laughed. "Sounds like you've had advance warning from Willy Billy," she said. Over our cokes last summer, she knew all about my eighth-grade super hero brother.

"Even without soccer, today might be that bad," I said.

"Not to worry. Elbows and feet will get you through. Let me see your class schedule."

That began my first day in middle school, and the first day I had a true friend for life. Rita led me though the maze, which had a sprawling but predicable order, she noted at lunch that my unfamiliar classmates looked as apprehensive as me, and she gave me a brief biography of my dragon teachers and confirmed that all but one, my social studies teacher, did not breathe fire.

"Ms. Abbott needs to be handled with kid gloves," Rita said. "I think she feels put down by those hard-core math and science teachers and she's out to prove that social studies can be just as tough."

I frowned into the salad on my lunch tray and it frowned back at me. It certainly wasn't as crisp and filled with the vegetables that our cook made, mostly lettuce with an onion ring and a single slice of tomato and a single slice of cucumber. Willy Billy neglected to warn me about the cafeteria food.

Rita bit into her hamburger, more bun than burger, and made a face. "Ask Ms. Abbott questions as if social studies completely mystifies you. I got through with a C."

"I'll be condemned to doing social studies with Nanny Bickel half of next summer if I get a C."

Rita giggled. "Nanny Bickel. I thank whatever passes as good fortune ol' Daddy never thought of a nanny." I knew that Rita, the single child of a business tycoon and his equally shark mother, "their mistake" as Rita said, felt no affection for either of her parents and might have been totally unloved except for her Aunt Zelda who had an art studio downtown. Rita had run away from home twice and ended up at her aunt's.

I thought of my own mother, glad to have Willy Billy and me under the watchful eye of Nanny Bickel. "Wouldn't your mother like you to stay at your aunt's?"

"Aunt Zelda would have let me stay, but that wouldn't look right if the president of Belanon couldn't manage his own daughter. Besides, Mother does not like Aunt Zelda, kind of weird since they're twins."

"Your mother and aunt are twins? I never heard that before!"

"I probably never told you. I was supposed to have a twin too, but my sister was stillborn."

"That's sad, Rita."

Rita shrugged. "Not sad for me since I didn't know about it at the time and I doubt it that sad for my mother. She just wanted to get back to running Beacom Real Estate and two kids would have been double trouble."

"Your aunt and mother sound as different as my mother and my Aunt Hetty."

Rita laughed. "Seems like we're more like each other than our mothers are like their sisters. Maybe we're more like our aunts than our mothers."

I took a bite of salad. Was I more like Aunt Hetty? Is that why Father's rules seemed especially aimed at me?

"We've only got a few more years before we can be who we want to be," Rita said.

"Then what will you do?"

Rita shrugged. "I have no idea. Right now, I'm thinking I'll be a bag lady. I'll live on the streets and tell myself stories out loud."

"You will not," I challenged her.

"No, maybe not," Rita conceded. "Aunt Zelda would kick my butt."

"I would too," I said.

"What will you do when you escape Nanny Bickel?" Rita asked.

"I don't know. Maybe we could go live at Windsong."

"And chop wood? I probably have better prospects as a bag lady."

As my first year in middle school went on, Rita and I devised ways of gaining a few extra hours past school time. We signed up for a Christmas pageant that the middle school held every December. When I told Nanny Bickel about after school practice, I stretched the practice time. Rita had no trouble with these subterfuges, but I had to have proof of my newfound after-school interests and when Father and Mother and Nanny came to the pageant, Rita and I were mentioned in the program in charge of the props.

Oddly enough, Ms. Abbott proved to be my next ally in after-school projects. Willy Billy's remark about Father's rules written in stone and his stories of the minotaur and other Greek ogres gave me just enough fuel to ask enlightened questions in class. When I brought up Willy Billy's phrase "written in stone," Ms. Abbott treated the class to a history of stone writings from Moses to Native American hieroglyphics. When I asked about the minotaur, we got Greek civilization from Alexander the Great to Plato. And when I asked about Michigan history that included log cabins and outhouses, Ms. Abbott's unit on Michigan history included not only the Upper Peninsula that Michigan had gained through a dispute over

Toledo, but the origins of Detroit down to the homes we lived in and the school we were destined to attend.

In spite of my underhanded reasons for my questions and the irritation of my classmates, I learned a lot from Ms. Abbott that year, and Ms Abbott thought me as gifted as Willy Billy. So, when I asked to join an after-school project to erect a diorama of Detroit for the front hall, she happily included me, and this time neither one of my parents had to attend the results of my extended after school activities. Mrs. Abbott gave each of us a snapshot of our efforts.

Over dinner, Mother said, "What a wonderful project!"

"You are making substantial progress in middle school, Sabrina," Father agreed.

"Thank you, Father," I said. I had worked on the diorama, but my after-school time took less than the project needed. In those extra hours, I learned the delights of strolling the mall with Rita, practiced putting on and taking off makeup and tried on clothes that would have given Father reason to put me into solitary lockdown for the rest of my life.

Willy Billy guessed at my time lapses from the beginning.

"You might want to find other friends," he said one night when I slipped in a little later than my allotted time. I had already made up a story about costume makeup for the spring pageant if Nanny caught me, but I didn't even bother with the story when Willy Billy blocked the doorway of the bathroom.

"You don't need to follow me like Nanny," I said as I scrubbed off the makeup.

"When she checked your room, I told her I was helping you with math."

I was stunned by his complicity. "Thank you," I said.

"You know Father would not give you permission to hang out with your friends at the mall after school. Rita doesn't have a nanny whose job depends on enforcing her father's rules. She can get away with a lot more than you can."

I frowned at him in the mirror. "How do you know?"

"I asked around," Willy Billy said. "Maybe Rita's parents don't bother to check, but Nanny Bickel is a little more thorough. I know you think you know enough about rules to break them, but you don't."

"It won't happen again."

Willy Billy shrugged. "I hope not," he said. "Next time Nanny will check my room for your presence, and I don't even want to think what Father will do if he catches wind that your projects include leaving school for the mall."

I never again stretched the time away from my 'allotted' schedule, although the time Rita and I went to Aunt Zelda's studio came close. Aunt Zelda met us at the door in paint-spattered coveralls.

"Rita!" she exclaimed. "My favorite niece."

"Your only niece," Rita said returning her hug, but I saw her as happy as I had ever seen her. "My friend, Sabrina," she introduced me.

"Sabrina!" Aunt Zelda hugged me in turn. "What a beautiful name! Come in, come in, we'll have tea and cookies. It's exactly the time of day for tea." I trailed behind Rita to a small table in the corner of the room, next to a kitchenette, the rest of the room devoted to Aunt Zelda's studio with art projects in several stages of completion; a sculpture with only a defined nose and chin, a collage with all but a corner missing, a breath-taking painting on an easel. I had never seen such a colorful disarray in one room.

Aunt Zelda busied herself making tea while asking me questions and before I knew it, she learned about Willy Billy, my parents, Ms. Abbott and Windsong. "I have to read your tea leaves," she said. "Rita won't let me read hers anymore."

"Why not?" I demanded of Rita.

"I don't want to know," Rita said.

"She doesn't ask many questions," Aunt Zelda said. She poured our tea from a fanciful teapot decorated with flowers and fairies that Rita later told me her aunt designed and sold. After we drank the tea, which smelled like cinnamon and tasted like heaven, Zelda peered into my cup. "You, on the other hand, have so many questions." She sat silent for a while. "You will spend many years looking for answers, Sabrina, and your life will take many unexpected turns."

"What does that mean?" I blurted.

"I don't know," Aunt Zelda shrugged and then laughed. "The damn leaves don't give details," she said. "They just fall together in a certain way and leave out a lot. But you will find your answers in time. Stay the course."

"Getting through high school," Rita said.

Aunt Zelda nodded. "The first step," she agreed. "You will do well in school, Sabrina."

I wanted to mention that I wasn't so good at math, but Zelda said, "You're better than you think you are." Aunt Zelda got up and collected our tea cups and packaged the oatmeal raisin cookies we hadn't devoured. "My tea leaves don't need to tell me you girls need to get back," she said, handing Rita the package. "Come see me anytime."

"She's awesome," I said to Rita when we left her apartment.

"She is," Rita agreed.

"She said you don't ask many questions."

Rita laughed. "Aunt Zelda says that's because I don't really believe a wet clump of tea leaves knows my future."

"I hope you're right," I said. "I don't want to spend years looking for answers. I don't even know the questions."

"I kind of spooked when Aunt Zelda said that," Rita admitted. "You spent half of your last summer at Windsong asking questions."

"They weren't questions that I'm going to spend years chasing around," I objected.

"Unless your life takes unexpected turns," Rita said in a voice that mimicked doom and gloom. Then she laughed, "I think Aunt Zelda gets her tea readings from what she finds out by asking you questions beforehand."

I didn't want to think that Rita's Aunt Zelda asked underhanded questions the way I did with Ms. Abbott.

Rita must have read my thoughts. "It doesn't matter either way," she said. "Aunt Zelda just gives you what she sees, however she finds it."

Four

The rest of my first year at middle school went off without a hitch. I aced social studies class and oddly enough, my math grades picked up. During our excursions, Rita compared prices, estimated time and distance to get us home by curfew and counted out change as if she had done it forever. Soon enough numbers were not ciphers dancing across a page but a reality and I learned to do the same. Maybe I was better than I thought I was. I didn't want to think of the rest of Aunt Zelda's tea leaf predictions. I didn't want a life looking for unanswered questions and unexpected turns, which sounded more ominous than a bad math test.

Father didn't find programs for Willy Billy and me that summer, thanks to Mother. "The children have done so well in school this year, perhaps they need time to pursue their own interests, don't you think, William?"

Father rose from the table. "I had the same thought, dear." He stared at both of us, particularly me. "It's time to see how well you two do with personal initiative."

I didn't know how to display personal initiative that met Father's standards without getting into trouble. I missed Rita.

Her mother had enrolled her in a summer camp a hundred miles away.

"An enlightened way to dump me into adult supervision," Rita said. "The camp encourages young women to the way of Christian commitment. Not that Mother has any such leanings herself."

"Will you run away?" I asked.

"I can't run to Aunt Zelda. She's in France for the summer sketching the Mona Lisa and feasting on baguettes and espresso at outdoor cafes. There's an artsy town a half-mile away from the camp. Cheshire. Just like the cat in Alice in Wonderland. Who knows—maybe I'll come back in September an enlightened woman."

"Maybe Father will let you come to Windsong with me."

"I don't think so," Rita said.

"Why not? He might like the idea of having a soccer player at Windsong to take me away from wading through swamps and collecting weird insects."

Rita picked up our pace through the mall, not even looking for the latest lip gloss. "You don't know?"

"Know what?'

"Your father is a shoo-in for the next prosecuting attorney, and my father will likely be his first case."

"What!" I stopped our rapid pace. Several shoppers looked at us.

I knew Father's important dinners had become more frequent in his bid for prosecuting attorney, but Rita's words were a revelation.

Rita resumed walking more slowly. "Yep, ol' Daddy is up on a fraud charge. I don't know the particulars, but Mommy's not too happy. Have you ever seen two sharks going at it in the same tank? At any rate, I don't think your bid for my Windsong appearance would go unnoticed."

"Willy Billy must have known."

"Maybe that's why he told you about my father to find other friends. If he told you, would you have found other friends?"

"Never," I said.

"I'm guessing he knew as much. He's kind of a nerd, but he's a pretty good brother."

"He could have told me," I objected.

Rita smiled. "You didn't ask the right questions."

I didn't ask the right questions because I didn't know the right questions to ask. Willy Billy had only told me to find other friends. If Father found out, he wouldn't have cared if I hung out with Rita at the mall or Angela or Francine. His wrath would have been the same. Now that Rita's father would be my father's first case as a prosecuting attorney, our friendship took on an importance that had nothing to do with unsupervised time away from school. Even though I worried about Rita's revelation, I didn't tell Willy Billy. I already knew he would only repeat that I should follow Father's rules and find other friends. I had other friends, but Rita was my best friend and that was that.

Willy Billy took on Shakespeare as his 'personal initiative' that summer, thanks to a PBS special. He decorated his room with posters of the great bard's plays and quoted him every chance he got. Nanny Bickel didn't question his new found interest. She took us to see Shakespeare at the Park, but I could see the fine points of Shakespeare's tragedies mystified her and completely eluded me. But when Father called Willy Billy to his office and asked for his chosen summer exploration, Willy Billy said that Shakespeare would be on Exeter's curriculum. Father harrumphed his agreement, since Willy Billy, anticipating Father's distrust, continued to play tennis at the country club. Willy Billy might be a nerd as Rita said, but a foxy one. He knew his way around Father.

Meanwhile, I researched the collection that I had found at Windsong. When Father questioned me about my summer plans, it started well.

"You have done rather well with your school projects," Father said. "I imagine you've made some new friends in middle school."

"I have."

"Do you have any summer plans with them?"

I didn't want to admit I had turned down an invitation from Angela VanBurton to spend two weeks with her and her tennis-playing sister as well as Brenda Althorn's invitation to ride horses at their dude ranch. I liked both of them, but both invitations extended past July 15th, and I didn't want to give up a Windsong summer.

"I haven't," I said.

I saw a shadow of disapproval in his eyes. "So what are your plans?"

"I thought I'd do some library work on my Windsong scrapbook."

"A Windsong scrapbook of bugs and leaves! What kind of nonsense have you chosen to fritter away half a summer?"

"Ms. Abbott said"—

"Ms. Abbott!" Father interrupted. "What business does she have with a scrapbook that's nothing but a bit of trash?"

I felt the heat of anger rise through me and I wanted to scream, "My scrapbook is not trash!" Willy Billy quoted Shakespeare's Cymbeline before my interview. I thought he was just showing off at the time, but the quotation saved me, "You leaned into his sentence with what patience. Your wisdom may inform you."

"Ms. Abbott said next year our biology class will focus on Michigan's plants and animals," I said with all the Shakespearean patience and wisdom I could muster. "I wanted a head start on research."

Father glared at me. "Why would a social studies teacher talk about the upcoming science curriculum?"

"Maybe because of our Michigan history this year?" I ventured. "Maybe that's how they plan it." I had no idea what I was talking about. I had just followed Willy Billy's example and pleaded my case for the upcoming year, although I didn't have the added weight of Willy Billy's tennis play. No way would I sign up for another summer of soccer torture.

"I will take that into account when I see what 'research' you are supposedly doing."

"Yes Father," I remembered to say.

If I didn't totally convince Father that my 'personal initiative' had any value at all, he didn't say more, more because of his busy schedule than about my less-than-forceful argument. His campaign took a lot of time.

"I don't think he even read all the stuff we did," I said to Willy Billy as we packed for Windsong, our 'summer initiatives' finished.

"We're going to Windsong, little sister." He started pulling down his posters of Shakespeare. "My last summer before Exeter."

"Why can't you go to high school right here?"

"You know why. Grandfather went to Exeter, Father went to Exeter, and I am William Denham the Third. That's how it is."

"That's how it is." My voice rose. "When I ask Mother why Father doesn't stay at Windsong, when I ask her why she never objects to all of Father's rules, that's how it is. That's the only answer I get."

"She married into a family of long-standing traditions. That's what tradition means."

"I'm not going to live with traditions bound up by a bunch of rules."

He turned from his bulging suitcase. "Father will be prosecuting attorney by the time I come back on break. Watch your step."

"Rita already told me about her father. My friends are my own business."

"Everything here is Father's business and, like it or not, go by Father's rules. I don't think the daughter of his next court case is in his plans for you."

I wanted to object, but of course he was right. "I'm going to miss you Willy Billy," was all I could say.

Five

Father's preoccupation with capturing a seat as prosecuting attorney cast a shadow on our trip to Windsong that summer. Mother didn't offer any comments on the passing scenery, not even when we crossed the Mackinac Bridge, her favorite place to offer a remark about the majestic tie the bridge gave to the two peninsulas. After Ms. Abbott's Michigan unit, I could have expanded on what it would have been like before Mighty Mac when we would have sat for hours waiting for a ferry to cross the straits, but I kept quiet as Father frowned at the line at the toll booth and the upcoming miles of uninterrupted forest that bordered the highway.

After Father left us at Windsong, I heard Mother say to Aunt Hetty, "It was so tiring, those dinners. I can't see why William can't be content with what he already has."

"Perfect couple," Aunt Hetty said. "What a joke." Then she saw me pretending to shuffle through the bookshelf in the corner of the front room, romances or murder mysteries. I learned two years ago to bring my own books to Windsong in case of a shut-in day. I liked books about Michigan wildlife or real adventures.

"Sabrina, go find your Uncle Lew and tell him dinner's ready."

"Father's going to be a prosecuting attorney," I said to get into the conversation. I had heard just enough to detect a crack in the crystal vase.

"Yes, Sabrina," Mother said, "but it's nothing for you to concern yourself with."

Father's new position meant more than nothing to me, if he found out my friend was the daughter of the man he would prosecute. Aunt Hetty might have liked to hear that story, but Mother wouldn't.

"Father will still bring us to Windsong?" I asked in an attempt to keep Mother talking.

She fluttered a hand, my question a worrisome gnat. "We come to Windsong every year. You know that."

"But maybe you'll have to stay and be at more dinners."

Aunt Hetty shot Mother a glance. "You worry too much," she said. "Your father will bring your mother and you two brats to Windsong even if he's President of the United States."

"Why?" I demanded.

Aunt Hetty laughed. "Because that's the way it is. No more questions, Miss Big Ears. Go find your uncle. I think he's in the tool shed with your Uncle Basil. Tell Basil to come in for supper too."

"Oh Hetty," Mother objected.

Aunt Hetty winked at me. "When your mother looks like she's ready to fall off her chair, Sabrina, question your Uncle Basil about the Bible."

"Why?" I demanded again.

"He'll go on and on and won't even notice when your mother escapes to her room." She laughed and pulled a roast out of the oven that had filled the house with a mouth-watering aroma. "Just chalk it up to your education. You never know when you might need a quote from the Bible, and Basil has them all. Get going, girl."

I remembered when Uncle Basil came to Windsong in past summers with a hangover or sometimes drunk and usually with a poached deer or other critter not in the hunting season. Aunt Hetty and Uncle Lew took his offerings and either fed him or sent him home with leftovers. Why would I ask Uncle Basil about the Bible? It made no sense at all, but Aunt Hetty's command left no room for further questions.

When I went to the tool shed to summon the men to supper, Uncle Basil greeted me with the words that would change

Windsong forever. "Sabrina, let me introduce you to my son, Borg. I know you haven't met before—a cousin you can call your own."

I remembered my manners and mumbled, "It's good to meet you, Borg."

"Likewise, cousin Sabina," Borg said as if he met unknown cousins all the time. "Your brother and I have already met."

Uncle Basil laughed. "Your brother and Borg were born on the same day a year apart. Borg is exactly a year older."

Willy Billy stood next to Borg and they looked as different as two cousins could. Borg was shorter, broader, ruddy-skinned. When he offered his hand to me, it was the size of a bear's paw and just as strong.

"Supper's ready," I could only say.

Uncle Lew, who looked as uncomfortable as I felt, immediately went to the door. "Can't keep Hetty waiting," he said and made his escape.

Supper went on much as Aunt Hetty predicted it would. Uncle Basil blessed the meal with an overlong prayer until the potatoes got cold and talked about the Bible as if he had written it. By the time Aunt Hetty dished out the apple pie, I saw that

Mother looked as cornered as she probably felt at Father's dinners.

"I don't think Adam and Eve started the human race at all," I said. "I think we evolved from." I floundered, "maybe amphibians."

Willy Billy stared at me, Borg snorted with laughter and five minutes into Uncle Basil's sermon, Mother escaped with her apple pie half-eaten.

The next morning Aunt Hetty was generous with a part of our family history that Willy Billy and I had never heard. Borg's mother left Uncle Basil and took Borg with her, but when she met an Ohio fisherman, she didn't want Borg anymore and dumped him on Uncle Basil's doorstep. Uncle Basil quit drinking, poaching and staying out all night, since that didn't seem the right way to raise a half-grown boy. He decided to be a minister, although it took some doing since he hadn't been in a church since he was a kid himself.

Aunt Hetty dished out our pancakes and bacon. "I hope Basil's new-found religion will work on his son," she finished. "Lord knows what that boy's been through with his mother and all."

"Borg seemed pretty bored with Uncle Basil last night," I said.

"You could have offered better arguments," Willy Billy said.

"You could have quoted Shakespeare once in awhile," I retorted.

"Stop it," Aunt Hetty said wielding her spatula. "Maybe you two will be good for him. Young people need other young people." She lowered her spatula and smiled at me. "Even if you do think we came from amphibians. Last I heard it was monkeys."

"I don't think Father needs to hear about this," Willy Billy said taking a careful forkful of a plump pancake.

"Of course not," Aunt Hetty said.

Willy Billy seemed to take Aunt Hetty's words about being a good influence seriously. He and Borg hit it off right away, but they left me out of their ramblings through the countryside that Borg knew well. At first, I tried to see Borg as an added member to our excursions but Borg had no interest when I suggested we loiter at my favorite spots and soon enough Willy Billy agreed with him. "You stay here and we'll catch up with you later," Willy Billy would say, but they never would, and I spent the day by myself. I still found new additions to my collection, not as much fun without Willy Billy and his notebook and his not-so-true stories. I noticed that Willy Billy didn't even take his notebook to the woods anymore.

"You aren't influencing Borg like Aunt Hetty said we should," I confronted him one evening when he got home late for supper. "He's influencing you. Aunt Hetty wasn't very happy tonight when you were late for supper. You've never been late for supper."

Willy Billy looked up from the little corner table in his bedroom piled with his books and notebook. "A strange twist in the order of the universe," he said. "Sabrina, the righteous."

"Where do you go all day?"

Willy Billy shrugged. "Borg knows his way around much better than we ever knew," he said. "Sometimes I don't even know where we go. His favorite hiding spots."

"What is he hiding from?" I demanded.

Willy Billy laughed. "Probably Uncle Basil."

I thought of Rita going to her Aunt Zelda's and my hidden friendship with Rita. Maybe everybody had to have a secret hiding place.

"You don't take your notebook anymore," I said.

"It just doesn't seem necessary," he said evasively. He picked up his notebook. "I just changed when I use it."

"I don't like it," I said, but I knew as soon as I said it that I had lost the argument.

"She fled from her wish and yet said, 'Now I may'—Othello,"
Willie Billy said. "I still know my Shakespeare."

I flounced out of the room but when I voiced my complaints
the next day, Mother said, "You are a young lady. You don't
need to chase around with boys as if you were one."

For once, Aunt Hetty didn't agree with Mother. "William has
changed since Borg's been around," she said. "He's always
back here when he's supposed to be. Borg doesn't seem to care
about what time he comes and goes. I'll have a talk with
Basil."

"Oh Hetty," Mother objected, "It will just worry Basil. He's
certainly better off with Bible verses than"— She stopped. She
didn't want to say that for years Uncle Basil's path was closer
to the rim of hell than a walk with angels.

Aunt Hetty must have regretted the morning she had given
Willy Billy and me Uncle Basil's history. "Perhaps you're
right, Elizabeth," she said. "William and Borg are young men
and Sabrina is a young lady." She looked at me. "I guess things
have changed, Sabrina." But I saw in Aunt Hetty's look that she
didn't like the change any more than I did.

I made a face and went to the Lake Superior shoreline and
threw stones at seagulls. Young lady indeed. I already knew I

would never be a lady like my mother. Although she had complained to Aunt Hetty about Father's formal dinners, she attended every one, beautiful and poised in her gorgeous gowns, and Father took care of her as if she was a precious flower in a crystal vase. I had never heard her disagree with him the way I disagreed with Willy Billy or Nanny Bickel. I forgot about Willy Billy and Borg as questions about Mother filled my head. How did Mother become that precious flower? She had grown here with an outhouse and a hand pump, carried firewood and chopped weeds in the garden. How had she become a fragile flower that never questioned Father's words and seemed content to live in his shadow except for our few weeks at Windsong?

Rita's dad had hit her mother, I had heard of other men who used physical or emotional abuse, but Father coddled Mother as he never did with Willy Billy or me. Was treating a wife like a hothouse flower also one of his family traditions? What would have happened if he would have married Aunt Hetty? The thought might have been laughable, except that I turned out to be the Aunt Hetty in his life, the shoot he'd like to cut from the flower in the crystal vase. I knew I'd never grow to be a lady like my mother.

Six

The following year home had also changed. Willy Billy's room stood empty, and I missed him even more than I had missed him on our jaunts at Windsong after Borg appeared; Willy Billy's ramblings with Borg, small when compared to his total absence. He wrote me a few letters, stiff and formal and devoid of Shakespearean quotes or the poetry that he wrote, and he always ended with "Sincerely, William". I didn't believe the sincere closing; Exeter couldn't have changed him that much. He mimicked what Father wanted to hear, as if he knew his words were not only for my eyes.

Father seemed oblivious to his violation of my privacy. "It was so good to hear what he said to you," Father said when he handed me the opened letters at dinner. "Please read his words to your mother." It angered me but if I objected, maybe I wouldn't get any letters at all. My correct thank you was as false as Willy Billy's reply to Father when he agreed to take up tennis.

When Mother pronounced Willy Billy's letters well-written and sounded so very much like him, that made me even angrier. Mother must have known Willy Billy better than that from our time at Windsong when he teased Aunt Hetty with rhymes about her stew or compared a local tragedy to Othello. Willy Billy and I were losing contact with each other and I didn't know how to fix it.

Rita had also changed over the summer. Her time at camp had not been a Christian enlightenment, but her stolen time at the village of Cheshire enlightened her nonetheless. "I'm going to be an artist," she announced at our first tea with Aunt Zelda.

"I knew it," Aunt Zelda said.

"I didn't," I said. "You said you were going to be a bag lady, Rita."

Rita smiled into her tea leaves as if she read them herself. "I didn't know either. All those artists in Cheshire-- When I came here, Aunt Zelda, I didn't get it."

Aunt Zelda looked pained. "You saw me through your mother's eyes," she said. "Messy, a little weird. At Cheshire, you found art untainted with family ties. You connected."

To my surprise, Rita nodded. "Maybe there's something in your tea leaves after all."

"How will you be an artist?" I asked Rita on our way home, her newfound interest as foreign to me as Willy Billy's quotes from Shakespeare.

"I already am. I've always had a notebook with doodles."

"Like Willy Billy's notebook!" I exclaimed.

"Like your scrapbook."

"You never told me you had a notebook," I said.

"I didn't want anybody looking." She grimaced. "Especially Mother."

I understood that. When Father didn't like what I did last summer for Nanny's home school, he called my scrapbook a piece of trash and, underneath my anger at his words, it hurt. Although I made up my defense for last summer's project, the research paid off. I aced biology, a silent revenge on Father's words, but it still hurt.

"I'm thinking Willy Billy's notebook never came up for your father's scrutiny," Rita said.

"No, I guess not."

"Willy Billy's better at keeping secrets than you are," Rita said.

"And you're as good as Willy Billy," I had to admit.

That fall neither one of us talked about her father's trial. As Willy Billy had predicted, Father became the new prosecuting attorney and as Rita had told me, Father took on Rita's father as his first case. By the time Willy Billy came home for Christmas, headlines in the Detroit Free Press screamed, Richard Gavin **Convicted of Fraud**. According to the tedious article, Rita's father skimmed funds from employee's pensions. Father was lauded in the news and the formal dinners increased.

I remembered Mother's complaint to Aunt Hetty last summer. "Perfect couple," Aunt Hetty had scoffed. At least Rita's mother told her father what she didn't like instead of pretending she did. Rita said the walls shook when her mother, fueled by a few cocktails, let her voice be heard, but I realized Willy Billy and I accepted Father's rules without complaint quite as much as Mother, except we found ways to escape after pretending we always agreed with him. Mother's only escape seemed to be Windsong but maybe she kept a secret notebook like Willy Billy. Rita said Willy Billy kept secrets better than I did, but if Mother had any secrets, she kept them better than either of us.

As autumn faded into December and Father entertained his distinguished guests downstairs, Nanny Bickel and I shared dinners together in the old school room, once filled with alphabet charts and later with maps and diagrams of evolution. The room had an enormous space of blank walls with only one small window that looked out on the driveway. Now Shakespeare posters and biological charts of flora and fauna decorated the walls. A table, big enough for art projects or scattered homework, stood in the middle of the room, and Nanny's desk and a book shelf filled the corner of the room opposite the lone window.

I learned to like the room that year, a cozier place than the huge formal dining room under Father's surveillance and Mother's compliance in the starched atmosphere of the lengthy dinners.

"You must miss Master William," Nanny said one evening as we ate chicken breast smothered with cheese and mushrooms and vegetable side dishes. I went for the dessert, a warm apple pie that wafted cinnamon and nutmeg, a dessert like Aunt Hetty would make.

"I do," I said between mouthfuls.

Nanny Bickel carefully picked at a broccoli side dish. "You've seen the headlines of your father's victory," she said.

"Yes," I said uncertainly trying to figure out Nanny Bickel's train of thought.

"When your father has more time on his hands after the holidays, he might be watching your friendships."

I swallowed a mouthful of pie without chewing. "You know about Rita."

Nanny Bickel pushed aside the broccoli and attacked the apple pie. "I checked with the school about the hours of your after-school projects," she said. "Your timeline was easy enough to trace."

I lost my appetite. "You told Father?"

"He hasn't asked." she said. "So far, with his busy schedule he's relying on me to keep track of your whereabouts. But I'm sure he'll get the word soon enough from some loose lips."

"I'm sorry, Nanny." Nanny had one more year with me. Her letter of recommendation rode on my hidden timeline. "Rita and I were friends before the headlines. I didn't know it would be any worse than running downstairs in my pajamas."

"It is worse, Sabrina. Not because your friend is Rita, but because you left school and we didn't know where you were. If you got in trouble, nobody would know."

I waved my hand and it came to me that the gesture looked much like my mother's. I hastily stuck my hand back in my lap. "I'll think of something," my words as evasive as Mother's fluttering wave of dismissal.

Willy Billy would be home next week but not even Willy Billy could think of something to keep my secret hidden. He had already warned me that my hidden time would be discovered and now Rita's father would be lucky to stay out of prison, according to the news reports.

Nanny Bickel must have felt the same way. "When you think of this 'something', would you find a way to let me know? I can't lie to your father if it comes to that."

I nodded. I should have known Nanny would find out first. She might only report what she was asked to report, but if asked, she wouldn't lie. In spite of my refusal to turn my back on Rita, I couldn't resent Nanny. She was probably the most honest one in the house.

"And promise me you won't go wandering off where I don't know where you are."

When Willy Billy came home, my school was already out for the holidays, and I ran to the taxi before it rolled to a stop in the drive. "Willy Billy!"

Willy Billy made a face at me and I helped him drag his bags up to his room bombarding him with questions at every step.

Nanny Bickel was less effusive, but I could see the sparkle in her eyes. "Your room is waiting, Master William," she said. "It's good to have you back."

To her surprise, he dropped his bag and hugged her. "You don't know how good it is to be back," he said.

I looked forward to three weeks of time in our old schoolroom, only occasionally interrupted by our downstairs dinner appearances but to my dismay as well as Willy Billy's, Father now invited him to his formal dinners, his less-formal luncheons and any other event that maximized press coverage. He was prosecuting another case that had gained interest and the city's public hero. The press photos displayed Father, Mother and successful son, now nearly as tall as Father and as photogenic, a set-piece of an ideal family. If a nosy reporter asked about 'the daughter' Father explained my absence as a wish to shield my minor status from public view, which endeared him further in the public eye. Evidently, Willy Billy's attendance at Exeter had put him in a status no longer minor.

In spite of Willy Billy's photo op appearances, Nanny Bickel and I heard about his real semester at Exeter. He had been homesick as he struggled trying to fit in with classmates who were equal or superior to him. Evidently, Exeter was populated with genius-level nerds. Willy Billy had never had that problem before.

"No matter what your life was like living at home," she said, "it's familiar. When you're out there on your own, it's like when I jumped off the diving board."

"A diving board!"

"I took a class in water rescue," she said. "I could swim but that diving board scared me worse than leaving home. I couldn't get my certificate until I jumped and so I jumped. After that, everything came easier. You will jump when you find what you want more than the fear of that diving board. Are you still writing in your notebook, William?"

Willy Billy looked surprised by Nanny Bickel's question. He thought his notebook as secretive as I thought my after-school projects were, but I learned a lot about Nanny in the past months. Under her prim exterior, she had the eyes of a hawk and the ears of a deer. She knew more about us and our parents than we had ever realized.

"Not that often, Nanny," he said. "Study takes most of my time." In his effort at camouflaging his surprise, he sounded just like Father and I suspected Nanny Bickel thought the same.

"Shakespeare?" Nanny pursued.

Willy Billy flushed. "I signed up for a class on Shakespeare this semester," he admitted. "And Father doesn't need to know. It's an elective."

Father, too busy with his new-found success and introducing Willy Billy as William Denham the Third, paid less than his usual vigilant attention to the 'errant shoot', and Rita and I spent time at Aunt Zelda's every chance we got. As I promised, I told Nanny where I went. She didn't like it but kept her silence when she knew we would be with Aunt Zelda.

Rita didn't have to coax her aunt into art lessons, and Aunt Zelda soon pulled me into their sessions. While Rita learned about materials and color and composition, I learned how to sketch a praying mantis, a lady slipper.

"Take your pad and pencil with you and record the things you see that won't fit in your scrapbook. Detail, detail, detail. It will be invaluable to your field work."

Aunt Zelda took my scrapbooks seriously and I felt a growing sense that my scrapbooks meant more than a mindless collection of bugs and plants that connected me to Windsong.

Seven

The holidays ended and Father's time as front-page news as well. After Willy Billy left, I felt more disconsolate than ever. Despite Nanny Bickel's silence, Father found out about Willy Billy's elective and asked him to take a government course instead. I could not imagine anything so boring, but Willy Billy's letter to Father and Mother dripped obedient compliance. "Thank you for your guidance, Father," he wrote, "the government class as an elective at this point is closer to the career we talked about." Father had decided that Willy Billy, William Denham the Third would follow a law career.

I wanted to spit. Willy Billy hadn't yet taken that run off the diving board.

"What if he doesn't want to be a lawyer?" I confronted Mother across the table the evening after Father had read Willy Billy's letter. How could she not know how it must have hurt Willy Billy to give up that Shakespeare class?

"William will make a fine lawyer," Mother said as if Father's parrot. "He has a proud tradition to follow."

Father glared at me. "I think it's time you find another pursuit more befitting a young lady than collecting bugs," Father said.

"Since your grades have improved enough, Grant Academy will take you next year."

"Grant?" I gulped. Grant was an academy for girls somewhere in Maine. Willy Billy had warned me to research girls' boarding schools and from my endeavors, Grant came as close to compliance with Father's rules as any could possibly be.

"I could go to a private school here."

"You need a more broadening experience," Father said. "Grant's a fine institution and they will guide you into a wholesome career."

"What about Nanny?" I blurted.

"I'm already making contacts for a future position for Ms. Bickel," Father said. "You're a little past having a nanny and Grant will shield you from the press. I've already made sure of that."

"That's important, Sabrina," Mother said.

"Father's shipping me to Grant next year," I wailed to Rita. Our after-school meetings had become more tenuous since her high school schedule and my ties with Ms. Abbott had altered our schedule to my supposed interest in girls' basketball. Rita's philosophy of elbows and knees had gotten her on the high-school team, although as a freshman, she warmed the bench more often than she played.

Before games, we hung out in the hall at the high school. "Five years without Nanny Bickel," Rita said. She did not sound as forlorn as I felt.

"I've learned to like Nanny Bickel," I said.

"The Stockholm Syndrome?"

I glared at her. "She's known about our after-school projects since last year, and she knows that my interest in high-school basketball is not all about team spirit." Nanny had actually gotten permission from Father, citing my summer soccer and my need to observe team sports.

"I'm kidding," Rita said. "Don't worry about Grant Academy yet. Things could change."

"I hope so." Inwardly I had little hope at all.

"I'll be here," Rita said flatly. She kicked a Coke machine, but it sat mute. I fished out change from my purse to coax a couple of cans from the bowels of the reluctant beast. "I'm sure you saw the headlines about good ol' Daddy," Rita said striding to an unoccupied bench. "Just like everybody else did." She waved at the hall as if it was thronged with every kid in high school, although the hall was largely empty. "It seems ol'

Daddy and Mommy Dearest are getting a divorce, and fortunately neither one of them remembered to ship me off to a boarding school."

"I'm sorry," I said.

"I'm not," Rita said. "I'll be at this high school playing basketball and escaping to Aunt Zelda's as often as possible."

Neither of us had ever talked about our fathers' confrontation in court before—neither of us cared—but today I saw our separate ways pulling us apart in the way Willy Billy and I were.

Rita took a long drink of her Coke. "You probably didn't need to read any headlines to get the news of ol' Daddy's sentence."

"I didn't," I said.

Rita nodded. "He's getting his share of photo ops too," she said. "For different reasons than those of your father. He's guilty as hell. Your father was just doing his job."

"My father is a control freak," I blurted.

"And mine is a crook," Rita said. "If Sigmund Freud was right, we're going to have an interesting time with the opposite sex, aren't we?"

"I don't believe in Freud," I said, although I didn't know much about Mr. Freud.

"I'm just saying. I saw you flirting with Kevin Ahrens. Watch it."

I felt my face heat. Kevin and I occupied the top rung in biology, my essays better, but Kevin aced lab.

"I wasn't flirting. I wanted to find out how he does his lab notes."

"His father works at the same law firm your father did. His daddy might be a control freak too, and maybe Kevin got the control freak gene."

"Not every son takes after his father. Willy Billy is not like Father."

"Are you sure?" Rita asked.

I took a small sip of Coke. I never could understand how Rita could gulp down a whole can of the stuff in two swallows. "I'm not sure of anything," I said.

Eight

In spite of Rita's hopeful words that things could change, Father's fixed position ensured that nothing would change for me. Grant Academy still loomed although Willy Billy's second semester changed at Exeter. His homesickness lessened, his grades soared, and he had made a few friends. Nanny said that now he would survive very well in his world away from home.

I should have been happy for my brother, but I felt left behind. When he came home for the summer, he made his usual face at me when I greeted his arrival. He hugged Nanny as usual, but as the summer passed, Father planned an agenda that took up even more of Willy Billy's time than the holiday season had taken. "I guess he has to learn how the system really works after that elective he had to take," Nanny Bickel tried to comfort me.

"He would rather have taken Shakespeare," I muttered.

Nanny Bickel smiled. "He might have learned as much."

"He'll take Shakespeare to Windsong. He didn't really take the plunge off that diving board."

"Maybe," she said. She turned away and I thought she looked sad. Maybe she felt as left behind as I did. "Now get yourself straightened up for dinner."

July 15th was only three days away. At least those dates written in stone hadn't changed; six weeks of freedom from Father and from checking off lists to get ready for Grant Academy. That thought made putting on a skirt and quelling my wild hair easier to bear. The only bright spot in Father's busy schedule for Willy Billy distracted him from arranging more soccer torture for me. I discovered Annie Dilliard and Rachel Carson that summer and even looked Father impressed.

When our Windsong day arrived, I dragged my bags downstairs, the first out to the car. Willy Billy soon followed, more carefully dressed and I saw he carried his own bag of books. On our trip north, Father aimed his conversation at Willy Billy with instructions on the reading material in Willy Billy's canvas bag from Father's own law library. He sounded as if he wanted Willy Billy to take the bar exam before the end of the next year. When Mother tried to comment on the beauty of the straits, Father interrupted her mid-sentence with a 'yes dear', and returned to his monologue aimed at Willy Billy who replied 'yes father' in much the same tone as Father used with

Mother, except that he more strategically placed his replies. Occasionally I stole a glance at Willy Billy or gave him a surreptitious kick, but he ignored my silent interruptions.

We were almost to Windsong when Father turned his attention to me. "You will be leaving for Grant Academy the day following your return to the city," he said. "I've instructed Ms. Bickel to pack the rest of your belongings before she leaves."

"I can help her when I get back, Father."

"After her vacation, she will be at her new position."

"But I didn't say good-bye to her," I cried, quite forgetting our back-seat code of quiet compliance.

"I'm sure you must have said something to that effect when you left today."

"I said that I'd see her in six weeks," I said. A chilling realization hit me. "You didn't tell her yet, did you?"

Father slammed on the brakes and pulled to the side of the road, much too close to a very deep ditch. I clutched the arm rest as a car whizzed past within inches, its horn blaring an angry warning. "If you wish, young lady, you may return home and spend the rest of the summer saying your good-byes."

Willy Billy's shoulders tightened and his fists clenched. He gave me a kick.

"I'm sorry if I spoke out of turn, Father. I was just surprised is all."

"Just surprised is all," Father echoed, wheeling the car back onto the road. "You may be sure if that mouth of yours gets you in trouble at Grant, you will find yourself in detention for a whole semester."

Not sure of the correct response, I said nothing.

"Have I made myself clear on your behavior at the best academy I could possibly find for you out East?"

"Yes Father," I said.

"I expect you to find friends there more appropriate for a young lady with a proper upbringing."

This time I was too stricken to speak. Father knew about Rita! Suddenly, his move to put me in a boarding school, in spite of Mother's objections, came into focus. The evening Father had broken the news about Grant, Mother said after I had left the dining room. "William, she's young. We have perfectly fine schools here."

I had stopped outside the door, surprised to hear her defend me, but I never heard Father's reply. His chair scraped as he stood up and I fled upstairs. In the few times I caught Mother alone, I tried to coax her into furthering her objections without letting on what I had heard.

"Your father's father sent him East to broaden his education."

"I don't need to do what Father's father did."

"Your father knows what's best for you and William."

"Why don't you ever say what's best for William and me?"

"Sabrina, both of you are doing fine under your father's guidance. It will be as he wishes."

"What is the matter with you? You never have any wishes of your own."

"That's enough, Sabrina. Go to your room."

I went to my room but I slammed the door. Grant to honor a family tradition or to ensure a head start on a superior education meant nothing to Father except a way to erase my embarrassing friendship with the daughter of the man he had convicted to win him fame. I choked down my fury, the only way to get to Windsong and out of Father's sight. Part of my anger was at myself. Nanny and William had both warned me that sooner or later, Rita's name would come up by someone in his circle. When I told Nanny I would think of something, I hadn't thought at all.

When we stopped at our usual rest stop on U.S. 2 and Father barked, "Fifteen minutes," I glared at the back of his head; fifteen minutes to let the dogs out for a run, I thought. I followed Willy Billy to the scenic view platform, but I did not follow him down the sandy trail to Lake Michigan's shore to look for treasures the lake may have brought to the water's edge. I sat on the slatted bench and stared at my toes. Sometimes the lake was blue with white lace, sometimes green-gray with crystals of light dancing from its surface but today it looked as flat and gray as purgatory, and I went back to the car before fifteen minutes elapsed.

"You knew!" I accused Willy Billy as soon as we got to Windsong and Father had left with a wave that I considered more a dismissal than a farewell. I didn't wave back.

I hauled my bags into my room and gave Aunt Hetty a cursory hug before I escaped to the woods. Aunt Hetty already had supper simmering, but I had to get away with my anger. The western sun cast long shadows across the forest floor and the great silence of the woods welcomed me, a quiet friend, too old and wise for small human tantrums to disturb the peace that slowly calmed me.

When Willy Billy found me under the branches of the ancient oak tree I loved, I could say nothing.

"Yes, I knew," he took up my words. "Or I guessed. Father didn't confide in me if that's what you're thinking. But I warned you."

"Nanny Bickel warned me," I said." I repeated Rita's mantra. "Only five more years."

Willy Billy shrugged and grabbed a handful of wintergreen leaves. "More than that for me if I'm going to law school," he said and shoved them into his mouth, our favorite Upper Peninsula chew.

"You aren't really going to read all that stuff Father sent, are you?"

"I suppose I'll try."

"What about Shakespeare? What about your notebook? You don't have to go to into law. You could be a writer. You can be anything you want to be."

Willy Billy looked pained. "We'll see," he said evasively. "Right now, Aunt Hetty said dinner's ready."

"I'm not hungry."

"Nothing worse than cold leftovers," Willy Billy said. I remembered last summer when he had missed dinner hanging out with Borg, but I didn't say anything. I didn't want to think about Borg right now.

I reluctantly got up. Willy Billy and I were allies once more and I didn't want to poison our first evening at Windsong with my anger at Father. I didn't want to poison six weeks at Windsong with anything that lay ahead.

The following evening Uncle Basil came to dinner dressed in his ministerial garb. Uncle Basil not only had a morning service on Sundays but an afternoon prayer meeting as well. He said he didn't have time to change, but as the dinner went on, I suspected he meant to continue his prayer meeting. Soon enough, Aunt Hetty gave me the look, which meant I should interrupt but I hadn't been paying attention to Uncle Basil's fervent prayers for the welfare of the family and the whole human race.

"Where's Borg?" I interjected when Uncle Basil paused to butter a slice of Aunt Hetty's homemade bread.

"I'm praying for his return to the fold," Uncle Basil said. "He's back with his mother. That woman would have caused Sodom and Gomorrah with her sinfulness."

I wanted to question Borg's mother's sinfulness, but now Willy Billy interrupted, "Where is his mother?"

Uncle Basil put down his bread. "You tried to be such a good influence on my son, William. You are an honor to your father and the Bible says"—

"Where is he?" Willy Billy demanded. Aunt Hetty and Uncle Lew stared at him. I even stared at him. "If you please, Sir," he added belatedly.

Uncle Basil waved his hand. "Someplace in Ohio from what I've heard."

When Aunt Hetty brought out her apple pie, Willy Billy said he ate too much for dessert, but I knew better and I could see that Aunt Hetty did too. After he excused himself, I continued questioning Uncle Basil about his sinful wife until he escaped with cartons of Aunt Hetty's leftovers, but I learned little more than that Borg's mother, Deborah, could have been a witch the way she cast a spell on Borg to follow her.

"Why did Borg go back to his mother?" I asked Aunt Hetty as we did the dishes. Although intrigued by Uncle Basil's accusation, I didn't believe in witchcraft.

"Borg was a trouble, but Basil's way of fixing him certainly didn't work," Aunt Hetty said.

"Now Hetty, Basil did the best he could," Uncle Lew said. He sat at the kitchen table with a last cup of coffee, his after-dinner ritual, the only time I saw him at rest, his big work-worn hands cradling the coffee mug, looking at the darkening kitchen window and usually not saying anything at all.

"Is Borg's mother as bad as Uncle Basil says she is?" I asked, my curiosity aroused. Father might describe me the way Uncle Basil described Deborah if Father used Biblical terms.

"I can't say," Aunt Hetty said and I could see she wanted the conversation closed.

"Deborah was a troubled woman," Uncle Lew said.

Aunt Hetty shot him a look.

"I'm just saying when a man and woman separate, it's hard on the kids," Uncle Lew offered. "I've seen it many times." He went back to staring out the darkened kitchen window.

Windsong changed that night whether Borg heeded the call of a sinful witch or not. Willy Billy no longer had the time for our hikes into the woods and if I invited a Shakespearean quote or a snatch of poetry from his notebook, he put me off like a worrisome gnat.

Without Willy Billy, my own interest in adding to my Windsong scrapbook waned as the weeks went by and the prospect of Grant Academy loomed. "Your brother is a young man at Exeter," Mother said. "You mustn't bother him if he needs to study. You'll understand when you go to Grant."

Aunt Hetty snorted. "You sound like Mr. William Denham the Second."

Mother waved her hand over her morning tea, a fluttery dismissal. "Of course, I do," she said. "That was what I agreed to with that little band of gold, wasn't it?"

"Birds come back to roost," Aunt Hetty muttered, "Band of gold or not."

I wondered if she referred to their last conversation I had managed to overhear. A fisherman who "didn't know the right end of a fishing pole" according to Aunt Hetty, arrived in Clareburn and spent more time in town asking questions than out on the lake. Mother seemed unusually interested in the incompetent fisherman and pestered Aunt Hetty for his description.

"There is no description, Beth. I'm just telling you about a city guy who doesn't know anymore about fishing than your husband did." That confused me. When had Father ever came to Clareburn to go fishing?

"Maybe he's from Detroit," Mother said. "Maybe I should invite him here to see if he knows William."

"I'll check around," Aunt Hetty said, but I could hear in her voice that she regretted bringing up the stranger.

As so often, I couldn't ask questions about what I had overheard. I didn't like the idea that one of Father's acquaintances had crept into Windsong. I waited for the fisherman to show up at a Windsong supper but to my relief, he never did.

Nine

Bloomfield Hills without Nanny Bickel felt as bleak and forlorn as the last day at Windsong when I stood by Lake Superior watching the clouds creep across the sky and turn the water a dismal gray. Willy Billy left for Exeter the same evening we arrived and my bags stood neatly packed outside my bedroom door for my departure the following day. My room already looked abandoned, stripped of my personal decorations, as sparse as a cloistered nun's cell. I looked for a final note of farewell, but Nanny had left nothing. I tried to call Rita, but an unsympathetic robot voice informed me the number was no longer in service. Willy Billy and I were being erased from Bloomfield Hills as if we had never been here, and I cried myself to sleep that night.

The next morning, Mother broke her pattern and shared breakfast with me, although neither of us ate more than a few bites of toast. "Your father had to leave early," she said. "But he said to give you his best."

I didn't believe a word. "Where did he send Nanny Bickel?" I blurted.

"I don't know," she said. "He assured me it was a good position."

"Don't you ever ask?" I demanded.

Mother looked at me and, for the first time, she forgot to wave her usual dismissal at my turn of the conversation. "I don't," she said. "I don't have your father's connections. I can't ask you to understand but your father knows what's best."

"You always say that."

"I do. It's how we get through."

A horn, lightly tapped, informed us the driver arrived ready to take me to the airport. Mother rose and hugged me before I was whisked away to Grant. "It'll be okay," she said but I didn't know if she meant her words for me or for her.

Grant Academy, in the middle of Maine, should have been a comfort, since its geography, close to an inland lake, resembled Windsong, but its geography had little to do with the freedom I always felt at Windsong, packed into a room with three other girls. Our close quarters left little room for privacy, something I had never experienced before.

Inwardly, I soon christened Ms. Shadrow, the head mistress of our dorm, Sergeant Shark. Her face thrust forward like a shark's nose, and her small mouth and eyes looked like an underwater predator. More to the point, she watched us, ready to bite at the smallest infraction of dorm rules. Rita would have appreciated the tag, but I didn't share my thoughts with my roommates, almost as foreign to me as a shark in Lake Superior.

The class regimen left me little time for outdoor exploration. What would happen if I ended up in detention? I remembered the first time Willy Billy had warned me that Father could jerk Windsong from summer break and a whole summer in my stripped-down bedroom kept me struggling to comply with rules even more rigorous than those Nanny Bickel enforced. As the semester wore on, I managed to stay clear of detention, but my grades would have earned me summer school back home with Nanny Bickel. I didn't find any 'appropriate' friends with my roommates. Soon enough, they ignored me, a shadow in the room with little to offer about fashion, music or theater, even if I knew some of Willy Billy's Shakespearean quotes. Now I knew how Willy Billy felt his first semester at Exeter and I wanted to cry. But I didn't.

When the holiday break came, I could hardly wait to get back to Michigan. When Willy Billy greeted my late afternoon taxi, I was so happy to see him, I forgot that Father would be wanting to know why I hadn't written, I forgot that my grades at Grant barely made the 'C' list, I forgot that my room would look as forlorn as if I had never been here, and I almost forgot Nanny Bickel would not greet me at the head of the stairs. I just never wanted to see Grant Academy again.

"You survived," Willy Billy said.

"Not well," I said

Willy Billy smiled and shrugged. "Believe it or not, it will get better," he said.

I grabbed my bag out of the taxi. "I'm running away."

"No you're not," Willy Billy said and grabbed the bag out of my hand. "Only five more years."

"Four and a half," I said.

"You can make it. I found Nanny Bickel. She'll give you the dive lecture just like she did for me."

"Willy Billy!"

Willy Billy put a finger to his lips. "Not a word. We'll talk later."

Father was already striding toward us with a reporter in tow. Now that I attended Grant Academy, he no longer shielded the young minor from the nosy press with a photo op in sight.

"Dinner is in an hour and we have guests," he said the minute the reporter left. He looked at my rumpled slacks and jacket. "You will need to dress. Your mother will be waiting."

"What's with the reporter?" I grumbled to Willy Billy on the way upstairs. "Father already got the job."

"He won another big one and he wants a seat on the bench," Willy Billy said. "Judge Ewell is retiring next year."

When I got to my room, a new outfit lay across my bed as surely as Nanny Bickel would have once placed it, the dress chosen by an additional maid Father had hired over the holidays. I wanted to rip it apart. Father drew me into his publicity vortex as surely as he had with Willy Billy the year before. I would look the proper young lady. I wanted two weeks without algebra and Mrs. Shadrow.

When the interminable dinner finished and Father's distinguished guests finally left, Father called me into his office. "Your grades are not what I expected," he said the minute I walked through the door.

The gown itched and Mother barely had a minute to envelop me in a scented hug and murmur Willy Billy's words, "You survived" before flashes exploded our brief reunion. I felt disgusted with the whole evening. "I'm sure my record won't be in the news," I retorted before I had the sense to keep my mouth shut.

Father leaned over his desk as if giving an argument to a doubtful jury. "You're right," he said. "Your first semester grades will not be public information." He shuffled a file, probably Grant Academy's record of my lackluster performance. "Grant sees you as capable of doing much better and so do I."

I remembered the proper reply to get me out of sight. "I will try my best," I said.

"I'm sure you will," Father said and for one fleeting moment, I think Father meant what he said. "If not, I will instruct Ms. Shadrow to supervise you more closely."

"That's not possible," I muttered before I left the room.

Two days later Willy Billy and I escaped to visit Nanny Bickel under the subterfuge of visiting the Detroit Institute of Arts. Willy Billy reserved tickets in the probable event that Father would check. Evidently, Willy Billy knew better than I how to plan an afternoon away that met with Father's approval. I felt a nostalgic pull when I thought how much Rita would have liked those tickets.

When Willy Billy and I got to the address, I was happily relieved that, as Father had said, he had found Nanny Bickel a place worthy of her talents, even more palatial than ours. A security gate guarded the entrance, but Willy Billy knew the code to get us in.

"Sometimes weird coincidences happen," Willy Billy said. "My dorm mate happens to be the nephew of Judge Fillmore, and wouldn't you know, Father got Nanny Bickel a position with the judge."

"That will no doubt be a favor that Judge Fillmore will remember," I snapped. Father even made Nanny Bickel's position a chance to advance himself.

"That's how it is, little sister," Willy Billy said. "And don't breathe a word about this visit to anyone."

When we crept through the back door to her room, I threw my arms around Nanny. "I miss you so much! I didn't know you would be gone." I blathered on and on and Nanny Bickel patted me and looked to Willy Billy for clarification.

"We didn't know you would be terminated before we'd get back from Windsong last summer," he explained.

"Didn't you read the note I left?" she asked me.

"There was no note!" I knew why there was no note and I shook with fury. "Father will hear about this. He's"—

Nanny Bickel grabbed me by the shoulders. "I don't know how you found me," She looked at Willy Billy. "But your father will not hear about this, or I might lose this job I have, such as it is."

Willy Billy shot me a look. "You've got our word," he said. "Is this position as good as Father said it was?"

"Only the pay. I doubt I'll get either boy past the fourth-grade reading level." She shrugged. "For whatever it's worth, your father would never have countenanced such bad behavior from either of you."

"Especially from me," I said.

Nanny patted me on the shoulder. "Especially from you," she said. "He knew a stone wall when he saw one." She turned to Willy Billy. "He sees in you a chip off the old block."

"I'm not," Willy Billy protested.

"I'm telling you what he sees," Nanny Bickel said. "I don't have soda, so let's have milk and cookies before the boys get back from school."

Ten

Willy Billy lock jawed about our visit to Nanny Bickel and ordered me to do the same and as much as I wanted to demand Nanny's note, I knew Nanny's tenuous position, but I could barely look at Father. Fortunately, his festive dinners did not often include either one of us, and I suspected that he did not trust that my appearance as a proper Grant Academy girl would hold up for any length of time.

"It might look a little odd if you were excluded now that Father put you in the public eye," Willie Billy said. "He probably regrets doing that the first day you came back from Grant."

"Father made a mistake?" I said sarcastically. Unlike our upstairs dinners with Nanny Bickel, we ate out at Sam's Pizza and Grill. Willy Billy's status as an Exeter student seemed to have earned us the privilege of dinner away from adult supervision, a welcome change in Father's rules.

"Not exactly a mistake," Willy Billy corrected, picking off the anchovies that I had insisted upon. "I'm thinking some nosy reporter had gotten a whiff of your friendship with Rita, and Father had to introduce the proper young lady from Grant Academy, the best he could do to dampen the story. Now he has to make excuses about our whereabouts for the rest of the holidays."

"That's crazy," I said, picking off the peppers that Willy Billy had insisted upon. "You're just guessing."

"I am. But I overheard him telling one of his guests about our visit to the Institute of Arts and how we 'young people' have so many interests of our own that keep us busy."

Willy Billy probably guessed right. Father's unusual appearance with a reporter in tow the minute I got out of the taxi that first day made sense. I felt a prick of satisfaction that Father had no idea that Willy Billy knew his manipulative moves as soon as he made them. "His little political games are disgusting," I said. "Rita was my friend before Father made a case against her father. Rita's father might be a fraud but that doesn't make Rita a bad person."

"You are the stone wall Nanny Bickel said you were," Willy Billy said.

"And the way you outguess Father, you're a chip off the old block."

Willy Billy's face darkened, and I regretted my words. The comparison was no compliment.

"Rita's phone is disconnected," I hurried on. "Can you find her like you found Nanny?"

"All I know, which you would know if you kept up with the local papers, her parents split up and her mother left town. I think she went South. No doubt Rita went with her."

"Where's her father?"

Willy Billy stared at me. "You didn't know?"

"Know what?"

"Somehow, he escaped the county jail and they haven't found him yet. They think it was an inside job."

"No!" I cried and a few customers looked up.

"Shh," Willy Billy said. "Let's get out of here."

All the way home, I begged Willy Billy for more details, but he could only tell me what he had read in the papers. Rita's home was up for sale, and Rita's mother would see nothing from the proceeds, since it had already been seized to pay extensive creditors. "Cover for me tomorrow, Willy Billy. I've got to go see Rita's Aunt Zelda. She'll know where Rita and her mother went."

"Watch what you're doing. Pursuing our own interests doesn't mean Father doesn't watch, and I'm sure Rita's aunt is not on his approved list either."

I knew how right he was. Father had found out about Willy Billy's Shakespearean elective and sent me to Grant when he found out about Rita, but I had to know what had happened. "Like you always say, it is what it is," I said, "and I don't like how it is."

Willy Billy shrugged and said no more.

The next morning Mother and I ate breakfast together after Father left for the office, one small change since my childhood days when Mother had coffee in the sunroom. Willy Billy was given the privilege of sleeping late on holiday, but evidently a Grant Academy girl did not accord the same respect. The maid, in lieu of Nanny, knocked on my door every morning at eight.

"You look a little pale," Mother said.

"I didn't sleep well," I said. I could hardly choke down the eggs Benedict that she had ordered. "I have so many things to do before I go back to Grant."

Mother was unusually curious. "Like what, Sabrina?"

I gulped down a glass of orange juice, searching for the right reply. "I promised myself to look over the syllabus for the next semester," I said. "I wanted to get a head start so my marks will go up."

Mother permitted herself a small frown of puzzlement. "That doesn't sound like you," she said. "After all, this is your holiday."

"Father let it be known my first-semester grades did not meet with his approval. Remember you told me that I would understand when Willy Billy hit the books last summer at Windsong? Well, now I understand."

The frown disappeared. "I'll be sure you are not disturbed," she said. "That new maid can be rather intrusive."

I escaped midmorning, my door tightly closed with a hastily tacked note on the door 'Do not Disturb'.

"Don't be gone too long," Willy Billy warned me. "Not even Mother will believe that note after a couple of hours."

I remembered Mother's unusual remarks. Did she suspect my unusual devotion to next semester's syllabus?

"I'll be back by lunch," I said.

When I got to Aunt Zelda's, her apartment door was locked and when I found the manager, he asked if I wanted to rent to the place. Aunt Zelda had disappeared and left no forwarding address. When I went back home, I told Willy Billy and then went to my room and left the warning on my door for the rest of the afternoon. Oddly enough, no one bothered me. That night horrific dreams invaded my sleep. Rita was kidnapped, Aunt Zelda murdered and reporters chased me down dark alleys accusing me of the crimes. When I awoke, I felt as guilty as if I actually committed the crimes. I hadn't kidnapped or murdered but my friendship with Rita made me an accomplice to their disappearance.

The holiday season ended on the cusp of those nightmares. Willy Billy left the next morning, and I packed up for my departure the following day. The intrusive maid, Susan, insisted on helping me empty my drawers and closet, and I had the creepy feeling that she would report the state of my underwear to the press as soon as I left. When I ordered her out of my room, Mother fluttered in shortly after. "You mustn't be rude to our hired help," she said.

"Susan is a snoopy bitch," I snapped.

"Sabrina! That language is horrible!"

"I'm sorry, Mother," I said. "I will pack my bags myself. Please apologize for my rudeness. Tell Susan I didn't have enough sleep or something."

"You must learn to accept who you are," Mother said. "You cannot wear your feelings on your sleeve. It will only disrupt your life."

Her words angered me even more. "What do you know about a disrupted life?" I cried.

"Every life has disruptions, Sabrina. Just remember your father and I want you to do your best."

I kept silent. Mother knew I had lost Rita, Aunt Zelda and Nanny Bickel within a few short months, and she had done nothing. She sounded like Father.

Eleven

When I went back to Grant, my second semester, whether fueled by rage or loneliness, my grades improved to a respectable 3.5 GPA, almost without my knowledge. I just liked the classes. Of course, biology was my favorite, but I had learned a lot about writing from Willy Billy's stories and this semester's English demanded a lot of essays. And, thanks to Ms. Abbott, I did well in social studies without asking leading questions. If I didn't have another semester of algebra, I might have had a 4.0 point.

As my interest in second-semester classes improved, I found an 'appropriate friend' almost by accident. Llewellyn McDermott and I were thrust together as lab partners. The boys, a recent innovation at Grant which had been a totally female academy, had dorms well-segregated from ours. As Llewellyn told me, the academy had fallen on hard times economically, and the board came to the conclusion that Grant looked a little out-of-date as an all-girls' institution. They flung open the doors to boys, although not many stampeded through the doors for admission, and the ratio of boys to girls remained woefully lopsided, but Llewellyn's mother, a Grant board member, enrolled him and Llewellyn had no other choice but to join the small group who also had the misfortune of being sons of board members. I wondered if Father had known that when he sent me halfway across the country to insulate me from maverick associations.

"It's okay," he reassured me. He pushed up the glasses on his long nose. "Girls are half of our species. My mother is a female."

I had never thought of myself in quite that way. "And boys are the other half," I said, although I didn't want to think of my father as the same half of the species that Llewellyn occupied.

"Exactly," he said. "And rumors are that male enrollment will grow. We might have a rugby team next year." He hunched over the lab table and stared bleakly into the microscope we shared, his shoulders too thin for his borrowed lab coat.

"Your father was a rugby star," I guessed.

"A polo player, a football fan and currently a local golf champion," Llewellyn agreed, and I knew him to be his father's errant shoot, as surely as I was.

He shoved the microscope over to me and changed the subject. "Microscopic life is fine, but I want to examine life we can see without a microscope."

"Like insects," I said peering at the protozoa slide.

"Like mammals. I want to be a veterinarian."

"Does your father know?"

"That has not been a matter of discussion between us yet," Llewellyn said. "I suppose your father has lofty aspirations for you, sending you to an academy reknown for its rigorous standards."

"My father wanted me out of the state," I said flatly.

"I see," he said and I saw in his eyes a glimmer of understanding.

As the semester went on, Llewellyn and I became an inseparable team. He got me through algebra, and I put his lab notes in legible form. His shorthand for his accurate observations rivaled a doctor's prescription scribbles. "I know what I mean," he objected.

"Mr. Fletcher won't," I said. "Writing is communication and right now, Mr. Fletcher is the one with the grade book."

My roommates suspected romance, a rare occurrence at Grant between the most unlikely couple on campus and took an inordinate interest in our study sessions. What did we talk about? Had Llewellyn ever kissed me? Who was his favorite movie star? Although Llewellyn looked the least likely idea of a Romeo, I learned that his father, one of the most important businessmen in Maine, had women all over the state at his beck and call. Somehow, his father's glamour had leached into my roommates' romantic imaginations, although Llewellyn, tall and too thin, wore glasses that hid his eyes, his only handsome feature. Nevertheless, not one of my dorm mates believed me when I told them we were only lab partners, and he tutored me into a passing grade in algebra.

Llewellyn would have been as horrified at their curiosity as I was, so I shared nothing of my dorm mate's romantic fantasies as we continued to meet and slough through my algebraic equations and his illegible lab notes. My friendship with Llewellyn, like my friendship with Rita, didn't fit, and the more it seemed that way, the more determined I became that no one, especially my father, had the right to define my friendships.

"It seems our study sessions have become a campus interest," Llewellyn said one afternoon as we gathered up our notes.

I said nothing. What could I say?

Llewellyn flushed. "I'm getting unwelcome advances from"--

"The female half of the species?" I supplied.

"Yes," he said.

"The girls in my dorm have been very curious about my private affairs," I admitted.

"Our study sessions."

I sank back down into the study room chair. Our corner table, always an area of comfort, now felt as stiff and foreign as Father's desk. Llewellyn stood over the table as I told him about the past weeks, as clearly and concisely as if I defended myself at one of Father's court trials and waited for Llewellyn to turn and leave.

Llewellyn took the chair across from me and collapsed into laughter. I had only seen him smile or chuckle and his laughter, something between snorts and guffaws, watered his eyes and took me by surprise.

"What's so funny?"

He took off his glasses and wiped his eyes. "Geek, by way of a friendship with one girl, is mistaken to be a chrysalis of stud father and pursued by females convinced he will one day be the mirror image of said father."

"That's crazy," I said.

"You know that and I know that." He stood up and picked up his folder of notes. "Who else needs to know? Tomorrow at four?"

I could only nod. Llewellyn had no more illusions about the new-found interest in him than I had about the dorm's interest in me. We were still friends.

To my relief, the dorm gossip waned as the semester ended. Monitored study sessions afforded little escape for amorous adventures, even if Llewellyn and I had been so inclined. Grant was as strictly run as Father knew it would be; he could have drawn up the code of regulations himself. In addition, a newcomer joined the boys' dorm mid semester, and the girls who had fluttered around Llewellyn, waiting for the chrysalis to burst into his father's image, now fluttered around Eric, who reminded me of Borg in the way he looked much closer to manhood than his years. He would probably be the captain of Grant's rugby team if such a thing ever came into being.

I wondered if Llewellyn felt the same relief that I did over the waning drama. Although Llewellyn won an award for top student that year, I remembered how Borg had taken over Windsong. The top student of the year might not compensate for being the alpha male. I didn't ask and I'm glad I didn't. At the end of the school year, I caught a glimpse of his father the day he picked up Llewellyn, and I knew the answer. He was as different from his father as I was different from mine.

Twelve

It should have been no surprise that Father knew about Llewellyn when I returned home for the summer. Dinner that evening did not include Willy Billy who would return two weeks later. Father had granted him permission to spend time with a friend.

"Who is this friend?" I asked, and I could hear the dismay in my voice.

"If you would communicate with your family more often, you would know about Gregory. His father, Orestes Thurman, is a state representative in Connecticut."

"He's a lovely man," Mother said. "He called and personally invited William on their family yacht."

"Good for Willy—William," I said, picking out the peppers from the summer salad.

"Your lack of communication can be forgiven," Father said, as if already dressed in a judge's robe, handing out his pronouncement from a very high rostrum. "Your grades reflect the ability of Grant Academy to encourage students to respectable achievement."

I took a bite of my salad and refused to say, "Yes, Father."
Willy Billy would have kicked me under the table.

"It also seems that your friendship with Jackson McDermott's son has been a good influence."

"Llewellyn," I choked.

Father permitted a smile. "Yes, Llewellyn. His mother's choice of a name, as I've been given to understand."

"Jackson dotes on her," Mother supplied.

"Yes, dear," Father said, but shot her a look. Mother had stepped out of the proper echo. "His great-grandfather on his mother's side had the unfortunate name."

I smiled at Mother. "Orestes Thurman must have also had a great-grandfather with an unfortunate name," I said. Llewellyn had only escaped my father's disapproval because his father was a successful businessman.

Father glared at me. "You also have the unfortunate habit of misinterpreting what has been said and turning a reasonable conversation into an argument."

"I'm sorry, Father," I remembered to say.

"Shall we ring for the entrée?" Mother asked. She had slipped back into Father's shadow. We lapsed into silence over lamb chops.

I had asked Llewellyn one time why he didn't just go by Lew.

"Because my name is Llewellyn," he answered and seemed genuinely puzzled by my question.

"My mother's name is Elizabeth and she goes by Beth. Aunt Hetty's name is Henrietta. Long names just get shortened." I didn't tell him my nickname for William.

"I wonder who invented names," Llewellyn mused. "What did they mean the first time they were used?"

Of course, I had no idea, except that many were passed down through families. If William ever had a son, he would surely be christened William the Fourth.

Llewellyn, unsatisfied with that thought brought a library book on names to our study session a few days later, and we spent half the time looking up the supposed meaning of the names of everyone we knew. Mine meant 'of the boundary line', William's meant 'determined guardian' and Mother's name meant 'oath of God' which made no sense at all.

Llewellyn's name meant 'lion-like', and he snorted with laughter. "Lion-like? Maybe my great-grandfather, but I'm more like the lion in *The Wizard of Oz*."

"Maybe we earn our names," I said.

"You're already on the boundary line with your father, but I've got a long way to go. Let's get back to algebra."

In the two weeks at home before Willy Billy left the Thurman yacht, I managed to visit Nanny, my only oasis. I had gotten the security code from him to unlock the back gate, but I would have climbed over the fence.

"You came back," Nanny greeted me.

"Of course, I came back," I said. "Susan, the maid, is"—I stopped. I would never call Susan a snoopy bitch to Nanny. "She's not you," I finished.

"You don't need a nanny anymore," Nanny Bickel said. "You just need somebody who knows you."

"I do. Willy Billy's on a yacht, Rita's gone, and Windsong is still a month away. You're the only other one who knows me."

Nanny smiled and poured me a glass of iced tea, a little concession, since she had never let us drink tea at Bloomfield Hills. "You were always the one who asked too many questions," she said. "If William had any questions, he kept them to himself—or maybe he found the answers by himself."

"I'm sorry," I said. "I never measured up to Willy Billy."

Nanny chuckled. "Oh, you measured up to William in your own way. You just didn't measure up to your father's rules."

"It seems Father likes me a little better now that I got a good grade-point average at Grant."

"That's no surprise. I saw your picture with him" –

"Don't," I said. "That was publicity for Father."

"I know. As William says, 'it is what it is'. I'm leaving here at the end of the month and going back to Alaska."

"No!" I cried. "Isn't what you have here better than Alaska?"

"It was with you and William, but this position is worse than the bar I worked at in Nome."

"Why? Father said this was a good position."

Nanny Bickel smiled. "Always the questions. Your father had his reasons for recommending me, but if you must know, the boys are basically spoiled beyond fixing and neither parent grants me an inch of discipline."

"But what will you do in Alaska?" I cried.

"That's not for you to worry about," Nanny said. "Now drink your tea and get back home before you're missed."

"Will you let me know where you are?"

"If I can." She hugged me. "You'll be fine, Sabrina. And I'll be fine. Just learn when to ask your questions."

"I can't!" I cried. "What happened to Rita? Why did Father make it a big secret where you went? Why doesn't my mother ever go against his 'wishes'?"

"Sometimes you just have to keep those questions to yourself. The answers don't always make things better."

Willy Billy came home on a wave of triumph as far as Father was concerned. The papers covered a huge charity event back East and pictures of Orestes Thurman's yacht with Willy Billy mentioned as well as Father, a small phrase, but the Denham name had now spread past Michigan.

"Father's probably already thinking of the Supreme Court," I said to Willy Billy after I had given him Nanny's news. "It's disgusting the way he used Nanny to make himself known to Judge Fillmore." We dined on pizza at Sam's Pizza and Grill on a fortunate night to ourselves. Father and Mother had been invited to Judge Rencourt's and this time Father didn't need us in tow for a photo op. Father made all the right moves, angling for a spot on the bench and it looked like he would get what he wanted.

"It is what it is," Willy Billy said when I made my observations. "We are living in one of the best areas in the country, thanks to the connections Father makes. We go the best schools. That doesn't come about by happenstance."

I stared at him. "Nanny's good position turned out to be with a couple of brats that drove every nanny crazy since the day they were born. Rita and I have been separated, you and I have been shipped out of state to be managed by people who only look at us as a statistic. Even Llewellyn"—

Willy Billy put up his hands. "Stop. Stop. What's this about your Llewellyn?"

"He's not my Llewellyn."

"Tell me about your friend, Llewellyn," Willy Billy amended.

"That's what I'm talking about. Llewellyn got me past a failing grade in algebra, and now it seems he's a good move on father's chess board, the son of the man who owns half the businesses in Maine." I took a ferocious bite of my pizza without bothering to pluck out the peppers. "If his dad takes a fall, Llewellyn will no longer be my lab partner. He'll be wiped off the map like Rita-- like Aunt Zelda."

"Jackson McDermott will not be convicted of fraud and wiped off the map," Willy Billy said. "He's actually a good businessman."

I didn't bother telling Willy Billy that Llewellyn never mentioned his status as the son of a good businessman. Llewellyn wanted to be a veterinarian.

"So what about Gregory?" I countered. "He's a good move on Father's chess board." The one picture I saw of Gregory, he looked shorter and slighter than Willy Billy and so fine-haired I figured that he would be bald by the time he was thirty.

"He's a good friend," Willy Billy said. "Good at tennis. Nothing more to be said except I'm glad Father pushed me into learning that game. I've learned to like it." He remembered to pick off the anchovies before he ate his half of the pizza. "Let's get back. I have some phone calls to make before it gets too late."

I didn't like the end of the evening. Willy Billy had changed, and Rita's question came back to me when I told her that Willy Billy was not like my father. "Are you sure?" she had said.

At Windsong that summer, I practiced sketching the bark and foliage of trees and insects. My additions to my Windsong scrapbook, which had now grown into a third volume, connected me to Rita and Aunt Zelda, but the saddened connection brought me little joy. Willy Billy no longer accompanied me in my explorations. He adopted Mother's pattern of coming to breakfast late and retreating to his room if Uncle Basil came around.

"Like father, like son," I overheard Aunt Hetty say to Uncle Lew one night when they thought me safely out of earshot. "Beth's kids are growing up. How will it all end when they're adults?"

"Now Hetty," Uncle Lew said. "Things have a way of changing,"

"Sometimes you almost sound like Basil," Aunt Hetty grumbled, "with his divine providence in change and all."

"Sometimes Basil is almost right," Uncle Lew said. He chuckled. "But don't let on I ever said that."

The exchange left no avenue for questions the following day. Anything I would have said would give away my eavesdropping. What did Aunt Hetty mean when she wondered how it would all end when we were adults? She seemed to have meant more than the change in Willy Billy.

I went back to Grant Academy that fall with the loose ends of the overheard conversation dangling with no resolution.

Thirteen

I endured my first year of high school, much as I had the year before with the exception of a new dorm room, new dorm mates and the freshman initiation. On hindsight, Grant Academy's vigilance probably kept the initiation relatively harmless, but to me, showing up on campus dressed in pajamas, my hair braided into little knots and my face painted white embarrassed me, even if other freshmen looked equally bizarre in whatever their dorm had decreed. Llewellyn met me at lunch dressed as a bad replica of a Mohawk, his hair bristled on end, his face smeared in war paint and dressed in oversized jeans, chopped in shreds in a bad imitation of fringed leggings.

"I think I'm supposed to be a zombie," I said.

Llewellyn put down his plastic hatchet between our lecture notes. "Then I'm probably supposed to either kill you or honor you as a spirit from the other world."

"I wonder how this fits in with the history of civilization," I said. This year we both struggled with Mrs. Berringer's history class. Her monotonous recital of material that she must have gotten from a PhD thesis proved so dense with dates and names that we spent most of our study time trying to organize our confused notes into a timeline we could understand.

"Tonight we have to eat dinner with a table of upper classmen" —

"Mostly women," I interjected.

"And they can order us to get up and dance," Llewellyn said, shuffling his class notes.

"Or recite nursery rhymes. This afternoon might not be a good time to figure out what Plato meant by the men in a cave looking at flickering shadows."

The evening's dinner turned out better than expected. Llewellyn and I both ended up at the same table. He had to dance around the cafeteria emitting war whoops and I had to stalk up to a neighboring table and steal a Coke and pretend to drink blood. But to our relief most of the evening's attention centered on Eric, dressed like Tarzan and called on more than once, since he hammed it up as king of the jungle.

"Not far from the mark," Llewellyn muttered

After our initiation as the under-class of Grant's high school, I determined to take Mother's advice and not wear my feelings on my sleeve or voice my caustic observations. At the very least, it would keep me out of detention. By the end of the year,

Llewellyn, who never wore his feelings on his sleeve, knew as much about western civilization as our textbook's author and again awarded for academic excellence, but he didn't sign up for Grant's budding rugby team.

His feelings about rugby didn't earn him detention, but it incurred his father's displeasure. He took little comfort when I reported dorm gossip that Eric, the newcomer and current campus star, had been dumped into Grant by his grandmother, who pulled a lot of political strings to get him there after he had been kicked out of two other private schools.

"I guess his grandmother will be happy he finally found his niche," Llewellyn said. "Father is not happy with mine." In spite of Llewellyn's refusal to play rugby, he was an excellent skater and competent at tennis. He just didn't like rugby.

"Doesn't a four-point-plus count for something in your father's narrow mind?" I demanded.

"Not so much. When I told him I wanted to be a veterinarian it was almost as if I told him I intended on being a beatnik poet."

"Beatniks were twenty years ago."

"That's what I'm saying,"

Llewellyn would go back home and I would go back home, but his summer had no Windsong escape. His sister, Wendy, two years older, trained for the Olympics in gymnastics. "My father may have preferred her to be a soccer champion," Llewellyn observed bleakly. "But at least she's a winner."

"It's disgusting," I said to Willy Billy the first time we had a minute to ourselves that summer. We sat in our abandoned schoolroom, snacking on chips and Coke before we had to attend an evening concert. The schoolroom still had Nanny's desk in the corner, and the times we once spent in the classroom that I once resented now seemed a cherished sanctuary.

Father lately became a supporter of Detroit's Symphony Orchestra, his new avenue into publicity, although I had never seen him interested in any kind of music before; his car's sound system sat mute on our trips to Windsong. Thanks to last semester's humanities class, I actually learned to like some classical music, especially Mozart, but tonight I dreaded listening to Wagner while dressed in a gown that accentuated my runaway red hair and freckles. After all those times at the mall with Rita, I knew which colors I wore best and maroon didn't make it on the list, but Susan had picked the gown, the current color of fashion before I had even gotten back from

Grant. She had no place putting a gown across my bed that made me look like poison, but my objections to Mother fell on deaf ears.

"It is what it is," Willy Billy said and plunged his chip into a spinach dip that was our favorite. "It's obvious Llewellyn's father thinks he's a loser. I'm sure that will come to a head in the next years."

If he meant his words to be a comfort, they didn't help.

"That's not how it is! Llewellyn is not a loser just because he wants to be a veterinarian."

"What will you do after Grant?" Willy Billy changed the subject. Or perhaps he connected my own aspirations with Llewellyn's unfortunate career choice.

"I'm going to be a biologist," I said. The words came out of my mouth as if I had thought them out beforehand, but as soon as I said them, they felt right.

"What kind of biologist?"

I sipped my Coke. "I don't know yet," I said.

"You might consider teaching science at university level."

"I don't want to teach it. I want to do it."

"Good luck with breaking that news to Father," Willy Billy said. "You and your Llewellyn might find yourselves out in the desert somewhere trying to cure insect diseases."

"In spite of myself, I had to laugh. "We'll hide out at Windsong," I said.

Willy Billy smiled. "And I suppose I'll be left to negotiate the legal and financial terms of your estrangement from your inheritance."

Since my first year of high school at Grant went off without at hitch and I had other 'appropriate' friends besides Llewellyn, Father was in a congratulatory mood when he drove us to Windsong that year. Thanks to Grant's influence and in spite of my earlier resentment, I proved myself worthy of the Denham name. Maybe Father had made the right choice. If I hadn't gone to Grant, I wouldn't have known Llewellyn, and if I hadn't known Llewellyn, maybe I would never have gotten through those math equations.

That feeling lasted until one night after supper Uncle Lew asked to look at my notebooks. "You know a lot more about the wildlife you're collecting than I can tell you anymore," he said.

I wondered at his strange request, since Uncle Lew never requested anything but his after-supper coffee that he drank in silence.

"You could do a kids' picture book," Aunt Hetty said, peering over his shoulder as he turned the pages. "Where on earth did you learn to do sketches like that? They're a lot better than what Lew's niece brings home from the library."

I dared not say that Rita's Aunt Zelda had taught me since Mother sat across the table from Uncle Lew, another aberration. Usually, she went for a walk or to her room after supper and left the after-meal cleanup to Aunt Hetty and me. "You're not helping, Hetty," Mother said. "Sabrina doesn't need to think of turning out children's books. Anybody can do that. Grant Academy expects more."

I stared at Mother. At Windsong she had always left Willy Billy and me to do whatever we wanted to do, the reason I had the notebooks in the first place.

"What do you mean, Mother? What does Grant expect of me? What do you and Father expect of me?"

Uncle Lew got up to pour an uncharacteristic second cup of coffee and Aunt Hetty stiffened behind his empty chair.

"Your interest in the surroundings at Windsong have been a summer diversion, Sabrina, but your father and I find this collection fixation a little disturbing at this point."

"So that's the sudden interest in my notebooks," I said. I suddenly realized that maybe Willy Billy's loss of interest in his notebooks and in Shakespeare hadn't been all about his disappointment with Borg's disappearance.

Mother fluttered her hand. "No, dear, I just thought it a good time to bring up what's best for you. You have to start planning your future." She may as well have been Father in that chair by the table.

More than that, I was enraged at Uncle Lew and Aunt Hetty's complicity in Mother's charade. "Good night," I said and slammed my notebook shut and went to my bedroom, too hurt to say more, too hurt to even confide in Willy Billy. Maybe he had been Father's informant. I felt betrayed by everyone. I felt betrayed by Windsong, my haven. The notebook stayed closed in the last few days before Father reappeared to take us back to the city.

"Your Uncle Lew and I didn't think it right," Aunt Hetty whispered to me when I stiffly hugged her good-bye, "but your mother thought it for your own good."

"Mother was my father's mouthpiece," I retorted.

"You're right," Aunt Hetty said. "Keep those notebooks."

Fourteen

My sophomore year at Grant proved as bleak as the Maine landscape in January. Llewellyn's father took him out of Grant and sent him to a boarding school close to Washington D.C. If Jackson McDermott's son was not going to be a sports star, his academic prowess would well be put into business management. Llewellyn sent me a letter outlining his own bleak semester at Blaine. "I cannot see myself running one of Father's businesses and hobnobbing with men like Orestes Thurman," he wrote.

I wanted to laugh at the thought of Llewellyn hobnobbing on the Thurman yacht with the suave Gregory, Llewellyn with his glasses slipping down his long nose and his intense frown at doing business as if attempting to explain an algebraic equation. It made no sense at all.

My bleak year when I had lost yet another friend, was compounded with my "blossom into womanhood", the term used by a euphemistic film Shark Shadrow had given us the year before but Nanny Bickel had told me what my body changes meant in much more detail than Shadrow's film. Nanny also included the part that the "male of the species', as

Llewellyn would have termed it, would play into the possibility that I could eventually be a mother. By this time, I knew enough about biology to know the accuracy of Nanny Bickel's explanation, but my need for bras that never seemed to fit and feminine napkins made one more miserable change in a bleak, gray year.

Willy Billy didn't come home at all over the holiday break. With Father's blessing, he spent the time with Gregory at a ski resort in Colorado. I got one postcard from him: "Skiing is the answer to man's mortal feet," he wrote. I thought I saw a glimmer of a possible notebook poem coming from that line, but the following line shut that down. "Making some important connections."

I went back to Grant with Rita's mantra in my head. "Only two more years—after this one." By now, accepted as the dorm nerd, I turned from my loneliness without Llewellyn by helping my dorm sisters with homework. After Llewellyn's help, I had learned to do the math I once avoided and found a certain comfort in its reliable logic. The girls that had seemed so foreign at first I found not that different after all. Most had a stake at staying at Grant, some with mothers quite like my father, some wanted their own versions of Windsong with freedom to do what they really wanted to do. After last summer's Windsong, I wondered how many of us would actually work at what we really wanted to do and how many of us would be shoved into a career 'that was best for us'.

The second semester Ms. Shadrow requested that I tutor Frances Wilkinson in freshman biology. "I've noticed that when you help others, you don't do their homework for them," she said with a hint of approval in her rare admission that she closely watched the dorm's study sessions. "That's very important in a proper tutor."

She was right on that point. Those who asked for help quickly learned that they either worked to improve their lagging grades or found someone who gave out answers for a price. I was probably the best deal. I didn't charge.

Proper tutor or not, one did not say no to a request from the headmistress, although I thought it unusual that the request came from her. Why didn't Frances Wilkinson just ask me herself like the other girls did? I would soon find out that my little niche as dorm nerd had its downside.

Frances and I met the following day at the same corner table that Llewellyn and I had once occupied, our backs against the wall to eliminate distractions. Frances would have preferred the center of the room with all her attributes on display, her blonde hair cut to perfection, her almond eyes accented with just the right touch of eyeliner and her manicured fingers worthy of a salon ad.

I soon found out that my gorgeous student had little interest in biology, her lab notes so sketchy I wondered if she had actually looked through a microscope at all, and she was genuinely puzzled if I used any scientific terms. She basically expected me to do the work for her. At first, she attempted flattery, accompanied with a winsome smile. "You are so smart," she said. "I'm sure you could come to an answer in half the time." Next came transparent excuses. "I tried so hard and just couldn't get the formula right. Could you write it out for me?" When that didn't work, sulky pouts followed. "You are not doing your job," she finally accused me.

I knew what that meant and told her mid semester to find another tutor. Not a good move. "Daddy said the headmistress would find a tutor who would get me through this semester! You will hear about this!"

When Shark Shadrow called me to her office, a summons no one wants to get, I expected the worse. I had only darkened its doors once, the day Shadrow had greeted me the first day of my arrival at Grant. A small room with only one window, too high to contemplate the sweeping lawn that met a forest of maples that flamed red and orange in a magnificent display every fall and even in winter held soft ridges of white with a stark beauty. A huge wooden desk took up half the office space and bookcases and file cabinets filled the rest that couldn't quite accommodate stacks of books and papers that stood on the desk and in the corners.

Shadrow stood behind her desk and did not invite me to sit on the lone chair that faced it. "I understand you've refused to tutor Miss Wilkinson any longer," she said without preamble.

"I'm sorry, Ms. Shadrow. I couldn't make it work."

Ms. Shadrow's heavy, dark eyebrows raised in silent question.

"We go through her assignments, I show her how to do them, but when she comes back, nothing is done."

"She doesn't understand?"

"She wants me to give her the answers," I blurted.

Ms. Shadrow looked down her long shark nose at me as if at a morsel to be ground up. "Do you have proof for your allegations?"

"What kind of proof?" I gulped.

"Did you keep a log of your sessions?"

The idea had never occurred to me. "No," I said. "I just did what I do with the other girls."

"I see," she said

I'm sorry I failed you, Ms. Shadrow,"

"You may go,"

I fled to my room, thankful I hadn't been put in detention or expelled and thankful that not one of my roommates knew of my summon.

When I came home for the summer break, I faced much more than the shark's icy dismissal. When Father called me into his study, he lost no time in confronting me. "You refused to tutor Benjamin Wilkinson's daughter!"

The fury in his voice so surprised me, I could only nod.

Father's voice rose. "Do you know who Benjamin Wilkinson is?"

I shook my head.

"Only Maine's recently elected Supreme Court judge if you bothered to look at a newspaper in the last six months."

"I'm sorry, Father. Frances Wilkinson expected me to do her work for her."

"You were just asked to do a lousy tutoring job!"

"Father, let me explain."

"Out." Father pointed to the door. "That mouth of yours needs no explanation. Ms. Shadrow should have put you in detention."

I fled. Even if the shark's report came at the end of the semester, it must have been scathing.

The minute Willy Billy came home and dragged his luggage upstairs, I blurted out my story and father's rage. "You would have won a star Father connecting with Frances Wilkinson," he said.

"I don't care about Father's star," I snapped. "She was a lazy bitch."

Willy Billy ignored my bad language. "Didn't you know who her father was?" he pursued.

"Father informed me. And I couldn't have put up with her even if I had known. It wasn't right!"

Willy Billy smiled a small, tight smile. "I'll see what I can do —for Windsong," He opened his suitcase. "But this is worse than running downstairs in your pajamas."

I wanted to rave on, but something in Willy Billy's tight smile and the disapproval in his voice kept me silent. I felt, as never before, the errant shoot that disturbed the right arrangement of life in Bloomfield Hills Willy Billy had become part of.

"I like your new car," I said in a half-hearted attempt to relate to Willy Billy's slant on Father's viewpoint. It was his graduation gift, but the first time I had seen it. Halfway through his final semester, Willy Billy requested that Father skip his graduation celebration from Exeter. "It's only one step toward a real graduation," he had written. "I would rather defer the celebration at the country club until I graduate from law school."

"That's odd," I said when Father had read the letter aloud at dinner. I would be so ready to celebrate after graduating from Grant, even if I knew that I too would return to school the following year.

But Father didn't think it odd. "William has a good head on his shoulders," he said folding the letter and pointing it at me as crucial evidence. "He's already looking ahead."

Father had rewarded Willy Billy's good head with a new car. Now I dared to ask Willy Billy, "Will you drive it to Windsong?" Perhaps he and Mother would go and I would be left at home with Father awarding me the detention I hadn't received from Shark Shadrow.

"Not this year," Willy Billy said shortly. "Mother's already asked that we go together as before. Now let me get unpacked before dinner."

I didn't have dinner with Mother and Father that evening. Father instructed Susan to serve my dinner upstairs, with the excuse that I needed my rest after Grant's last semester. Snoopy Susan saw through the flimsy excuse and asked me about my supposed symptoms, which almost made me as upset as I was supposed to feel.

Willy Billy reported that Mother remarked that perhaps it might do me good if I came down for dinner, but Father did not relent. "It's more important that Sabrina meditate on how to behave in the world she's in, dear," he said. "She became a little high-handed with certain of her dorm mates. That attitude is not befitting our daughter."

"I'd rather stay upstairs," I said to Willy Billy, but the thought that I would be left upstairs for the rest of the summer loomed a real possibility.

The next two weeks were filled with tension until Willy Billy found the right ammunition that mollified Father. Frances Wilkinson had been expelled from Grant at the end of the semester for not only failing grades but for being found in a compromising situation with Eric, Grant's rugby star. Eric, although severely censured, whatever that meant, would be at Grant next year. Willy Billy did not tell me how he got this top-secret information, nor how he had found Shadrow's report. The scathing words that I had envisioned only contained one brief line: "Miss Sabrina's work with other dorm mates shows initiative, but her attempts at tutoring Miss Frances Wilkinson proved unsuccessful."

After Willy Billy's discovery, I ate dinner downstairs, a mixed blessing. I would be going to Windsong, but with Father's pointed refusal to include me in the stiff dinner conversation. I hadn't been forgiven—only tolerated.

Fifteen

Our first night at Windsong, Aunt Hetty and I just finished the dishes when a police car, lights flashing, lit the dark kitchen window. "What the hell!" Uncle Lew exclaimed. He jumped up and threw open the front door before the officer had a chance to knock. Aunt Hetty stood as if frozen at the kitchen sink, a damp dish towel in hand.

"Is Mrs. William Denham here?" the officer asked.

"Yes sir." Uncle Lew opened the door wider and a state policeman stepped inside and removed his hat.

"May I speak with her?"

Mother and Willy Billy came down the hall from their rooms, as if summoned, and the look on Mother's face frightened me more than the police officer's strange intrusion.

"Mrs. William Denham?"

"I am," Mother said.

"I'm afraid your husband's been in an accident, Mrs. Denham."

"Where is he?" Mother asked as if she expected Father to appear behind the officer.

"He was killed, Mrs. Denham. I'm sorry for your loss."

Mother took a step sideways and Willy Billy caught her before she fell.

I ran to her, but Aunt Hetty brushed me aside and pushed the damp towel on Mother's forehead. "The smelling salts in the bathroom cabinet," she ordered, and Willy Billy hurried to comply.

"I'm so sorry," the officer said.

"Help me get her to the couch," Aunt Hetty commanded. "Then you'd better leave."

"Thank you," Uncle Lew managed when the reluctant officer retreated.

When Mother revived, the whole evening seemed a surrealistic scene, a bad dream. Uncle Basil and Borg arrived shortly after the police left, alerted by a neighbor's scanner and I was too numb to be surprised at Borg's appearance. He stood behind Uncle Basil and stared at us, not knowing what to say. Even Uncle Basil seemed at a loss to summons the right Biblical quote and just asked what he could do to help. Aunt Hetty sent him to find out what the sheriff knew. For once, my curiosity deserted me. I didn't want to know. When we finally went to bed, reality still hadn't hit me. The evening would melt away when the first rays of the morning sun would put our lives back to its predictable pattern, but the world had shifted. Our lives would never be the same again. The following morning we left Windsong with a car and driver Uncle Basil had found, both a little dusty but dependable.

The next days were blurred confusion. When I saw Father for the last time at the funeral home, his body seemed smaller, his sharp features softened in death. How he got there, how Mother managed arrangements, I had no idea. I had never attended a funeral before and had nothing with which to compare the flowers, the muted organ music and the hushed atmosphere, attended by a kaleidoscope of father's associates, most unfamiliar to me. I struggled to follow Mother's composure, accepting hugs of condolences, sitting through the ritual of the Presbyterian minister who delivered a eulogy that must have been a formula for such occasions when he presided at funerals for those who seldom attended church.

I felt an immense relief after everyone left the luncheon after the service. Uncle Lew and Aunt Hetty did not attend, the only faces I wanted to see. Now I just wanted to be alone, but when I fled to my room, I felt an enormous guilt. Father had never forgiven me, nor I him, and now we would never make amends. I cried then, but not for Father's absence but my own guilt. I had never been what he expected and now I never would be.

After the tsunami of Father's death and funeral, Mother and Willy Billy often met with Father's attorney. To his credit, Father had left a sizable trust to get William through law school and me through college. I'm sure if I had ever told Father of my career choice, he would have disapproved unless I aimed to run a major lab for a pharmaceutical company or opted for a sedate position as a university professor. But after Mother's little speech last summer at Windsong over my 'collection fixation', I think he guessed I wanted to wander the forests of the Upper Peninsula and add to my notebooks until I had a room full of them. Now he would never hear of my impossible dream, and I felt another wave of guilty grief, but I kept it to myself. Neither Willy Billy nor Mother needed to hear about impossible dreams.

We continued to have dinner with Mother every evening. After she had fainted at Windsong, she seemed unusually composed. Her voice took on Father's tone as if she simply slipped into taking his place at the table. We would return to school and finish what Father had given us.

"That's good," Willy Billy said one evening before summer ended and we sat by the pond. "She'll be able to handle things herself when we're at school. I worried about that until I saw Father's attorney."

I disagreed. After the shock of Father's death subsided, Mother touched on the unfortunate accident that robbed the world of a judge, who would have been fair, even in the face of enemies. What enemies? I had always thought of Father garnering praise, not enemies, and thought that Mother had always felt the same.

"Father was an excellent driver, Willy Billy. The accident doesn't make sense."

"I think it's time you dropped the Willy Billy. I'm too old for that nickname."

I refused to react to his reference to his position as the man of the family, another change brought about by Father's death. This evening our walk to the pond the first time I had a chance to have him to myself. "What happened, William?" I insisted.

"According to the police report, Father braked and swerved and went off a steep embankment thirty miles out of Clareburn. It couldn't have been a deer. High rocks on one side, steep embankment on the other. Deer don't cross there." That evening at Windsong I didn't want to hear details, but I had heard them anyway.

"He wouldn't have swerved for a rabbit or a possum," William admitted.

"Something else distracted him. Mother said he had enemies."

"Little sister, you don't want to be getting like Uncle Basil, looking for hellfire and brimstone around every corner."

"The name is Sabrina," I said. "I'm too old for nicknames too."

"I stand corrected." He stood up. "Let's go back to the house."

"Why weren't any of Mother's family at the funeral?" I demanded as we walked back.

"Mother asked them not to come," he said. "Uncle Lew had to identify Father's body. I think Mother's choice was meant to be compassionate."

I thought of how Father must have looked before presented at the funeral home. Perhaps Mother meant they be spared. Or perhaps neither would fit with Father's well-heeled associates. I tried to brush aside the uncharitable thought. Tomorrow we would be leaving to finish the schooling Father's trust had set aside for us. What advantages did Mother have growing up at Windsong? Did her advantage of marrying father have to be kept separate from her early years? Was that why Father never stayed at Windsong?

"The fragile flower in a crystal vase," I quoted William's long-ago poem.

He stopped and stared at me. "You have the memory of an elephant." I had learned from Llewellyn to fix words and ideas in my mind with a picture. I would never have William's quick wit, but his compliment kept me from elaborating on my uncharitable thoughts.

Before I went to my own room that evening, I crept down the hall and slipped into Mother's room. Still downstairs, perhaps ordering Susan to let me pack my own bags; perhaps meeting with the cook for the next day's menu. What sort of dinner would Mother order when she would be the only one at the huge dining-room table? Or would she take her dinner in the kitchen, cozy in contrast, looking out over the side lawn with its manicured shrubs and gardens of marigold and azaleas, a cheerful burst of color against the late summer sky?

Mother's room left no clues about her. The queen-sized bed with a white headboard and a white chenille bedspread looked as if no one ever slept in it. The pristine vanity table held a brush and comb mid center. Matching dispensers of lotion and perfume looked more decorative than used. Even the small corner desk looked untouched. Nothing personal. Nothing out of place.

"Sabrina!"

I jumped. "Mother! I--I thought you might be here," I stammered. I felt as guilty as the day Father caught me in my pajamas in the sunroom.

Mother stood in the door. "You needed to see me?"

"I just wanted to see how you were. You know, before we go back to school."

Mother walked in and put an arm around me. "I will be fine, Sabrina. And you will do fine too. We've never expected anything less from you."

I wanted to ask, why didn't you really want Uncle Lew and Aunt Hetty at the funeral? Who were Father's enemies? Will you miss us when William and I go back to school? Where will you eat dinner?

But Mother was already turning away. "I'll see you at breakfast before you leave."

Nanny Bickel had said sometimes I had to keep my questions to myself and learn when to ask them. It seems this was one of those times.

When I went back to Grant, news of Father's death had spread across campus. Mrs. Shadrow made it a point to call me into her cramped office and offer her condolences. "Despite your unfortunate experience with Miss Wilkinson, I would certainly recommend you for a tutor again."

"Thank you," I said.

"Just be sure you keep a log," she said. "That will be all." I later heard she had almost been fired over Wilkinson's dismissal. Mrs. Shadrow was not a shark after all.

Now an upper classman, I shared a new dorm, and the girls tried to be comforting, but I felt I didn't deserve their comfort. I hadn't been a good daughter. My most cherished of condolences came from Llewellyn in his haphazard penmanship. "I have had no occasion to write such a letter before," he wrote. "Nothing in English class prepared me, so if this lacks your approval, please send back an edited form. I will not say that I'm sorry for your loss, since that's what everyone else says. I have a hard time fitting into what everyone thinks appropriate, and being who you are, I most valued your refusal to always be appropriate. I'm not in a position to offer much, other than a sincere hope that you will go on being who you are."

Sixteen

William enrolled at the University of Michigan and I finished my years at Grant. Perhaps Father and all his rules had been right after all. I could have ended up like Frances Wilkinson or Judge Filmore's boys that Nanny could not bring up to a fourth-grade reading level. Or Father could have been a man like Rita's father and misused his power to blow our lives apart.

Such was my reasoning when I finished Grant and finally won an award, not for the top student, although I came close, but for outstanding citizenship. It seems helping my dorm mates without charge won me points. Although I once thought I would mark my last days at Grant with a wild celebration, I had to admit, I more appreciated Mother's gift of a car. My college years at Michigan State University would be filled with freedom to travel the state, find Nanny Bickel, go South and find Rita, visit Llewellyn, and I could spend the whole summer at Windsong!

But as my college years spun by, none of that happened. Cars need gas, oil changes, insurance. Mother's strict allowance kept our cars running, but needless trips through the country did not fit into the budget. William found the strict allowance challenging and learned to keep enough of his allowance to lend out with interest. I had no such entrepreneurial skills although I now charged for tutoring and learned to put my allowance in envelopes: gas, clothes, miscellaneous. The miscellaneous envelope always emptied first.

For the first time, I worried about money and wondered how much Mother had left. She not only bought me a new car, but bought a new, silver Lexus the year after Father's funeral. When she asked us to choose a university in Michigan, I thought she wanted us to spend more time with her than if we had gone to some Ivy League college out East, but maybe Mother's budget didn't allow for the extra tuition. William could have gotten into Harvard, but he enrolled at the University of Michigan without question and undeniably proud of his alma mater. He never failed to ask me how life was at the "cow college," Michigan State's unfortunate nickname. Michigan State had been my first choice, even before Mother let her wishes be known, one of the first agricultural colleges in the country with an excellent biology department. Since we saw so little of each other, I didn't mind William's teasing, but the only time I watched a football game was when the two Michigan titans clashed.

William and I did get home for weekends occasionally in our college years, although seldom at the same time. To my relief, Susan left, but Mother retained the cook and insisted on dinner in the dining room. The huge table still echoed with Father's presence. "Maybe you should downsize," I suggested one weekend, my mind on the considerable upkeep of a house with rooms Mother never used and a lawn the size of a park.

"I'm fine, dear. This place meant so much to your father."

"Father's not here anymore," I said but when I saw the look on Mother's face, I wanted to bite my tongue off. I had slapped Mother's memories of her marriage as if it meant nothing. If William sat across from me, he would have kicked me.

"I don't think that was called for," Mother said getting up from the table.

"I'm sorry, Mother. Please sit down. I'm just worried about you here all alone."

Mother sank back into her chair. "I said I'm fine, and I will make the decisions about where I live and how I live."

I would have liked that answer if I felt her life her own instead of still harnessed to Father's memory, but I knew better than to say more. Father had always treated her like the 'flower in a crystal vase', as William said and from everything I had ever seen, she never had much of a life at all.

"It's ridiculous," I complained to William the next time we happened to be home on the same weekend. We ate lunch in the old schoolroom and left Mother to herself except for breakfast and dinner. "Mother acts like Father still runs the place and we're still kids."

"You exaggerate. Mother went to the club this afternoon."

"The club. This place. Dinner in that dining room. She acts as if Father is still here. His money can't keep her forever."

"The allowance that Mother arranged for us has got you going, hasn't it?" William teased. We both had the same stringent allowance. "You could double it if you did more than tutor and listened to me."

"It's more than that," I said. "The maid dusts Father's study every day, Mother eats dinner in that damn big dining room every evening, and cook admitted Mother still orders a meal as if we were all here."

William frowned at his turkey wrap. "Mother has plenty of money to live on. Our educations are taken care of all the way through grad school, and the Lexus was covered by the insurance on Father's car. Father's inheritance in itself is worth a fortune. I know that much."

"She's not even fifty yet," I said. "Thirty more years living in this mausoleum?"

"Mother needs to live here right now, Sabrina. Psych 101. Everyone goes through the grieving process in their own time."

"And sometimes people get stuck," I retorted. "It hasn't been months. It's been a few years."

"Some take longer. She was always our father's shadow and it must be harder for her."

"Why?"

"I don't know why but that's how it is."

I wanted to throw my turkey wrap at him, but Nanny would sit me in a corner writing an apology and her presence still inhabited our old schoolroom. 'That's how it is' didn't always relate to that's how it was or that's what it will be, but I didn't go there.

"I heard from Nanny Bickel," I said.

William stared at me, surprised by my abrupt change of subject.

"She somehow heard about Father's death and sent us a letter separate from her condolences to Mother." In spite of my concerns that Mother lived in Father's shadow, she left any mail addressed to me untouched.

"After all this time! What did she say?" William seemed truly pleased that she remembered us.

"Her father died or killed and they found his body out in the wilderness weeks later. She moved in with her mother and whipped her brothers and sister into shape. Except for one sister, they're all gone now working in Alaska somewhere. Only one brother seems to be take after her nasty father. I'll give you the letter."

"She's still living at home with her mother? That's awful! Maybe Mother could make some connections"—

"She likes it there, William, and she's proud that her family is making it because of her. I'd like to visit her someday. Maybe I'll take Mother with me," I teased.

Seventeen

Despite my ambitions at connecting with long-lost friends, Llewellyn visited me first. In an unlikely turn, his father had finally given in to Llewellyn's career choice. "Father's not happy, but I am," he had written when he got into Penbrook University. In the spring of my junior year, a seminar on animal husbandry at Michigan State brought future veterinarians to the campus from all over the country.

"Sabrina!" he greeted me halfway down the sidewalk before I even got to our arranged meeting place by the clock tower, the most obvious place for a stranger on campus to find.

I hardly recognized the Llewellyn from our first years at Grant. He had grown some and he didn't just walk. He strode. The skinny shoulders I remembered hunched over a microscope in an oversized lab coat now straight and broad and the worried frown gone. With his wavy, dark hair and glasses that did not conceal his expressive, brown eyes, he looked almost handsome. "Llewellyn!" I broke into a run and we collided in a hug. The girls at Grant should see us now. We had never hugged even at the end of the year before summer breaks.

"Michigan State is good for you," he said simply. "You look wonderful."

"So do you," I laughed. "Llewellyn the lion-hearted. You got what you fought for."

"It seems there's been a change of heart with our male progenitors"—He stopped in embarrassment. "I'm sorry," he said. My male progenitor was gone, erased before I ever had to do battle, although he must have known of my intentions. I had told Llewellyn of the time at Windsong when Mother enlisted Uncle Lew and Aunt Hetty to steer me away from my "disturbing fixation" with my notebooks.

"No apology necessary," I said. "Mother decided it doesn't matter if I'm in biology or English literature. She figures I'll find a suitable mate before I'm through."

"And have you?" Llewellyn asked as we strolled past the tower, past the campus.

"No. Girls interested in butterflies and lady slippers do not attract high interest to the male of our species unless I write poetry. Not good if you write about the female spider devouring its mate."

"Sabrina from the boundary line. By the way, I looked up Frances Wilkinson's name after your tutoring incident. It meant 'free from France'."

"Maybe free from underpants."

Llewellyn laughed his guffaw snort. "Maybe names are more accurate than I thought."

"Maybe," I said. "But I have not been on any boundary lines since I've been here. My degree in biology is impeccable."

"I'm only here for four days," he said. "Can you enlighten my spare moments with your macabre observations on the mating habits of the insect variety?"

"I will be honored. Your time at Michigan State will be well taken. You will get two seminars for the price of one."

By the time Llewellyn left, I knew I fell into an impossible love. He had given me no indication that he felt anything else than our enduring friendship, and I couldn't bring myself to hint that, according to Michigan State's legend, I would not be a proper Michigan State Spartan unless I kissed in the shadow of the clock tower. When I dreamed of him naked, coming down on me, I tried to discard my wild lust as biology taking over common sense. He had years to go before he established a career and so did I. I had seen other girls drop out of college and leave their aspirations to marry before ever reaching their goals. Not one of my arguments with myself would have worked if Llewellyn didn't live several states away.

I wished I could confide to Rita my turmoil. Somewhere I read that people have three circles of friends: the very close, a small circle, a larger circle of friends, social with similar interests, and a yet wider circle of friendly acquaintances that cooperate in shared projects. I had friends in circles two and three, but only Rita and Llewellyn occupied orbit one, and I still missed her, but she and her mother had disappeared without a trace. She once told me that her mother had come from a life quite as bleak as Nanny Bickel's and clawed her way to a better life with nothing more than catching the eye of Rita's father at a strip club where she worked in the sleazy side of Atlanta. He recognized her ambition, not to mention her feminine charms, and appointed himself as her knight in shining armor, paid for her education and eventually married her.

Rita had learned about her history and her own unwelcome arrival from listening to the virulent wars between her parents, but never learned where Aunt Zelda fit into the family picture and never understood why her mother held such animosity toward her sister.

"It must have been that my aunt and mother both ended up in Michigan doing well, but Aunt Zelda never got there stripping for a rich guy." Rita said. Her reasoning made sense. Rita's mother could have been fearful of what Zelda might say if the media tracked her mother's background to Zelda's door. Was that why Mother's family had never visited Bloomfield Hills, not even for Father's funeral?

Was Rita her Mother's errant shoot? Had she pursued her art? Was she a street artist scrawling caricatures for money enough to eat? Was the street all she had wanted, free of her father, her mother's rejection? Had Aunt Zelda been erased from Rita's life, as she had been erased from mine?

Eighteen

Windsong in the years while William completed law school and I finished my degree in biology no longer held the same allure as a retreat to freedom of our young years, often, our stay shortened by summer classes or part-time jobs. When William finished his law degree, he got a position in Father's law firm and moved back home. I knew living back home would not happen in my life and I applied for jobs in a hundred different directions. If I found a good man to marry, as Mother hinted, I wouldn't have to count the dollars garnered from tutoring and a part-time position at the university bookstore. I might not have wanted to live home, but I never missed an opportunity for a good meal, and I took advantage of Mother's invitations to dinner as often as I could.

"You're not helping," I told William after one such meal after I attempted to convince him to move our Wind Wong visit up a week when the book store would be closed.

"That's your agenda for changing the time Mother goes to Windsong," William said, "but you have to understand Mother Is comforted by the dates staying the way it has always been."

"You're enabling her."

William halted our evening stroll around the pond and ran his hand through his hair in quite the same way I remembered Father doing when I had become a problem. "I'm making sure she's not being victimized," William said. "That's all I know how to do."

I couldn't say more. William did more for Mother than I did. He probably would have preferred his own apartment, but he had grown as worried about Mother's tether to Father's memory as I was. She acted as if Father still occupied his seat at the table, and she predicated almost every move she made with "your father said" or "your father wishes". William's attempts at pulling her into new interests proved fruitless.

William, Mother and I each occupied our own little islands in the middle of a lake of uncertainty. Sometimes William stayed at Windsong for a few days and returned to drive us home. Sometimes he stayed longer, but spent his time in his room as if back at his law office. Our companionship in our younger years had disappeared and William had taken the place of Father, and I the errant shoot without a job.

Uncle Lew and Aunt Hetty still welcomed us and fussed over Mother as they always did. Uncle Lew now asked me as many questions as I once asked him and collected insects and plants ahead of our visits to fuel his questions, although his tool shed had never held such collections before. Aunt Hetty too took an unusual interest in my lab notes, always asking to see the sketches in my Windsong notebooks. They did their best to let me know they accepted me as much as they once accepted the messy, young niece who invaded Windsong every summer, but Aunt Hetty no longer teased William for a poem or a quote from Shakespeare.

Uncle Basil made his usual appearances around supper time. I had seen a change in my fire-and-brimstone uncle. His church opened a soup kitchen and he contributed to their efforts with his dubious meat sources. The women in his church made quilts for veterans, held ambitious bake sales and community festivities around the holidays and formed a youth Bible study group. Uncle Basil's burgeoning church had been taken over by the women and changed his message from hell and damnation to love thy neighbor. Oddly enough, Uncle Basil went along with the changes. Maybe Borg's brief return had mollified him.

"Uncle Basil doesn't talk about Borg," I said one evening as Aunt Hetty and I cleaned up one evening after a chicken dinner that could have rivaled Frankenmuth's claim to fame. "He was home that summer Father was killed. I thought he came back to Michigan to stay."

"He stayed for awhile," Aunt Hetty said. "I hear he's out west working on a cattle ranch and doing okay."

Mother no longer escaped to her room at his appearance. Mother seemed to forget my presence and I heard reminiscences I never heard before. Uncle Basil once rescued Mother when she broke through thin ice. She covered up the evidence when he wet the bed in his younger years, and later he covered for her when she snuck out at night. I listened to the stories, so different from the mother I knew that I could hardly believe them, as unlikely as William's long-ago tales about real people in Clareburn. And that's when I learned that Deborah, the witch of Uncle Basil's damnation, had once been a part of their escapades.

"Deborah got crazy after her brother disappeared," Uncle Basil said at one of his reminiscences. "After we married, she kept talking, talking, talking about finding him."

"Yes," Mother murmured.

"I couldn't help her. I wasn't with you guys the night he disappeared."

"You had the flu," Mother said. "You gave it to me the next day if I remember. What was that awful concoction Mother gave us every time we sneezed?"

But Uncle Basil was not to be sidetracked. "Somehow Deborah thought I should know."

Mother waved her hand. "Let's not talk about Deborah," she said. "It's too painful."

I wanted Uncle Basil to talk. He had never talked about his ex-wife before in such a way. Deborah no longer sounded like an evil woman but a woman in pain. If William ever disappeared, I might go crazy too.

"When did Deborah's brother disappear?" I asked.

Aunt Hetty frowned and attacked a pan with a scouring pad. "I don't really remember. About the time your mother and Basil were up to their tricks. I was already married to Lew."

"Hetty wasn't up to no tricks," Uncle Lew said from his corner at the table with his after- supper cup of coffee. "We married right and proper. Your mother and Basil"—

Aunt Hetty waved a scoured pan. "Lew--"

"I'm just saying, Hetty, Elizabeth and Basil were different than you. Maybe your folks got tired of watching so close."

Aunt Hetty lowered the pan. "They were the youngest two," she said, "and Basil was the boy that father and Mother always wanted. A boy before me died a crib death and when Basil came along, he could get away with almost anything and your mother hooked unto that star."

"My mother hung around with other kids?"

"Basil and Deborah's friends," Aunt Hetty said. "Your uncle Lew is right on that point. Deborah's brother was a year older than those kids and a roughneck. He probably toppled into a river somewhere when he got too drunk to pull himself out, but Deborah could never accept that."

She swished the dishwater down the drain. "That's all I know," she said.

But I wasn't done. "I'm worried about Mother. She's holding on to Father's way of doing things way beyond sense."

"She seems the same to me," Aunt Hetty countered. "Except she doesn't run to her room when Basil comes to supper."

"At home, she sits at the same spot at the table, orders Father's favorite meals and keeps the place exactly like he left it. From

Uncle Basil's stories, she was so different. Why can't she get a life now that Father's gone?"

Aunt Hetty wiped the counter that had already been wiped. "You ask too many questions."

"This is important, Aunt Hetty. You know Mother better than I do. Better than William does."

"You and William are overreacting to your own memories of your father, and it's to be expected. He treated you two with an iron hand, but he doted on your mother and she figured he knew more than she did about how you and William should grow up right in the city. I didn't always approve of his ways, but you and William turned out all right. Get on with your life and don't worry about your mother."

In her own way, Aunt Hetty could be as evasive as Mother. I looked at Uncle Lew for support, but of course he stayed firmly rooted in Aunt Hetty's camp. "How about a game of checkers?" he suggested.

Nineteen

Although Windsong gave me no answers to Mother's reliance on the ghost of my father, I did get on with my life, and it twisted in unexpected ways as Aunt Zelda's tea leaves once said it would. Michigan's Department of Natural Resources, the DNR, hired me to oversee the trout planted all over the Upper Peninsula's lakes and streams, a job dealing more with data than wandering through woods and collecting additions to my notebooks. But I now had job as a biologist in the real world.

Mother said that Father wouldn't have approved and she urged me to get into a pharmacy lab or teach at Michigan State as a full-time professor, much as I knew Father would have wanted. Even William agreed with Mother when I moved from East Lansing to St. Ignace. "We have computers now. You can work here."

He had a point, but I wanted to be closer to the little fingerlings released into the wild in a way that didn't match data spitting out of a computer. I knew that my move put distance between Bloomfield Hills with my new home, and William would be left alone at the dinner table with Mother and Father's ghost, but I could no longer deal with my own complicity in enabling Mother. William had guarded against her victimization, but he had become a shadow of Father guarding the fragile flower in a crystal vase, almost as painful to witness as Mother's reliance on him.

I settled in an apartment over a store housed in an ancient building that rattled and shook with anything from a passing semi to a full-scale Michigan gale, but I spent most of my time on the road investigating the lakes and streams that we planted. I wanted to know firsthand the DNR's effect on the area I had learned to love from my years at Windsong. Soon enough, my reports to the main office included local DNR officer's observations as well as those of fishermen I came across in my ramblings.

"Your reports are a little unusual," my supervisor noted in one of his emails, "and I for one, find the anecdotes you include entertaining and sometimes enlightening." I made a face at the email. I had hoped enlightening would be the more important word, but at least he recommended I stay on when my internship was over.

Autumn already covered the Upper Peninsula in a wild burst of color when someone knocked on the wooden door of my apartment that would have yielded to a good push. I hadn't yet figured out the intricacies of the old lock, which seemed engineered more to locking me out than keeping anyone out who didn't have a key at all.

"Who are you and what do you want?" I yelled.

"It's Llewellyn."

A heroine in a romance novel would have opened the door and fell into his arms. Instead, I opened the door and we stood looking at each other like a couple of frightened deer blinded by the headlights of an oncoming vehicle. We had kept in touch with emails after we both had computers and I confessed my few affairs; Eric who loved my intelligence but had none of his own, Benjamin who had all the intelligence and personality of a textbook and an encounter with Corwin who collected affairs like I once collected specimens for my notebooks. But in my candid confessions, I had never once admitted to my lusty dreams of him after we met on campus, nor the fact that every short-lived relationship I attempted had been measured against him, and none had ever come close.

Llewellyn had had one relationship that had turned him upside down when it ended, but our email exchanges seemed devoid of the angst of our earlier letters and I had already resigned myself that we were drifting apart. One day I would send an email that would never be answered.

"I got a job in Michigan," he finally said. "I didn't want to say anything until I was sure."

I burst into tears.

"Maybe not a good surprise."

"I-I thought I'd never see you again."

He pulled me into his arms. "Sometimes the female of the species are difficult to understand," he said. "I always knew I would see you again."

That was the beginning of the rest of my life. The next year, we married. We might have married the day after he knocked on my door, but Mother insisted on a wedding that would come up to Father's expectations, although a small affair, "according to the bride's wishes", the Free Press reported. Llewellyn and I had given Mother our list of friends, a little less than an affair of 150 people that Mother insisted William scare up from father's connections. And my wishes far less than the proper fitting for a bridal gown that rivaled a queen's, the proper flowers and the right Presbyterian minister for a church wedding.

I chaffed at bowing to Mother's wishes. I enabled her, as surely as William, but oddly enough, William and Llewellyn were allied in complying with Mother's elaborate plans with the "small affair".

"Planning this wedding is the most Mother's done since arranging Father's funeral," William said. "This is good for her."

"If it was my mother, she'd be doing the same thing," Llewellyn said. The sorrow that flickered in his eyes stopped my objections. His mother died a few years before and although she hadn't been an affectionate woman, she had twisted her husband into agreeing to accept Llewellyn's enrollment into a veterinarian's program.

As we curled up in my bed in the drafty apartment that shook with the winter winds, I agreed. Mother would have the wedding she wanted for me. "I'll put up with the rest," I reluctantly agreed. "Just as long as you're there."

"And your Uncle Lew and Aunt Hetty," Llewellyn said. "I'm already a given." Although he hadn't yet been to Windsong, he had certainly heard enough about it.

"And your family," I added. His sister and father planned on witnessing yet another of Llewellyn's unfortunate decisions.

Bad enough Llewellyn moved to Michigan to care for farm animals instead of the over bred pets of his father's friends, but a woman who chased fish did not seem a suitable mate for the heir to Jackson McDermott's fortune. I wondered if William's connections assured Llewellyn's family's appearance.

"We are the errant shoots," I said. "Can you live with an errant shoot?"

"Could I live otherwise?" He twisted around me. "I have all I want."

That June we went to Brenda Althorn's wedding, my second-best friend in middle school and my chosen maid of honor—I guess my matron of honor, since she beat me to the altar by a few months. Our wedding would be in November. 'You'll like her," I said to Llewellyn. "She likes horses."

"Good discussion at the bridal table," Llewellyn said. "Give me a kick when we go on too long."

"If you look too interested, I'll knock you off your chair," I said.

In the receiving line, Brenda greeted me as if we hadn't seen one another for years. It had been a while, but our friendship rekindled when we both ended up at Michigan State. "I'm so glad you came," she said. "God, this dress feels like a torture chamber. I hope you have the good sense to get married in slacks and a tee shirt."

"Not likely," I laughed. "It will be your job as a proper matron of honor to make sure I'm as uncomfortable in my beauty as you are."

"I'll do my best, but I think, in spite of all, I'm playing second fiddle. I remember how close you and Rita Gavin were. Have you ever kept in touch after she left?"

"No, I could never find her."

Brenda's brown eyes were sympathetic. "That must have hurt. When Angela moved, I felt ripped in two, but at least I knew where she went." She put her arm around Angela. "She's a pretty good maid of honor even if she would rather be out playing tennis."

I had been wedding guests of other friends I seldom saw anymore, and so much had changed in my life, but Brenda stirred memories of Rita that had not been left behind at all.

After Brenda's wedding, Llewellyn said, "We've invited your friends, my friends, our friends. We have to find Rita." I should have known Llewellyn had noted Brenda's words.

"You're crazy," I murmured and trailed my finger across the body I had lusted for since our meeting at Michigan State. "I've looked for her."

"You didn't have a computer."

Llewellyn had a point. My frantic searches for Rita and her aunt had been when I still attended Grant Academy. Since the computer had come into common use, Llewellyn used it as if he invented the thing.

"I'll find her," Llewellyn said.

I loved Llewellyn for taking an interest in a friend I thought lost forever, but when Llewellyn saw a knotty problem, he went to work to undo the knots. His outspoken analysis of factory farming had already earned him publicity he abhorred, publicity that either glorified or vilified him. He wanted neither. He just wanted to undo the knots he saw in treating animals he knew inside and out. I didn't want to tell him that Rita's disappearance could not be analyzed like in science. When he located her six weeks before our wedding, I couldn't believe it.

"A little more difficult than algebra," he laughed. "She's done everything to keep herself off the grid. Have you ever heard of outlier art?"

"No."

"Artists outside the mainstream. They just do what they do and sometimes they get 'discovered' by trolling art collectors. From what you told me about her, that's where I started my search, but I think we might have to go to her in person."

"I'll call her."

"I tracked her to a New York art dealer, but he isn't talking. No phone. No computer. She's serious about keeping to herself."

I felt a chill of trepidation. Was Rita the same friend I remembered? Was she a bag lady? "Maybe she won't be happy that we found her."

"Too late for second thoughts. I found an address. We're going to New Orleans to deliver an invitation in person."

"Thank you for finding her," I murmured.

"Don't thank me yet." My lion-hearted Llewellyn had doubts too. Confident with science and computers, he wasn't so sure about the female of the species.

Twenty

New Orleans vibrated with music, the smell of Cajun cooking, the push of tourists and the welter of voodoo shops, strip clubs, and blues bars. The lacy architecture, the walled gardens and Jackson Square seemed a page ripped out of history and if Llewellyn hadn't led me, I would never have found Rita's address at all. Her place, away from the noise and glitter, was low, flat and gray, sandwiched between others quite the same, although each had their own touch of flowering plants and yard decorations. Rita decorated her front door with a frame of blue lights, and painted with black women holding drums, washboards and skillets in a tumble of bright color.

Llewellyn knocked on the door once, twice and a third time.

At his fourth knock, an irritated voice yelled, "Go away."

"Rita, it's Sabrina!" I yelled. "Let me in!" A long quietness ensued before we heard a lock click and the door opened against a security chain. Rita's black face peered through the crack in the door.

She threw open the door and hugged me. "I knew this day would come! I just never knew when."

"I tried so hard to find you! If it wasn't for Llewellyn"--

164

Rita let me go and hugged Llewellyn. "Thank you," she said. "Whoever you are, thank you. Come in. I'll scare up some tea and cookies just like Aunt Zelda always did. We've got a lot of catching up to do."

Rita's front room, quite like Aunt Zelda's had been, was filled with her art projects but the surreal collages, fanciful costumes and masks looked nothing like what I had seen in Aunt Zelda's studio. If Llewellyn was surprised at Rita's riotous home studio, he didn't show it. In her tiny alcove of a kitchen, he listened to Rita's story as if he had known her all her life.

Shortly after she and her mother had moved to New Orleans, Aunt Zelda followed "like a bad dream according to Mother", Rita said. Her mother tried to get up a real estate business like the one she left in Michigan, but soon found that her business had been largely propped up by Rita's father's connections. Her after-dinner drinks soon stretched into drinking straight vodka shortly after her morning coffee.

At first, Rita struggled to hide her mother's bottles, but in her mother's alcohol-riddled reasoning, Rita had become the cause of her downfall. One night when she took a broken, jagged bottle after her, Rita fled to Aunt Zelda who already guessed what was coming. Rita finished high school and her mother finished her life in a bar brawl. "Mother and I were oil and water, but I never wanted that for her," Rita finished.

"Why didn't you let me know where you went?"

"Mother said we had to stay hidden and later I had to hide Mother's bottles. After Mother passed, I figured you weren't at Grant anymore and I knew better than to ask your whereabouts from your parents."

"Sometimes you just have to save yourself," Llewellyn said. I thought of his struggle with his powerful father, not the same as Rita's story and yet similar. He had to save himself from his father's iron hand, just as Rita had to escape her mother's rejection. My own escape from Father's disapproval came through no struggle of my own.

"My father was killed in an auto accident," I said.

"That must have been hard for your mother," Rita said. I saw in her eyes she knew my only grief had been the guilt I felt.

"So where is Aunt Zelda?" I asked anxious to change the subject.

"She's on the other side of town and doing well. When she figured I got good enough, she sent me on my way and I'm up to my neck busy."

"You're off the grid," Llewellyn objected. "I had a devil of a time finding you."

Rita grinned. "A little marketing ploy. Art dealers like to discover artists, don't they? Aunt Zelda said after she taught me all she had to offer that I wouldn't make it as her knock-off. If some big art dealer finds me, a talented outlier, and puts together my connection to Aunt Zelda, we're going to be the best of enemies. It'll add a little heat. Even the art world likes a little gossip."

"Rita!"

Her grin widened. "I bet you thought only our fathers knew about manipulation. I wondered when we met again if you had changed, but you're still Sabrina, who wouldn't even know how to cheat at cards. Your name might mean out of bounds, but it's not about manipulation."

"You know the meaning of names!"

"I had to research names to get a feel for one of my clients." She looked at Llewellyn. "You're lion-like. Believe me, you'd better be, hitching yourself to Sabrina."

"And you're the pearl," Llewellyn said.

"In an oyster," Rita said. "Oysters are in a shell. I like my shell."

"Llewellyn and I are getting married, Rita, and we want you and Aunt Zelda to come to our wedding."

Rita laughed in a way I had never heard in our young days of angst. "I doubt if we're on your mother's guest list."

"You're first on mine," I said.

"I'm not sure it's such a good idea, Sabrina. Bloomfield Hills has a long memory, and I don't want to ever see the place again."

"You and Aunt Zelda were my friends when I needed friends. At Brenda Althorn's wedding she brought up memories I hadn't talked about for years."

"Back in school, she was the one with the horses?"

"That's Brenda. We both ended up at Michigan State, both in biology. She's my maid of honor instead of you. She mentioned that."

Rita laughed. "Believe me, Brenda's a better choice. I'm guessing your mother's been planning your wedding for months."

"Please, Rita," I said. "You don't have to be a maid of honor. I just want you and Aunt Zelda there."

"Please, Rita," Llewellyn echoed. "I do not want to marry an unhappy bride."

Rita smiled and put her hand over mine. "I guess we owe you that much after leaving like we did. We'll be there."

Twenty-One

Our November wedding day turned sunny and almost warm after a week of November gray. Llewellyn and I had driven down from St. Ignace the day before and although I was certainly not a blushing virgin, Mother reserved a room for Llewellyn at the hotel that included the other out-of-town guests, so he would not see me until the grand moment when I came down the aisle. "At least, Mother didn't say that was what my father wished," I grumbled.

"You'll get a full night's sleep," Llewellyn said nuzzling my ear. "The female of the species knows a thing or two."

I didn't get a full night's sleep. I woke up at the crack of dawn to get my hair done, to get a pedicure, a manicure and a facial followed by a late breakfast with Brenda who would later help me dress. I couldn't eat more than a piece of toast.

"I feel like a piece of polished furniture," I complained. Brenda laughed. "You're the third bride I've been a bridesmaid for. You should have eloped to Las Vegas."

When it was finally time to dress, Mother came in shortly after Brenda had slipped my gown into place and gave my hair an extra spritz of hairspray. Mother touched my cheek. "You're beautiful," she said and her eyes misted. "I know I haven't always been the mother you needed, but you're my wonderful daughter. I love you."

I turned and crushed her to me in a burst of emotion. She said three simple words I had been waiting for all my life. "I love you too," I choked.

In spite of my grumbling compliance at Mother's elaborate preparations, that moment made it all worth it and later when the organ broke into the wedding march and I took Uncle Lew's arm, my heart raced. In spite of my complaints, my two favorite people from Windsong were here.

"You clean up pretty good," Uncle Lew said. "Don't be stumbling in those shoes. I'm getting too old to catch you."

Uncle Lew's banter quelled my nerves and I managed to get down the long aisle in heels, but when Uncle Lew gave my hand to Llewellyn and stepped back, and I saw the love- struck look in Llewellyn's eyes, I felt the full impact of the ritual. Before all these people in a church bedecked with fall flowers, Llewellyn and I would announce to the world our commitment to each other. It was a moment like none other.

My wedding bliss followed me back down the aisle on Llewellyn's arm and lasted until the receiving line. The first clouds appeared when I saw that Mother almost lost her composure when my two long-lost friends came through the line, the only black faces in a sea of white. Either Mother had not seen their names on my amended guest list or thought they would never appear. Aunt Zelda, now in her seventies as far as I could calculate, strode through the line like an African queen, taller than most of the people to whom she offered her hand. Rita followed with none of Zelda's imperious carriage. She had inherited her father's short, muscular stature, and I had to smile when I remembered her on the soccer field or kicking our cokes out of the machine meant to take our quarters. The queen and the warrior.

"What do you think you're doing?" William hissed at me as we sipped champagne and mingled with the guests at the reception. "Father convicted Rita's father, for god sake."

By this time, I had already heard the murmurs: "Can you believe it?" "What nerve, those two showing up". "It must have been Sabrina's idea. She always was a thorn in her father's side".

"Rita is not her father," I said.

"She's a bad memory of her father. Some lost a lot of money because of him. No one in this town has forgotten."

Didn't William remember how Father separated Rita and I when neither of us could protest? Didn't he remember how devastated I was when Rita disappeared? How had we grown so far apart in the last years?

"This is my wedding, William, and I wanted all my real friends here."

"This will be the gossip all over town tomorrow," William said. "You might have thought of Mother."

I felt my blood rise, but I kept silent. His words struck home. After Mother said she loved me, she had remained icily apart from me the rest of the evening. It hurt me to see she didn't seem to be any closer to Uncle Lew and Aunt Hetty. Uncle Lew wore a tux for walking me down the aisle, but Aunt Hetty, in her best blue dress looked almost as out-of-place as Aunt Zelda and Rita.

Brenda, my loyal matron of honor, was the only one who understood in her own way. "You and Llewellyn are like horses," she said. "They know the people they trust. It'll be okay."

"I'm sorry," Rita said when they left. "I had to come to your wedding because I love you, but maybe it wasn't a good thing for you."

"Rita! We've been friends since middle school!"

"And if you remember, you had to keep our excursions to the mall top secret when my father made front-page news. Seems like nobody forgot those headlines."

Aunt Zelda hugged me and chuckled. "Remember. Rita is an outlier artist. She stays under the radar."

"Not for long," Llewellyn said. "The computer is like nothing we knew ten years ago. I found her, didn't I?"

"I know," Aunt Zelda said. "I'm not looking forward to pretending we're enemies when the art collectors 'discover' her and start beating down her door. So far, only one New York collector tracked her down, but it's only a matter of time."

Rita hugged me. "It's hard to be an oyster," she said. "But you will know if and when you need to reach me."

Our wedding scoured deep marks in one day. As William had foreseen, Aunt Zelda and Rita's appearance gave the gossip mill better news than the roster of guests that Mother and William had secured.

Rita and Aunt Zelda's appearance also struck a note of hideous bigotry in Llewellyn's father that Llewellyn had never seen before. His father had disapproved of Llewellyn's career choice, had openly disapproved of his stance on factory farming, but it was nothing compared to his rage at his son's bride. His parting words were filled with alcohol-fueled rage. "You are no son of mine, I will make sure of that. Stay in Michigan and rot with your wife and her black, law-breaking friends."

In spite of my rage, I felt a little sorry for Llewellyn's sister, Wendy, who stood behind her father and turned her head in embarrassment. She probably had black friends that she kept away from her bigoted father.

"It's all my fault," I apologized when we were safely back in St. Ignace.

"It's not your fault," Llewellyn said, "I never knew Father to talk that way. I'm not like that, Wendy's not like that, and William's not like that. Things change."

"For every one of us, there's a hundred like your father or others like William, so worried about Rita's father's history, he'd like to pretend she never existed. He knew Rita when I was in high school."

"I can't fathom Father's rant. He deals with black businessmen all the time."

"Maybe he just wanted one more excuse not to like me."

Llewellyn put his arms around me. "We'll fix the world tomorrow. Let's go to bed."

"It's not even nine o'clock."

"I love these long northern Michigan nights," he said.

Twenty-Two

Soon enough, Llewellyn's prediction that things would change happened in an unexpected turn. Less than a year after our wedding, Michigan State University invited him to a teaching position. He knew how I loved the Upper Peninsula and decided to decline, but I wouldn't let him. His work against factory farming would have so much more impact at the university than the articles he had written. Once again, I would be living down below, and even East Lansing seemed too close to my alienation with William, too close to my conflicted relationship with Mother, but I insisted that Llewellyn take the job.

Our move met with silence from Bloomfield Hills, and it hurt that William and I could almost be as far apart as I had once been from Father, but my job kept me busy and I was often out of town. I loved those times, especially when Llewellyn accompanied me, not as a silent visitor but as an extra set of eyes. Soon enough, he grew deeply interested planting trout into a natural habitat, a positive move, that soon led him to investigate the impact of other species introduced into an environment with less desirable results. His first interest in the abuses of factory farming had spread to a wide range of concerns from chemical insecticides to animals still used unnecessarily in lab experiments. "Life in all its forms is one great tapestry," he said. "If you pull out one thread, it will eventually unravel."

"Right down to the insects?" I teased.

"Right down to the insects," he said. "Humans don't get along well with the cycles of life on this planet. We have the science to know better." His extra set of eyes saw so much farther than mine. Before long, he knew as many lakes and streams as I did and imagined the planted trout growing in the wild as if he had hatched them himself.

In my spare time, I also helped him with student papers and his own research reports. We knew each other's strengths and weaknesses. I knew all about clarity and conciseness with the written word.

"You're my right hand," Llewellyn said one evening after I had edited his latest article.

"Maybe you're left."

"Don't get conceited. I'm left-handed."

When Mother called one day and asked us to dinner the following evening, saying that William would like to see us again, I was too surprised to do anything but accept. "I can call her back and say I have to be out of town," I said to Llewellyn after I hung up. "Or you have to be out of town. Or both of us have to be out of town."

"The female of the species are difficult to understand," Llewellyn said. "Neither one of us are going to be out of town. We'll go to dinner."

Of course, dinner with Mother was quite the same as it had ever been, although William now sat at the head of the table. Llewellyn and I sat opposite Mother, me in my usual spot, Llewellyn to my right, which caused our arms to collide until I insisted we change positions.

"I don't wish to admit discord, Sabrina," Mother said. "Why must you always be oppositional?"

"Llewellyn is left-handed," I said.

Mother looked at me, puzzled, but William laughed. "I remember those days back at Exeter sitting on the wrong side of a leftie."

"I didn't know," Mother said. "There is so much we don't know about you, Llewellyn. But we were happy to hear of your position at Michigan State."

"How is that going?" William asked.

"It's a lot different than helping a cow calf."

Mother gasped and Llewellyn turned scarlet at his breach of polite table conversation, but William again took away Mother's edge with a laugh. "I bet," he said. "I've heard that you have quite a following at Moo College."

Llewellyn's flush deepened. "I don't know if it's exactly a following," he said.

William acted more like the teasing brother I once knew. Was it his way of forgiving me for inviting the daughter of my father's enemy to our wedding? His forgiveness because of Llewellyn's 'following'? Or were my conjectures about his motives my left-over feelings now that William sat in the seat Father had once occupied?

The rest of dinner, we spent catching up on life since the wedding. In spite of the excited after-wedding gossip, William's practice flourished. Mother, on the other hand, looked shriveled. In spite of her impeccable dress and makeup, she couldn't hide her body, once slim, now almost skeletal, or the vague look in her eyes. After her first reprimand at my change of seats, she added little to the conversation and when she did, it usually prefaced with 'your father said' or 'your father would have wanted'. Shortly after dinner, she excused herself and left to go lie down without eating more than a spoonful of her parfait.

Llewellyn looked at me and I could see in his eyes the same alarm that I felt at her changed appearance since the wedding. Evidently, William saw the look too. "I have a favor to ask of you," he said. "Mother insists we go Windsong next month, and she's so frail, I'm not comfortable about taking her there by myself."

"Is she seeing a physician?" Llewellyn asked.

"Yes," William said but I heard a note of uncertainty in his voice.

"What's the matter with her?" I demanded. "She looks like she's aged thirty years."

"She assured me her doctor says she's fine—just a little underweight. And before you ask, she insists on her privacy, and I haven't been able to talk to her doctor myself."

We went to Windsong on July 15th, the date Mother still insisted upon, even though Llewellyn would have to drive up later, since he had a seminar scheduled through the first two weeks of our departure. Despite Mother's frailty, she weathered the trip well and even talked more than usual about all the other trips we had taken, although I noticed that some of her recollections were out of order and some events I didn't recognize at all. William had never starred in a Shakespearean play in town, and I had never been asked to submit my notebooks to a local publisher. "I guess I did the right thing leaving Windsong to marry your father," she said. "You children were very fortunate for what you had."

"Did you want to leave Windsong?" I asked.

"Oh, I had to, you know." She fluttered her hand as if it was a question not worth asking.

"Why?"

She looked at William with a startled expression as if someone had just pulled her out of a dream. "It was the best way," she said vaguely and lapsed into silence. William's eyes met mine in the rear-view mirror, and he raised his shoulders in a small shrug that silently said, "It is what it is, Little Sister."

In spite of my concern at Mother's strange stories, I had faith in the restorative energy the trip would have for her. If she thought leaving Windsong was the best thing, she still came back every summer to the comfort of Aunt Hetty and Uncle Lew's quiet kindness. But when we arrived, Aunt Hetty and

182

Uncle Lew looked as alarmed as Llewellyn and I had been. Nevertheless, Aunt Hetty cooked her usual best and distracted Mother with local gossip. Unlike our visits to Windsong in the last few years, both William and I stayed the whole time and Aunt Hetty seemed relieved we were there.

When Llewellyn arrived, I took him to all my favorite haunts. We hiked through woods, we splashed through swamps and came back to the house as disheveled as I had once been when I was ten years old. "I don't care if you did come from the East," Aunt Hetty said to Llewellyn. "Sabrina found the right man."

"I found the right woman," he said. "And I don't care if she didn't come from back East."

Uncle Lew laughed. "Then I guess you like bugs and flowers."

"As much as you do," Llewellyn said. He had seen Uncle Lew's collection in his work shed from back in the days when he wanted to make sure I hadn't lost my way.

Uncle Basil came for dinner a time or two, but he seemed less enthusiastic about Llewellyn. "Too smart for his own good," I heard him grumble to Uncle Lew. "I bet he questions the beginning of mankind."

"Sometimes I'm tempted to question it myself," Uncle Lew said.

William and I watched for every sign of improvement in Mother. She talked more. She ate more. She listened to Uncle Basil's stories about his ex-wife's long-lost brother with more compassion. Didn't her eyes look less washed out and vague? Even as we compared notes about perceived flashes of improvement, Aunt Hetty dashed our conjectures toward the end of our stay. "She's dying," Aunt Hetty said. "You two have to deal with that. I don't care what she told you her doctor says, she's putting up a smoke screen."

"She could do that," Uncle Lew said. "That was how she got through."

Aunt Hetty frowned at him

"I'm just saying," Uncle Lew said. "She made sure you kids were all right."

"I won't believe it," William said, but his voice sounded strangled. "Mother has always been fragile. Windsong has been good for her."

Although I wanted to agree with William, Llewellyn had already told me that he saw little improvement during Mother's stay.

"When you take her back, insist on talking to her doctor," Aunt Hetty commanded, "even if you have to threaten him within an inch of his life."

Twenty-Three

When we got back home, I lost no time invading the privacy that Mother insisted William honor. I found the day of her next appointment, and William and I showed up in the waiting room before she even sat down. "What are you children doing here?" she demanded, as if we had just walked into one of Father's dinner parties with shorts and tee shirts, but she kept the anger in her voice low.

"It's time we have a family conference with your doctor," I said, matching her low tone. "We aren't going to leave."

"Please"—William said and I figured he worried about me causing a scene as much as Mother did.

"I will never forgive you for this," she hissed and turned on her heel and took a seat on the far side of the room but we took seats beside her. Thankfully, our stiff waiting-room silence only lasted a few minutes before the nurse called Mother's name. We trailed behind her, and the nurse looked at Mother in surprise, but Mother said nothing and neither did the nurse.

When the doctor came in and saw us crowded in the small exam room, she looked more relieved than surprised. I had pictured Mother's doctor to be an elderly, patrician gentleman that would fit well into one of Father's gatherings, looking over his eye glasses to deliver ponderous lectures to any hapless guest who circled into his orbit. Dr. Lee, a young Chinese woman, came up to William's armpits in height and wore loafers and a smock with an oriental calligraphy pattern. When Mother stiffly introduced us, Doctor Lee held out a hand unusually large for such a small woman.

"I am so glad you have come," she said. "This is not comfortable. We will go to my office where we can all be seated."

We relocated to her office, more spacious but with little more adornment than the exam room offered A framed photo of an elderly woman hung on the wall with her certificates and the erect posture and regal tilt to her head bespoke confidence and authority. The woman was no doubt Dr. Lee's mentor and inspiration, probably Dr. Lee's mother.

Dr. Lee said to Mother, "I am happy that you have brought your son and daughter into our conversation on your well being."

"They are here against my wishes," Mother said stiffly.

"I see." Doctor Lee said. I felt sorry for her as she looked at us with both compassion and resignation in her eyes. She could say no more without Mother's permission and evidently she knew Mother's position.

"We came here today because we are both very worried about Mother," William said. "I've asked her for your diagnosis and she says she's a little underweight."

"Your mother needs to gain thirty pounds for a woman of her age and height," Doctor Lee agreed. She had just emphasized that Mother was much more than a little underweight.

"Why has she lost all this weight?" I confronted the doctor.

Doctor Lee looked at Mother. "Shall I continue, Elizabeth?"

"You may," Mother said as if at a party accepting a refill of her champagne glass. I might never be forgiven, but William and I would know the answer to our past weeks of anxiety.

Mother's untreated cancer had spread since Doctor Lee's diagnosis months ago. When I told Llewellyn the devastating news that evening, he agreed with Doctor Lee's advice that the major intervention William and I wanted for Mother was too late. He put his arms around me. "She didn't want to go through cancer treatment when Doctor Lee advised it," he said. "That was her choice. Get hospice in. They will help her die in peace."

"Why couldn't she tell us?" I cried. "Why would she live with that awful secret for months?"

Llewellyn took me in his arms. "From what I've seen, she's lived with more secrets than that one."

Since Father's death, I had been more concerned with Mother as stricken with obsessive grief than a mask for secrets. "What do you mean?" I said, but I already knew that Llewellyn had seen farther into the distance Mother had always kept.

"Just a feeling when we went to Windsong"-- his voice trailed off. "Right now, you've got more important things to do for your mother."

We didn't have long to do those important things. Mother insisted that the bed Hospice brought in be installed in her upstairs bedroom and in an unexpected turn, she asked for Aunt Hetty after all the years when Aunt Hetty hadn't been invited to our home. Even for my wedding, she and Uncle Lew stayed at the hotel Mother reserved for out-of-town guests.

"William died in a car accident," Mother cried when Aunt Hetty came to her bedside. "That's all it was, wasn't it?"

"An accident," Aunt Hetty said. "It's over Beth. Now rest."

"None of this would have happened if William hadn't come to Clareburn."

"Hush now. I'm here. You rest."

After Mother's frantic greeting, she said little, and Aunt Hetty took over like a one-woman hospice. She bathed her, drenched her parched lips with water, slathered her with lotions, changed her sheets and sat mute at her bedside after she lulled Mother to sleep. William and I crept in and ordered Aunt Hetty to rest, but she could not be persuaded to leave Mother's bedside for more than a few scant hours, and she was there with William and me when Mother took her last breath two months later.

We all stood transfixed as the hospice nurse called the doctor, the undertaker and whisked away the pain killers that one of us had to witness as she flushed them down the toilet. She took over the awful details of death that we were too numb to handle. None of us cried. I don't thing we had any tears left.

Aunt Hetty was the first to urge us out of the room. "Your mother would want some privacy with the rest," she said, "She's already way beyond what we can do for her now."

"Funeral arrangements," William choked. "I couldn't bear to talk to her about it."

"She knew that. She arranged to be laid to rest in Clareburn. Your Uncle Basil will do the rituals."

"But Father's grave site is here!"

Aunt Hetty put an arm around him. "I can only tell you the written instructions she left with Basil her last time at Windsong."

Mother's last wishes did not come to me as the thunderbolt surprise that hit William. I had heard Mother's last words to Aunt Hetty and I expected Mother to leave us with unanswered questions. Her choice to be buried miles away from Father was her last. Although neither of us disputed the unusual arrangement Mother had requested, we insisted on a closed casket. No one needed to see the ravages of the delicate beauty Mother had once been. Aunt Hetty objected to our decision. "Everyone will wonder what you have chosen to hide."

"You said Mother would want her privacy," William said, "and I'm sure she would not like an open casket. We will keep Mother's dignity." I admired William more in that moment than I had since our early days when he comforted me after my pajama episode, when he found Nanny Bickel, and when he got me to Windsong after my tutor standoff with Frances Wilkinson. I didn't add that I too wondered what Mother had chosen to hide.

"I hope he'll be okay when it's over," Llewellyn said. "Right now, he's running on man-of-the-family duty. That takes

William a long way." Throughout the last months, Llewellyn had listened to me, comforted me and even did some of my computer work. I ached for William, who did not have an arm of love holding him up like I had. Man of the family in an empty house echoing with memories would hold no warmth.

Twenty-Four

The funeral offered us little comfort in Uncle Basil's church, a rented hall that had once belonged to the Veterans of Foreign Wars. Despite a mild October day, the place was chilly and Uncle Basil's service, in a departure from his recent mellow demeanor at Windsong, thundered the hell fires of damnation that would afflict those who chose wayward living. He seldom mentioned the prospect of peace for the departed.

Mother's final resting place in Clareburn was in a cemetery that looked as if it had been there since the first voyageurs arrived. Many of the headstones dated back a hundred years, some so overgrown with lichen and moss, it proved impossible to read the names of the people they were meant to remember. A memorial at the cemetery's entrance stood more imposing than the rest for a Clara Burns that I later found had given the town its name.

After Basil's final words at the grave site, Borg came up and hugged William and me like a long-lost brother. "Don't mind Father's fire and brimstone," he said. "That always comes out when he's taking things hard. He didn't like that closed casket, and he wanted to impress us heathens with what's in store if we don't mend our ways."

Uncle Basil could have taken into account others who also took things hard, but I was too surprised at Borg's reappearance to frame a caustic reply.

"The closed casket was Mother's wishes," William said, something neither of us knew to be true. "I'm sorry if Uncle Basil couldn't accept that."

Back at the church, the funeral luncheon was a full-scale dinner of ham, baked beans, sausage and sauerkraut, a bounty of side dishes and a dozen different pies for dessert. I wondered if half the mourners that filled the church came for the October feast that wafted alluring aromas through the congregation as Uncle Basil commended Mother to eternal rest.

Borg sat with us through the meal. His work out west came to an abrupt end when he got in a fist fight with his ranch boss. Then he worked for a trucking company until they found out he didn't have a license to drive eighteen wheelers. "I don't know what all that fuss was about," Borg said. "It's just like driving a very big car when you're going down the road. A little trickier when you're backing up though."

"What are you doing now?" Llewellyn asked. I noticed that he had been silently taking Borg's measure throughout the meal. Uncle Lew and Aunt Hetty had left the table and Borg's stories to talk to friends and neighbors. Neither seemed interested in eating, and I saw William didn't eat much either. It almost made me ashamed of my ravenous appetite. Would I be one of those people who appeared on talk shows, broke the scales at 300 pounds and confessed I ate to fill a void? That stupid thought filled my head and continued to circle around my head, so I never heard Borg's answer to Llewellyn's question, although I heard William's response.

"You can't be making much sorting nets. I could offer you more as a grounds keeper at Bloomfield Hills."

I think that's when I lost my appetite. To be honest, I had never outgrown my juvenile dislike for Borg, and I didn't see much in his recent history to change my attitude. What was William thinking?

"Eventually you could work into something more than a hand-to-mouth job," William went on. "There's all kinds of training schools for truck mechanics down below, anything you want."

Borg squared his wide shoulders. "I'm not a charity case just because my last jobs didn't work out."

"Of course not," William said. "I'm just offering you an opportunity. Cousin to cousin."

"Let me think on it," Borg said, "though I have to admit, cousin to cousin, it's the best offer that's come down the creek in quite awhile."

On our way back home, I argued, beseeched and begged William to think about his offer to Borg. "He would fit in as a grounds keeper like you would fit in mending nets. It can't work, William. You must have seen that."

"He hasn't even taken up my offer yet," William said. "I know you've never liked Borg, Sabrina, but I know him better than you do. He's had some bad breaks, but he's our cousin. I'm just offering him a chance at a better life than any he'll ever have in Clareburn."

Llewellyn squeezed my hand and I dropped my arguments. That evening Llewellyn said, "William must have felt he could fix something when he couldn't fix the unfixable."

I accepted the explanation and reasoned that neither William nor Borg would pursue an impulsive offer made in a moment of funeral stress.

Twenty-Five

Three weeks later I went back to Windsong when Mother's head stone was set and I went alone. "Wait until I can go with you," Llewellyn objected.

"I have the time now. It'll just be a long weekend."

Llewellyn frowned.

"Sometimes my road trips for work are longer."

"This is different."

"I know you want to point out the absurdity of driving across the state to see a polished piece of granite that will be there long after we're both gone."

"I don't want you alone."

"I won't be alone. I'll take Aunt Hetty to the cemetery with me." I didn't know how to explain how I needed to feel Mother truly put to rest, alone and separated from Father that kept her like a flower in a crystal vase. I should have known better than to think a block of carved and polished granite would give me that assurance, but the reality of her last wishes had not yet settled in my mind.

"Your mother's life with all your unanswered questions is gone, Sabrina. That's how she wanted it."

"You know me too well. I can't stand unanswered questions."

He hugged me. "Only in algebra. Call the minute you get there."

The drive to Windsong proved desolate and sullen after the beautiful colors of autumn had fallen from the trees after Mother's funeral. I stopped at the rest stop on Highway 2 that I remembered from our trips with Father, a necessity for using the restroom, but I didn't go to the shore line of Lake Michigan as William and I always did. I had already seen that the lake looked as gray as the sky. When I drove through Munising, dusk had already fallen but I didn't stop. Clareburn was not far. Windsong was not far. I only wanted the trip over.

"What on earth are you doing at Windsong!' Aunt Hetty said when I called her the next morning. After an uncomfortable night in a chilly bedroom with a small electric heater and no morning coffee, I could understand her point.

"I came to see Mother's head stone," I said.

"Oh for god sakes!'

"And I want you to come with me."

"You could have waited until summer."

"That's what Llewellyn said. This afternoon?"

After I went to Millie's Diner for breakfast and several cups of coffee, I picked up Aunt Hetty at one. The sun shone without much warmth, but the naked trees looked a little less dark on our drive to the cemetery.

"I saw to it the stone was set right without you driving up here," Aunt Hetty said as we got out of the car.

"I know, Aunt Hetty," I said. "It's just something I had to see for myself."

Mother's grave still looked like a raw wound surrounded by the serene grassy plots nearby, and my heart lurched. Maybe this trip was as mistaken as Llewellyn thought it would be. The simple head stone sat firmly anchored on a cement base, simply embellished with an adornment of ferns and the words, 'Elisabeth Denham'—

"The fools! Her name was spelled with a 'z'!" I exclaimed.

"It was," Aunt Hetty said but she didn't seem as indignant as I was. "Great-aunt Elizabeth's name was spelled with a z."

"It has to be fixed."

Aunt Hetty gazed down at the head stone and smiled a little. "Your mother never liked her name with a z. We called her Lizard, we called her Lizzie, even Liz. She was finally okay with Beth."

I thought about the time Llewellyn looked up names and their origins. "You and Mother were named for great aunts. My father and my brother were named for Grandfather Denham. I'm the only one in the family who doesn't have a namesake."

"You were named after your mother's imaginary friend. When we were kids, she went to that big oak tree where Sabrina supposedly lived and jabbered at her for hours."

I knew that oak tree well. I never had an imaginary friend living there, but I sat under it when angry, sad or happy. My eyes misted over. My mother once took refuge under that tree just as I did.

"She loved this place more than she ever loved Bloomfield Hills," Aunt Hetty said in a moment of candor. "I think that's why she wanted to be here at the end."

Aunt Hetty's words comforted me more than the misspelled grave stone, but on the way back to East Lansing, I had to pull over and cry as I never had in those long weeks before her death or at her funeral.

Twenty-Six

The following weeks cart-wheeled around getting back to 'normal', stitching up the hole Mother left. In spite of her silent withdrawal through much of my life, I felt her absence more keenly than I had ever felt Father's. Father's death filled me with guilt that I had not measured up to what he wanted for me. With Mother, so many other things had been left unsaid.

I worried about Llewellyn's prediction that after Mother's caretaking, William's grief might crash over him, but he seemed genuinely glad for my phone calls and finally invited us to dinner. I could not refuse, even though I knew that dinner in that huge dining room, echoing with memories, would rip open the pain of those last months with Mother.

"If it's too soon, we could meet William for dinner somewhere else," Llewellyn suggested.

"Better sooner than later," I said. Our warm bed seemed an island of refuge away from the 'sooner or later'. I kissed him. "Thank you for understanding."

"Maybe I don't. I never went back home after Mother died."

"But you must have missed your mother."

"I missed having a mother who wasn't always trying to improve me. Jacklyn, that's what she preferred to be called, could bend a steel rod with her will, and she willed that both Wendy and I would be the best, better than all her socialite friends' offspring. She and my father were a well-matched pair."

"I didn't know," I said. "She sounds a lot like my father."

"In the long-term outcome, she pulled all the strings when she realized I would be a failure as a business magnate and did her best at damage control. I have her to thank for getting me into Penbrook. But I never fit at home. I guess we were both looking for the mothers that our mothers could never be."

I had never thought of Mother in quite that way before, but Llewellyn's point struck home. I was always asking Mother for more than she could give.

"But I miss Wendy," Llewellyn went on. "Even though Wendy proved to be the star child, she looked after me in her own way, something like William did with you. I got a call from her shortly after our wedding. She said she realized that day she had bought into being what Father demanded and said she was glad that I hadn't. She moved to New York and she's living with an artist."

"So now your father never wants to see her again either."

"You'd think so, but instead he kept calling her, begging her to come back until she got her phone number changed."

I put my arms around him. "I'm so sorry. I've been wallowing in my family problems. You've been there for me, and I haven't been there for you at all. I didn't even know she kept in touch with you."

Llewellyn twined his legs around me. "You were the best thing that ever happened to me. Wendy's news came out of left field and I didn't say anything because I didn't know if it would last, but she's still in New York and she says she's happy. In spite of our parents, you had William and I had Wendy, but our lives have shifted, and you and William's lives are shifting too."

"Wendy's choice makes more sense. William should dump that mausoleum. He doesn't need three stories of rooms and two acres of grounds to live in."

"I don't think that's going to happen yet," Llewellyn murmured, "He's still holding on." He kissed me then and both of us forgot about our shifting lives.

However, when we arrived at William's for dinner the following evening, Llewellyn's words about shifting lives jumped into focus. William had neglected to warn me that he hired Borg as groundskeeper, replacing Carson, who left when he reached the age of Social Security. At the very least, William had not sent him out the door to make way for Borg.

But that was the very least. Borg joined us for dinner in a shirt and sweat pants that looked as if he dragged them out of a laundry bag. I had never liked our formal dinner dress code, but Borg's appearance seemed a slap in the face to good manners. Surely, he still had the shirt and slacks he wore at Mother's funeral. More upsetting, he hugged William when he came in and put a hand over William's whenever he made an important point in his monologue about all the improvements to the grounds since he arrived. Borg made it obvious that his position at Bloomfield was much more than a grounds keeper.

When I looked at William, he chose to ignore me during Borg's recital and after dinner invited us to walk the grounds to inspect Borg's handiwork. From what I gathered, Borg had added dormant indigenous plants that would blossom next spring and transform the gardens into a showcase of Michigan plant life, an idea I would have loved if it I could believe Borg's extravagant claims. Nothing much could be seen past the after-dark lights, and a cold, November rain pelted us before we returned to the house.

"This would be snow up to my nuts if we were in Clareburn," Borg said.

"There's a lady present." Llewellyn's voice was as cold as the November rain.

Borg made an exaggerated bow. "Pardon me, Cousin Sabrina," he said.

"I think it's time we leave," I said.

"Don't go, Sabrina," Borg said. "I'm not too good at proper manners yet. I still talk like where I come from."

Llewellyn took my arm. "Thank you for dinner, William," he said. "But as Sabrina said, it's time we leave. This rain may turn to ice."

Llewellyn knew it wouldn't. The forecast promised to stay in the low forties all evening. William probably also knew, but he agreed with Llewellyn and we left while Borg was still bemoaning Clareburn's weather in November.

"What is happening?" I finally broke our stricken silence on the way back to East Lansing.

"Your brother and Borg are in a relationship," Llewellyn said, "Maybe going back to the Windsong year you told me about."

I started crying. "I wanted William to have somebody to love, but Borg!"—

Llewellyn took my hand. "Borg put on a display for our benefit. William wanted to admit his relationship to us, but I don't think he expected the way Borg chose to announce it."

"But how can William care for such a Neanderthal?"

"Don't insult the Neanderthals," Llewellyn said and squeezed my hand. "My guess is that Borg's very difference freed up William after all his years of being locked into what he was expected to be."

I remembered William's early interest in Shakespeare and the stories he wrote in his journal. "Then he should have a writer or an actor for a partner," I said.

"This is his first love, as far as you know," Llewellyn said. "It may not last."

Twenty-Seven

Two days later Wendy called Llewellyn and told him that she and her artist friend would be in East Lansing the next day for an art show and conference.

"You have to invite them to stay here," I said. Our apartment had an extra room, although we used it as an office space instead of a guest bedroom. We had never had overnight guests before.

"How will we do that?"

"I'm thinking they don't have a king-size bed in a New York apartment unless Wendy's lover is another Andy Warhol. Go get a couple of the best inflatable mattresses you can find and I'll get extra bedding."

"What if they're vegetarian? Or gluten free? We've been so different. I don't know how she lives." Llewellyn was as flustered as I had ever seen him.

"I'll pick up some green stuff. She's your sister and she wants to see you. That's all that matters."

"The female of the species are difficult to understand but maybe you're right." He kissed me. "Anyway, you're the best thing that ever happened to a cow doctor."

"You're the best thing that ever happened to a gal who chases fish. Now get going—inflatable mattresses."

In spite of my brave words, I didn't admit to Llewellyn my own inside quivers. I only met Wendy once at our wedding and she looked the proper heiress who had never seen an inflatable mattress stuffed in a room with desks and book shelves. Even if she had moved out of Jackson McDermott's orbit, after seeing our makeshift accommodations she might think, like her father, that Llewellyn made a very bad choice. We'll manage, I scolded myself as I picked up bedding and groceries. How long could an artist show and conference be?

By the time Wendy and her friend, Fulton Donovan, arrived, we were as prepared as we could be for house guests. Wendy looked as fit and stylish as she had at our wedding, but her casual slacks and corduroy jacket reassured me that she did not expect a formal reception.

"We couldn't come to Michigan without seeing you two." She hugged us both, then turned to me. "I heard about your mother. I'm sorry."

"Thank you. We're glad you're here."

They stayed for three days but my concern over the living arrangements soon faded. Both left shortly after breakfast and didn't come back until evening. They ate salads and steaks as well as bacon and eggs and slept on the inflatable mattresses without comment. It would have been a good reunion for Llewellyn and Wendy except for Fulton's habits more disturbing than where to sleep or what to eat. He used cocaine and didn't hide it from us.

"His little tic," Wendy said. Lots of people we know do something."

I didn't want to rock the boat, so I said nothing. In those brief days, I had learned to like the big sister that Llewellyn knew. She quizzed him, teased him and lectured him on everything from college politics to proper exercise.

"You take care of my baby brother," she said when they were leaving. "He gets too intense."

Llewellyn said, "Look who's talking."

She hugged us. "I'm so happy. I'm not Daddy's little girl with all that gymnastic stuff. Thanks to Fulton, I've taken up watercolors. What would Daddy think of that?"

"It's almost as bad as being a veterinarian," Llewellyn said and Fulton laughed and clapped him on the shoulder.

"Way too intense," he said. "You gotta just let life happen."

After they left, I said, "I like Wendy, but she doesn't need to be with someone with his little tic."

"I think this is Wendy's first big love," Llewellyn said, "but she's always had her head screwed on straight. It might not last."

I hoped Llewellyn was right, but I always thought William had his head screwed on straight. Llewellyn had said our lives had shifted and if Wendy was happy, if William was happy, I had no reason to believe that the shifts were tectonic plates that would cause earthquakes, but I couldn't help but feel earth tremors, and I saw in Llewellyn's eyes that he felt them too.

Twenty-Eight

Not long after Wendy's visit, William called and asked me to lunch. "Anywhere you name. Even Sam's Pizza and Grill we did back in the day."

"It's closed," I said. "I'll meet you at Delaney's Bistro." I guessed he wanted to apologize for Borg's behavior, but I didn't look forward to a second-hand apology.

"Good choice," William said when we met the next day.

"The only place I knew in the vicinity of your office," I said. "I 've had a few luncheon meetings here with my supervisor so I know the food's good."

Delaney's flavored their menu with Detroit's music, the Detroit Tigers, and the food of the men who had assembled the sleek cars Detroit once produced. The menu offered a taste of soul food, cuisine of the immigrant labor force that once kept the city humming and hot dogs and beer for Detroit Tiger fans.

William gazed at a framed and autographed picture of Marvin Gaye that hung over our corner booth. "This place is a food trip through Detroit's history."

I picked up the menu, determined not be sidetracked from our reason for being here. "I'm going to have Stanislaw's sausage and sauerkraut," I said, opting for the labor force menu.

"No pizza?" he teased

"I never liked the peppers you insisted on ordering," I said

William studied the menu. "I guess a Tigers hot dog and beer," he finally said.

"Does Cook have hot dogs on the Bloomfield menu now? Maybe sloppy joes?"

It was a preemptive slap at Borg, and I regretted my words as soon as I said them. William had never criticized my choice of Llewellyn, even though Llewellyn's outspoken stand on factory farming and chemical insecticides had earned him as many enemies as allies. In an op-ed page in last week's news that decried Llewellyn's movement against 'progressive' farming, William's connection to Llewellyn was mentioned. My relationship with Llewellyn affected William's life more than his relationship with Borg had affected mine.

"Sorry," I said. "Borg is none of my business."

"He tried too hard to impress you and Llewellyn that he worked hard on his job."

William knew very well that was not the only thing Borg impressed on us. "Just to set things straight, William, it's not the gender of your partner I object to. It's his character."

"I know you've never liked Borg, but there's a side of him you don't know. He played the fool the other night, but that's what I love about him. He keeps me from taking everything too seriously, and he knows more about what grows in Michigan than I ever knew."

"I have to admit, serious has always been one of your flaws," I said. "I'll try my best to be civil to him."

A black waitress appeared, dressed like a backup singer for Diana Ross. Other wait staff dressed in Tigers uniforms or factory workers' garb. Our waitress was supposed to urge us to soul food, just as the Tigers waiters urged patrons to hot dogs and beer, but she must have picked up on the sparks between William and me and only raised her eyebrows when she took our order.

"Whatever you think of my relationship with Borg, that's not why I needed to talk with you," William said after Diana Ross left. "Mother's attorney called. We need to settle the estate."

"Oh," I said. Unlikely as it seemed, I hadn't thought much about the estate.

William smiled. "Unfortunately, you will now have to navigate money matters past sorting your earnings into envelopes. Mother's attorney wants to meet with us, but I can already tell you Mother left all her assets to be divided between us. I don't have a dollar amount, but that means both Bloomfield Hills and Windsong will be sold and divided, as well as anything in her bank accounts."

"Windsong sold!" I exclaimed.

"It's part of the estate," William said. "Father bought it some years ago."

"William, we can't sell Windsong!"

William's eyes shifted up to Marvin Gaye. "Borg thought it might be better if we would," he said.

"Borg!" I cried. "Windsong was Mother and Aunt Hetty's home. It was Borg's father's home. What is he thinking? What are you thinking?"

"We only use the place six weeks out of a year, and the place needs a new roof, the washer died last summer"—

"William, you are living in a place with more rooms than you ever see, three workers paid year around and two acres of ground you probably haven't walked across since you've been there."

"I guessed you would say as much," William said.

"And I especially resent Borg telling you what we should be doing with Windsong."

Our lunches came, but I had lost my appetite. In spite of William's words, I couldn't comprehend his relationship with Borg unless Borg was William's Shakespearean Falstaff. Shakespeare's plays may have a way of echoing real life, but Borg's eagerness for us to give up Windsong would put a wedge between William and me as well as the rest of our family in the Upper Peninsula. Borg was only thinking of himself and his new-found position as far away from Clareburn as he could get.

"He probably thinks you should hold on to his place in Bloomfield Hills too," I said.

William threw down his napkin and got up. "We haven't discussed it, Sabrina. Our appointment with Mother's attorney is next Wednesday, and I hope we can come to an equitable agreement without histrionics."

He left before I could reply, but I didn't have a reply anyway.

Twenty-Nine

In spite of William's parting words at Delaney's lunch and Borg's objections, I bought Windsong from part of my share of the estate, and we agreed to put Bloomfield Hills up for sale without histrionics. Even though William had an attachment to it, he was too smart with dollars and cents to keep a place that size, but Borg would no longer have a job. Not one of us was happy with the final settlement, Borg least of all. From what I gathered, Borg thought William had enough money to buy out my share and keep Bloomfield Hills.

In spite of William's invitation to Borg to move with him to a condo, their relationship soured in the following months before the place sold and by spring Borg went back to Clareburn. "The ill-begotten gains of the father will rain hell and brimstone down on his offspring," Borg roared before he broke a few pieces of furniture and left.

"So much for William's claim that Borg lightened things up," I said to Llewellyn. "He sounds like his father." But I saw that Borg's comments about ill-gotten gains had hurt William deeply. Although both of us had chafed under Father's rules, neither one of us had ever believed him dishonest. "Borg was the one after ill-gotten gains wanting to live at Bloomfield Hills with William."

"He could have lived with him in the condo."

"Like a caged gorilla," I muttered.

"William will move on and so will Borg in his own way. Meanwhile, you're the proud owner of Windsong."

"More confused than proud. I've never been the owner of anything in my life, other than the car Mother bought for me and the clothes on my back. I have no idea what comes next."

"We move there," Llewellyn said. "Michigan State is unlikely to renew my contract. They're downsizing theoretical biology."

"Llewellyn!" I cried.

"Not to worry," he said. "I think I already have a job lined up with the National Veterinarians for Health."

"You never told me!"

"I was waiting to have something definite to tell you. I'll be traveling a lot, but my home base can be anywhere. It may as well be at Windsong and you will be even closer to your job."

"We will not move to Windsong," I said. "You have established connections here. You have friends and colleagues. My acquisition of Windsong was a sentimental attachment. We will just keep it as a family cabin as it always was."

As if by some strange wheel of circumstance, two people I valued in my growing years reappeared early that summer to fuel Llewellyn's argument. Rita's letter came first.

"I don't do email .," she wrote, "but I heard of your mother's passing and wanted to be with you. Unfortunately, Aunt Zelda would have none of it this time. I never told you how she dragged her feet when I insisted we come to your wedding. This time she was adamant that my appearance would only cause more hurt than help.

But now Aunt Zelda crossed over as well, and I have to do what I think I should have done in the first place. Aunt Zelda told me the enmity between our fathers had nothing to do with the court case. My father found out something about your father and wanted to get back at him, but never had a chance to say what he had found out. She feared our appearance would stir up old questions and she worried you asked too many questions. But at the end, she wanted me to warn you to let sleeping ghosts lie.

I kept silent for so long. This is all conjecture, but lately my bones (or Aunt Zelda's ghost) have been nudging me to deliver Aunt Zelda's warning.

You are always on my mind and in my memories."

I cried over Rita's letter. Aunt Zelda had given me what I needed to sketch my notebook entries that were just now being considered for a children's book. More than that, she had given Rita and me a warm spot in our young years and gave Rita an avenue to do the art she had always loved.

I didn't want to believe Aunt Zelda's words of warning, but I remembered the day at Windsong when Aunt Hetty had laughed at the stranger in town that pretended to be a fisherman and Mother's unusual curiosity about him. I tried to reason it was nothing but Mother's boredom, but I also remembered the stranger came to Clareburn the summer after Father had won the case against Rita's father. Rita's father had committed suicide before they had tracked him down after he had broken his bond. Let sleeping ghosts lie, Aunt Zelda had said, and I resolved to follow her advice and only remember the good times I had in her wonderful, disorderly studio.

Nanny Bickel's visit came second. She called me one evening to say she came to Detroit on family business and could we meet for lunch. I almost dropped the phone before I had the sense to suggest Delaney's Bistro the next day. We had exchanged a few letters through the years, but she had moved after her mother died, and I had moved more than once. Somewhere, we had lost contact.

"Aren't computers wonderful!" Nanny Bickel exclaimed after we hugged so long at Delaney's entrance that we blocked foot traffic. "When I got back to Michigan, I just had to see how you and William were doing."

"It's so good to see you, Nanny!"

She laughed. "I'm not Nanny anymore. In fact, I'm not even a nanny. I'm Jennifer."

She certainly didn't look like Nanny Bickel anymore. If it wasn't for the same small figure with the erect posture, I might not have recognized her in a light and flowery dress, quite different from the sober, solid colors that she used to wear. She no longer wore glasses over her gray-green eyes and her cropped hair had now grown to wavy shoulder-length.

"You look wonderful!" I said when we were seated in a booth at the back of the room.

"It's probably love," she said. "I'm also no longer Bickel. "I married Derek Ellis a year ago He gets better every day."

"That's wonderful!" I said again and thought maybe Nanny would reassert herself and ask if that was the only adjective I knew, but she only smiled and said, "It is wonderful. And you also married. I still pick up the news from the Michigan papers. Is your Llewellyn wonderful?"

"I think I loved him since Grant."

This time our server was a young, blonde boy in a Tigers uniform and, since both of us ordered a hot dog and beer, he didn't have to urge us to his specialty.

"I'm sorry about your mother," Nanny said. "It makes us orphans, doesn't it? No matter the age."

"Yes," I said.

"You have a man to stand beside you, but I worry about William. How is he doing?"

"We sold the place in Bloomfield Hills. He has a condo"—

"It hasn't been good for him, has it?" Nanny interrupted.

"No, it hasn't," I said. Our food arrived and I don't even remember eating it as I blurted out all the history that had happened since she had left.

"If only your parents would have done things differently," Nanny Bickel said when I finished. "Your mother knew about William's fascination with Borg. She knew about you and Rita's friendship when all that court stuff was happening. She never said a word to you and William, but she told your father every little thing. She just gave it all to him, as if she didn't dare do a thing herself."

"Why?"

She grasped my hand. "Always the questions. I don't know why, but I always thought it went back to something that happened at Windsong. She always insisted on going every year to Windsong, the only thing that she took upon herself."

"What do you mean?"

Nanny Bickel shrugged. "I have no idea what I mean almost as if she had to know what happened there every year. Your mother's position as your father's first lady came at a price. I don't think she was a happy woman the rest of the year." Nanny stopped. "I shouldn't have run my mouth, Sabrina," She picked up her purse.

"Don't leave!" I cried.

She leaned over and hugged me. "I've told you what I think and most of it is nothing more than my opinion, but I know you still have questions that will probably never have any answers. Some things are just best left to history."

"That's what Aunt Zelda said. That's what everybody says. I just want to know why Mother didn't have a life of her own. She wasn't like that when she was at Windsong."

"I worry about you. You can't be consumed by questions that can never have any answers even if you're the stone wall I always knew you were. Believe it or not, you've got a streak of your father in you." She bent over and hugged me. "Right now, I have an appointment with my niece. My brother, the one most like my father, passed, and my niece needs some help putting his affairs in order."

"I'm so sorry! I didn't know"--

"Not to be sorry, Sabrina. My brother was not a good man. I have some questions about my own family too, so I understand. If I don't find the answers, the questions will be lost to history. I just don't want you getting hurt asking your questions."

Llewellyn's job came through a week after my reunion with Nanny Bickel and three weeks after my letter from Rita. "We move to Windsong," he said. "You love the Upper Peninsula more than I love East Lansing, and we have to settle on a home of our own before we start a family."

"Start a family!"

"Don't you want to see how a little Llewellyn or a little Sabrina turn out?"

This time my objections wavered after Rita's letter and Nanny Bickel's visit. Somehow, the reason for my mother's sad life stemmed from Windsong.

Thirty

We moved to Windsong late that summer despite William's objections. "The place needs major renovations," he said. "And both of you are throwing away your careers to live in Siberia." The roof and washer did need to be replaced, but Uncle Lew lined up local workers who managed all that, and I had never considered turning Windsong into a shadow of our home in Bloomfield Hills. In spite of my new status as land owner, my job went on much as before—actually I was closer to my physical job than I had been in East Lansing, and my laptop took care of the rest. On the other hand, Llewellyn's new job took him away from Windsong much of the time but, as he reasoned, if we still lived in East Lansing, it would have been the same, and I knew better than to complain. I might be Llewellyn's first love, but his burning desire to right the problems in the world of human intersection with the world of biology came a close second.

I reassured William that our move to Windsong did not meet his dire predictions and urged him to come up, as he had in our younger years. "Not even July 15th to August 29th," I teased him. "Windsong is open all year around."

William made excuses and although he never said as much, I suspected Windsong had changed for him from a getaway to a tangled web of too many bad memories, and those memories had buried the good ones when he wrote stories and read Shakespeare.

Windsong had changed for me as well. Uncle Lew, my quiet ally, helped us with repairs Llewellyn couldn't do himself, but he didn't come around otherwise, and Aunt Hetty stayed away as if she had never known the place. She turned down invitations to dinner with flimsy excuses: She had a meeting, she had a cold, the roads were bad. "It isn't you," Uncle Lew offered one day. "This place reminds Hetty of your mother."

William's disastrous affair with Borg had also made him a victim of grief's repercussions, but shouldn't our shared grief bring the family closer together? Instead, my move to Windsong had driven a wedge into my family.

"We shouldn't have moved here," I said to Llewellyn on one of his fortunate weeks home. "I seem to be an albatross."

He smiled. "A huge seabird in the Southern Ocean. Of the 22 species, three are endangered"—

"Stop it," I said playfully slapping his head. "That's not what I'm saying."

"I know what you're saying, but you are not the harbinger of horrible things to come."

"It feels like I am." I had tried to connect with people in Clareburn. I joined a small book group the library held, I even joined a craft group at Uncle Basil's church, a humbling experience. I did much better drawing than making wreaths or potholders. The women acted polite, friendly, even helpful, but none invited me to lunch or to neighborhood bonfires. With my family ties to Windsong I felt I belonged here but evidently they didn't feel the same.

"People up here take a while to warm up," Llewellyn admitted. "Or maybe those questions your Nanny Bickel and Rita's Aunt Zelda warned you about might be the questions that somebody in Clareburn doesn't want you asking."

"I've never asked anyone questions except Uncle Lew and Aunt Hetty and they're family, but sometimes I think they're hoping I'll just go back to collecting insects for six weeks out of the year." I snuggled up to him. "Maybe I should do just that."

"You can't do that," Llewellyn said. "We've made this place our home and if you leave, you'll always have questions unanswered. Whatever your Aunt Hetty is avoiding here, I believe it's more than your mother's absence. If I'm right, it makes me worry about you when I'm not here."

"I don't feel threatened by what she's avoiding here, I just feel ignored. I guess I miss a warm body to talk to sometimes."

After Llewellyn left to conquer the world of biological disasters, I regretted my words. He didn't need a whiny partner trying to pin his wings to my sentimental memories of the Windsong I once knew. Llewellyn insisted we move because he knew I loved this place, but he had guessed right. Now that I came back, unanswered questions haunted me. If Mother had kept hidden something she knew, what did she know? Why had she cried to Aunt Hetty that nothing would have happened if Father hadn't been in Clareburn? When? Why? Why had she questioned Father's accident?

Against Aunt Zelda and Nanny's advice, I had to find answers before Windsong would truly be our home. I couldn't ask those questions of Aunt Hetty in Mother's last days, but I could ask Aunt Hetty now.

By November, I knew it wouldn't be long before snow would maroon Windsong between the winter blasts that kept the snow plows too busy to get down our road until they cleared the town. Llewellyn and I had stocked enough supplies and emergency equipment to survive a siege, and I traded in the car Mother had given me at graduation for a four-wheel drive, but even a four-wheel drive had its limits. Physically ready for an Upper Peninsula winter, possible days without human contact worried me. I needed to talk to Uncle Lew, to reconnect with Aunt Hetty, with Uncle Basil, even Borg. My family.

I went to Uncle Lew and Aunt Hetty's and banged on the door of their small gray-shingled house. From inside, their dog, Benjie, responded with frenzied barking but no one else appeared. Uncle Lew once told me that they should have named Benjie Killer. Evidently his German Shepherd heritage made him a fierce guard against all intruders. I didn't even try to open the door.

I went to the lumber yard where Uncle Lew worked, but he didn't work that afternoon. I questioned three people before their trucker told me to look in Billy's Bar and Grill. "He takes a half day every few weeks, and he and his wife hang out there for a couple of hours," the young man said, throwing a box into the truck. "The boss just lets him do it. I'd be fired."

The young man's words made no sense at all. Uncle Lew and Aunt Hetty at a bar? I went back to my car. Maybe I should just go to Uncle Basil's church, but the thought of running into

Borg drove me to Billy's Bar with more cars and trucks around it than any other place in town. I might meet half the people I had met at the book club or the craft workshop. Maybe Uncle Basil's church that was hosting a food basket giveaway made better sense, Borg notwithstanding.

In spite of my dithering, I walked into the only bar in Clareburn. Bruce Springsteen blared "Born in the USA" from wall speakers. No hip hop here. A drunken man came up and sang in my ear. I recognized Ingersoll, the fisherman that Borg once worked for, and a few husbands or brothers to the ladies I knew from the book club and craft workshop. Then I saw Uncle Lew and Aunt Hetty at a corner table and made a beeline to their table before Ingersoll could ask me to dance.

"What are you doing here?" Aunt Hetty demanded.

"I-I came to see how you were doing," I stammered.

Uncle Lew stood up and waved me to an empty chair. He signaled the bar tender. "We're doing fine," he said when I sat down. "I see you've met Clyde."

Aunt Hetty ignored Uncle Lew's attempt to make light of my unexpected appearance. "What are you doing here?" she repeated after I ordered a beer.

Her unexpected greeting sparked anger in me. "You haven't come to Windsong since I moved in."

Aunt Hetty waved her hand in an eerie resemblance of Mother's hand of dismissal. "I don't need to be at Windsong all the days of my life."

I thought of all those days when Aunt Hetty had taken care of Windsong and Mother's last days when Aunt Hetty had taken care of not only Mother, but William and me. Something didn't fit.

"But I'm at Windsong."

"It was always from July 15th to August 28th," Uncle Lew agreed. "Your father was firm on that point."

Aunt Hetty pointed a finger at him. "Sabrina doesn't need to hear"—

"I'm just saying what she already knows. Every year, July 15th to August 29th."

"I need you to tell me what Mother meant when she said my father's accident wouldn't have happened if he hadn't been in Clareburn."

"Beth met your father on July 15th right here in our fine city," Uncle Lew said.

"Lew"—

"I'm just saying Mr. William Denham the Second came up here one summer with a few of his buddies looking for fish or who knows what and met Beth. When his friends left, he stayed all summer chasing her like a lovesick dog. That's how it all started."

The thought of my stern father hanging around Clareburn and chasing a local girl posed such an odd, jagged picture, I could scarcely believe it. "Why Clareburn?" I could only think to ask.

"Such a simple thing," Aunt Hetty said. "He came up here to try his hand at fishing. It seems your Grandfather Denham had once been a pretty good fly fisherman in these parts. Your mother could have told you that much."

"I didn't know"—

"Most of your questions have simple answers," Aunt Hetty said sharply. "Just old history that doesn't mean anything."

I wasn't satisfied. "What did Mother mean when she asked if Father's accident was only an accident?"

Aunt Hetty stood up. "Exactly what she said. Your mother was very sick and she never got over your father's death. You know that."

"It seems she meant more."

"Leave your mother in peace. Come on Lew, we have to go."

"We're doing fine, Sabrina," Uncle Lew said and I could see he felt bad about Aunt Hetty's sharp words, but he said no more.

I finished my beer staring at the neon sign for Budweiser over the bar. Aunt Hetty's reaction at my appearance hurt me, but it confirmed Llewellyn's words that maybe her avoidance of Windsong tried to warn me away from my inquisitive nose. Let sleeping ghosts lie. Why leave my parents' history behind? Wasn't I part of that history? Wouldn't my children someday be another link in that chain of history? Perhaps the beer helped me decide to visit the food giveaway at Uncle Basil's church. Maybe he had more transparent answers.

I found Uncle Basil busily sorting cans and packages into sacks. Fortunately, Borg was nowhere in sight.

"What are you doing here?" Uncle Basil greeted me. It seemed to be a family greeting, at least where I was concerned.

"I was in town and just thought I'd drop in."

"Oh," Uncle Basil said. "That's nice."

On a sudden impulse, I said, "I thought you might be too busy to cook. Come up to Windsong for supper."

"That's very Christian of you, but I won't be done here until six." I guessed I had taken him by surprise and he couldn't find a better excuse to turn away a niece's hospitality with all those Christian ladies within earshot.

"That's fine," I said. "Do you need some help?"

"Thank you. We're fine."

When I left, rewarded with smiles from all those good ladies, as well as a coffee to go, although none who knew me from the craft club invited further conversation. I drove to the grocery store to pick up the makings for spaghetti and a salad. Uncle Basil would probably call later to cancel, and I would eat spaghetti and salad for the next three days.

Contrary to my pessimistic expectations, Uncle Basil arrived at six-thirty with a sack of leftover groceries from the food giveaway. "Got to be prepared for what's coming," he said. "You've never been through an Upper Peninsula winter. You really ought to move south."

I tried to reassure him by showing him the supplies Llewellyn and I had stocked, but when Uncle Basil sat down to dinner, he didn't seem impressed. "A Windsong winter is no place for you," he said. "And that man of yours. He's not around half the time. That's not right. A good Christian husband"—

I recognized a sermon coming on the duties of a Christian husband that would wilt the salad and mush the spaghetti. "Uncle Basil, did you know Uncle Lew and Aunt Hetty hang out at Billy's Bar every couple of weeks?" I interrupted him.

"Of course, I knew." He put a forkful of spaghetti in his mouth as if to block further conversation.

"Why?"

Uncle Basil glared at me. "Billy is Lew's brother. Hetty is my sister. My church is about the true word and Billy's church is a bar of idle gossip. They chose Billy's Bar."

"I'm sorry. I just never knew"—

"My sisters were a disappointment to me, Sabrina. Always whispering about my Deborah. After Deborah left me and I found my way, I tried to bring your mother and Hetty to the true path, but they stuck together like glue. Every July, here was your mother at Windsong. Every July, here was Hetty at Windsong like some kind of conspiracy."

"July 15th to August 29th," I supplied.

"Does that make any sense?" Uncle Basil flared. "Your father was a little obsessive, but every year? You could set the calendar."

"You didn't like my father?"

235

"Nobody in Clareburn liked your father. I wonder why your mother liked your father."

"I'm trying to find that out," I said.

"Some things are best left to the Lord. Borg's mother never found the answer to her brother's disappearance, and it made her crazy. I took in our boy when he didn't know where he would be from one day to the next."

We finished dinner with Uncle Basil asking so many questions about my preparations for the winter ahead, I had no chance to ask any of my own but when he got up to leave, he had a final admonition. "You need to stop searching and take the Lord's path Leave it His hands."

"Take home the rest of the spaghetti for you and Borg," I said.

"He's not living with me," Uncle Basil said.

That gave me a chance to ask, "Where is he?"

"I don't know. When he came back to Clareburn, he sorted nets for Ingersoll, but he wouldn't accept my invitation to live in a Christian home. I don't know where he went, now that the nets are pulled. Probably up to that shack he hid in when he was a kid."

I gave Uncle Basil the rest of the spaghetti anyway. In spite of that little nugget of information, I felt truly sorry for him. All his admonitions to me about being unprepared for winter were his worries for the only son he had living in a shack in the middle of an Upper Peninsula woods. From what I knew about Borg, he could survive a winter in the Arctic.

Thirty-One

Soon enough the November gales of Gitchee Gumee hit land with a force so hard, I thought Windsong, despite all our preparations, might be blown to pieces or buried under snow until spring. I secured all the shutters, rechecked the generator twice and, between storms, clambered up and shoveled snow off the newly-installed roof. With the shutters closed, days seemed endless nights. I did crossword puzzles, read half the books I had brought with me and sent emails to Llewellyn and every friend I had, but neither books nor electronic messages filled the hours. Maybe Uncle Basil knew how ill-equipped a girl raised in Bloomfield Hills was to live through an Upper Peninsula winter.

Before Christmas, Llewellyn followed the snowplow with his SUV filled with supplies and whimsical gifts that could only have come from Llewellyn—a first edition book of algebra, an 1800's guide to the insect world, a framed existential rendering of a question mark. I gave gifts to Llewellyn more practical: a pair of snowshoes, a woolen shirt and a parka I had seen online that claimed to withstand subzero temperatures.

In spite of our light-hearted reunion, Llewellyn wanted me to close Windsong for the winter. "I worry about you. Stay with William. Or we'll find an apartment. Windsong this time of year is not the summer Windsong."

I couldn't admit defeat. I had lived in St. Ignace over winter, but I didn't bring that up. A winter in St. Ignace suffered in comparison to Windsong. "We decided this would be home for a little Sabrina or Llewellyn someday. Will we take them away from their home for half the year, so they never belong here or anywhere else?"

"But we don't have a little Sabrina or Llewellyn yet."

"No. All I have are questions about their history."

Llewellyn made a face and stirred the chili, his only claim to culinary fame. "You know how to turn my own arguments back at me," he said.

"I'll be fine," I said. "After I get some answers to my questions, I wouldn't mind a little Southern sun."

"I think we'll be here for quite awhile," Llewellyn said.

I felt bad. I won the argument, but hadn't erased Llewellyn's worry, not all about the Upper Peninsula winter but at the questions I had. After the holidays, Llewellyn reluctantly left me to my stubborn ways with a hug and his sad observation that the female species were difficult to understand.

After he left on a bright January day, I ventured into town again, determined to make my time at Windsong more than a stubborn standoff from the difficult female of the species. Llewellyn deserved more than a worrisome albatross around his neck, a harbinger of danger because I couldn't stop asking questions of ghosts who only wanted quiet.

The lumber yard closed in January and Billy's Bar had only a few trucks sitting in its parking lot. I drove past Uncle Lew and Aunt Hetty's. Benjie was cavorting in the snow and I figured my appearance would be as welcome to the dog as a good bite of ham. Uncle Basil's house a block away from his church, which hadn't yet shed its VFW sign, looked occupied. His truck stood in the drive as well as another vehicle, but today I had no inclination to bang on my relatives' doors.

I picked up a few random groceries, mostly to gab with the gal at the check-out and then went to the Clareburn County Historical Museum, housed in an old one-room schoolhouse. In a streak of luck, the place, thanks to dedicated volunteer, Elaine Burns, stayed open every day from one to four. Her great-grandfather, Fulton Burns, founded the museum, a fact she shared that with me as soon as I stepped in the door. Evidently, I had been the only visitor in days of her vigil. She underlined the importance of the museum and its archives to the preservation of Clareburn's history. "We aren't computerized yet," she apologized. "I don't know how to work one of those things, and these young people leave the county before I can get any help."

After her effusive greeting, she guided me to shelves of stacked files and left me alone. I waded through Clareburn County history the old-fashioned way. Fortunately, Elaine Burns, a meticulous archivist, kept every clipping, every photo, every piece of information in pristine order. I spent the afternoon looking for anything at all about the Halbert family, my mother's maiden name. I found that the town had been named after Fulton Burns' beloved wife, Clara, whose impressive monument stood at the entrance to the town's cemetery, but in a surprising twist, I also found my mother's family related to the founding mother.

When Elaine brought me a cup of hot tea, I mentioned that we could possibly be distant relatives. Elaine agreed. "Great-aunt Elizabeth had the misfortune to marry Mr. Benjamin Halbert, a bit of a scoundrel, and it seems our side of the family split with the Halbert side. Kind of like the Hatfields and McCoys for awhile."

The archives bore out her admission. Benjamin Halbert built Windsong and then disappeared after cheating local trappers who stormed Windsong, but had the decency to leave without burning the place down. Not a good piece of family lore about my maternal great-grandfather.

I found little more than that, except that Uncle Basil's wife's brother, Harry Borgendorf, had never been found, and the local newspaper clipping hinted at foul play, although nothing in the coverage said any more about that speculation. Borg must have been named for the Harry and Deborah's last name.

"Harry Borgendorf was my Uncle Basil's brother-in-law," I said to Elaine when she came to refill my teacup.

"I remember when that happened," Elaine Burns said. "I always wondered. Those young people hung around together, some Burns, some Halberts. Harry was a rowdy, a little older than the rest, but he hung around with them. Wouldn't you think one of those kids would have known something when he went missing after one of their beer busts? Deborah kept yelling foul play, but the law treated her as a distraught sister. Nothing could ever be proved."

Except for a few short clips about an ongoing search, Elaine was right. The local search for Deborah's brother yielded nothing.

Shortly after those news clips, the local paper announced Mother's marriage: Elizatbeth Halbert to marry William Denham the Second, although the reporter responsible for the particulars of the actual nuptials could only relate the pedigrees of Elizabeth and William Denham the Second. That came as no surprise. In going over Mother's papers, I knew they had been married in a private ceremony at my paternal grandfather's, the august Judge William Denham the First. Mother's marriage to Father took place far from Clareburn County's reporter. I knew little of my father's father or his mother. Both had died when I still wore diapers but for the first time, I wondered about my paternal grandparents. How did they feel about my father's choice of a bride? Did they think her a flower plucked from the Upper Peninsula to reside in a crystal vase? More likely, my grandfather Denham thought of my mother much as Llewellyn's father thought of me, an unsuitable mate to his only son. Mother must have felt the weight of that disapproval, so far from Windsong and everything she knew. Tears stung my eyes. Her whole life had been trying to fit where she didn't belong.

  When I finally left the museum, the bright January day had already turned to dusk and Elaine Burns followed me out the door and locked it behind her.

"I'm sorry I kept you so long," I apologized.

"No apologies necessary," Elaine said. "I hope you found all the answers you were looking for."

I hadn't found many answers at all, only a sad feeling that I might never fit here as surely as Mother had never fit in Bloomfield Hills.

Thirty-Two

When I got back to Windsong and emailed Llewellyn about my discoveries, his email came back so fast I didn't even have the chance to reply. Don't ask any more questions until I get there. The brooding dusk that peppered me with warning bits of snow on my way home burst into a full-blown storm, and the power went out. I silently thanked Llewellyn who had shown me how to start the generator that would keep Windsong from becoming a dark island in a world of white rampage.

When the January blast subsided after two days, the drifts around my SUV, protected only by a tarp, stood hip-deep. We needed to build a garage next summer. By the time the power flickered on and the snowplow came through, the driveway remained buried, but I first needed to clear the roof. We should have had the sense to install a roof with a 45-degree angle like Uncle Lew's. Why hadn't Uncle warned me?

As if I had called, Uncle Lew's truck appeared and he got out and grabbed a snow shovel from the truck bed. "Get off that roof," he yelled.

"I'm younger than you are," I yelled back. "I'm almost done."

He said no more as he tackled the drifts in the driveway. By the time I joined him, we made short work of my snow-bound condition.

"Come in. I've got coffee and stew," I said.

"Seems you've got power," he said when he came in.

"Just a couple of hours ago."

He looked around as if expecting to see melting icicles hanging from the living room ceiling. "Guess your man had the sense to get a generator for the power outages," he said.

"That's Llewellyn," I said.

He sat down at the table, but when I put a plate of stew in front of him, along with his coffee, he objected, "Hetty's probably got supper going. You don't need to be taking care of me."

"You took care of me," I said, ladling out a bowl. "Payback."

"That was nothing," Uncle Lew said, but he ate and I ate in a companionable silence that stretched back to my early days at Windsong.

"Good stew," he said when he finished. "You must have been watching Hetty."

"How is she? I haven't seen her since that afternoon at Billy's Bar."

Uncle Lew frowned at his coffee. "That took her by surprise, Sabrina. That wasn't good catching us at Billy's."

"I wasn't catching you, Uncle Lew. I just wanted Aunt Hetty back in my life—the way it used to be."

Uncle Lew nodded. I went on, "I didn't know Billy was your brother."

Uncle Lew chuckled. "I got four brothers. Billy's got the bar, Dan's got the lumber yard, Caleb's got the fish-packing outfit and Frank's got the grocery. I'm the only one who doesn't have a business in town."

"I bet your great-grandfather was a Burns," I said.

He shrugged. "My grandma was a Burns. Not likely I'll have a monument like the old gal they named the town after."

"Why was Aunt Hetty so bothered when I showed up at Billy's Bar?"

"Hetty's always been afraid of people talking."

"Talking about what!" I exclaimed. Questions without answers, an undercurrent of history that had been kept veiled.

"I always figured it was about the Burns and Halberts. She don't want people talking about you. You are a Halbert."

"That makes no sense," I objected. "That was generations ago."

"People's memories go back a long way around here, and I did have a couple of old aunts who didn't like Hetty. She got kind of haunted looking for gossip, so we got in the habit of going to Billy's. All he ever tells us is what we read in the paper the next week, or stuff about Borg or Basil and Basil's wife, and Basil usually filled us in on that when he showed up at Windsong."

"Something doesn't fit," I said.

Uncle Lew got up. "It's just one of Hetty's little tics. Maybe just keep the peace. That's what I do."

"I won't come to Billy's when I see your truck there," I promised.

"One piece of that old history is this place," Uncle Lew said. "Old Halbert built it so far out of town because he and Fulton Burns were at odds."

"It must have been hard on his wife," I said.

"Women always get the worst of men's bad behavior," Uncle Lew agreed. "Thank you for supper."

Llewellyn drove into my newly shoveled drive not long after Uncle Lew left, and I was so happy to see him, I forgot all about his last email which had been left unanswered. I flew out to meet him the minute he got out of his SUV.

"You're supposed to be in California," I said, cuddling into his arms like a love-starved puppy.

"I left on the first flight home."

"You can't be leaving your job every time the power goes off up here."

Llewellyn held me so tight I almost lost my breath. "I had to be here," he said. He dragged his duffel out of the back seat and followed me into the house. He looked around as if he too was worried icicles would hang from the front-room ceiling.

"I'm fine," I said. "The generator works great. You shouldn't have left your California conference. I was going to email you after Uncle Lew and I shoveled out."

"It was time to leave. Those characters out there don't have a clue when I warned them a drought was coming. I might as well have been your Uncle Basil preaching at a Windsong dinner."

"Your email sounded almost as ominous, minus the Old Testament references," I teased.

He lifted the lid on my kettle of stew, and I shoved him to the table and ladled out a bowl. "My stew is almost as good as Aunt Hetty's," I said. "Uncle Lew said so."

He gazed down at my offering. "I wasn't worried about the generator or your ability to make a good stew," he said. "I insisted you come here. I was wrong, and I put you in danger."

Thirty-Three

Llewellyn had read the local police reports that concluded Father's death an accident. The car, going too fast to stop for a deer perhaps, lost control and rolled into a ravine and the car burst into flames. We already knew that story. I had found the same story that Elaine Burns had clipped from the local newspaper. But Llewellyn found Father's insurance investigator by way of intrepid computer searches. Mike Conroy, now retired and relocated in California, finally agreed to meet with him in the middle of California's wine country at a local wine fest. "Just like in the movies," Llewellyn said. "We're walking around like a couple of spies under cover."

However, Conroy proved a reluctant accomplice. Before Llewellyn could even open the conversation, Conroy said, "I don't know why you even insist we meet, Mr. McDermott. My job as insurance adjustor assessed the dollar amount of the damages, and we settled that claim years ago."

"I know," Llewellyn said, "but there were a few phrases in your report that differed from the Clareburn County sheriff's report."

Mr. Conroy shrugged. "The police on the scene had already ruled it an accident."

"I know," Llewellyn repeated, "I just want your real thoughts from your observations."

Conroy took a drink from his plastic cup of wine. "In my younger years, I worked for Friedmont Insurance and saved them some big dollars with my investigations. When Atmor bought them out, they wanted to avoid litigation, settle fast. Right or wrong, I guess they figured it saved them money. I'll give you an example. A woman who claimed a neighbor's dog bit her and she wanted thousands for treatment and emotional distress. Her supposed doctor's visits were not for dog bite. Pretty obvious to me. Atmor settled for a lot less than she asked, but they settled nonetheless, and off she went to find another sucker."

"So William Denham's accident was like the dog bite?"

"A little more serious," Conroy said. "When I got there, the car had already been removed from the scene, but the skid marks indicated it would have been enough to stop Denham's car if it had been going a hundred miles an hour. The car seemed to have stopped before it toppled off into that ravine and in that kind of rollover, a car like his would not have burst into flames. The ravine was not that steep. I think it was set on fire."

"But that could be proven."

"Maybe," Conroy said. "If they had a better forensic team than the local sheriff back then."

"So you thought the accident was not an accident at all."

"That's what I think." Conroy took another drink of the wine they were supposed to be taste testing. "But that's just me. I did the best I could to raise questions with the Clareburn sheriff, but he figured I was just trying to get Atmor off the hook, and Atmor paid the claim. As my boss said, I'm no crime detective." He shrugged. "And I could be wrong."

I was shaken by Llewellyn's story. Nanny Bickel, Aunt Zelda, even my own conjecture after Father's death pointed to Conroy's suspicions. Why had my mother pleaded with Aunt Hetty that it was an accident?

"You can't stay here asking questions," Llewellyn said. "I never thought what you wanted to find out might involve murder."

I thought of Uncle Basil's Deborah and her outrageous claims about her brother's disappearance. "My questions have been about Mother and Father's history, their ties to Windsong that kept us coming back every year and the reason Mother wanted to be buried at the local cemetery. I never said anything about murder."

"But you had your suspicions."

"Never enough to suggest it. Besides, if Father was killed, it doesn't mean his killer came from Clareburn," I objected. "He had enemies in Detroit, and I don't know of any here. Nobody liked him much when stayed around that one summer, but he never even stayed at Windsong as long as I can remember."

"It's not worth the risk," he said. "We'll close Windsong. I already checked on an apartment close to your brother's condo."

Something fierce in me arose. He sounded like my father who made decisions for me, decisions he expected me to follow. Our first horrible quarrel ensued. I would not pack up Windsong and leave on a moment's notice.

Llewellyn threatened to leave his job and stay at Windsong.

He would do no such thing because Mike Conroy, a would-be detective, might have gotten his clues wrong.

I put myself in harm's way because I stubbornly thought myself a better detective.

Llewellyn had no right to question my family's loyalty if they suspected a killer in Clareburn.

And so we ranted.

Llewellyn slept in William's old bedroom that night and I didn't sleep at all. I wanted him in the worst way, but I would not be another Mother to my father's orders. When I got up the next morning, I had no idea how we would get through the day. I started a pot of coffee and decided I would just sit mute at the table and drink the whole pot looking out at the snow drifts past the driveway.

When Llewellyn appeared, he went to the refrigerator and started breakfast. The aroma of frying bacon filled the kitchen. He didn't say anything either, just slid a tempting plate under my nose when he was finished.

"Thank you," I muttered, too hungry to push the plate away.

"You're welcome," Llewellyn said and we tackled our bacon and eggs in silent unison. When I got up to wash the dishes, Llewellyn came up behind me. "I'll clean up my mess," he said. "I'm sorry I came on like gangbusters last night."

I turned and grabbed him. "I never want to sleep alone again when you are in the same house," I said.

We did the dishes together, but neither of us felt ready to reopen last night's contention. I hadn't changed my mind and I knew that he hadn't either. He busied himself with bringing in wood for the fireplace and checking the generator, batteries and supplies. I put together a batch of oatmeal cookies and fiddled in the kitchen straightening cupboards that didn't need it. What was I to do with Llewellyn's contention? Should I abandon Windsong? Would Clareburn harbor a killer? Who in Detroit would come here to kill my father in a staged accident? How could my questions be answered?

I had almost talked myself into reopening my argument when the telephone rang. "Is Llewellyn there?" William demanded.

"Yes," I said. "How are you, William?"

William's next words struck like an Upper Peninsula snowstorm. "His sister, Wendy, didn't have Llewellyn's phone number and found me. His father passed away. She's here and wants to talk to him."

Why she didn't have Llewellyn's number? I called Llewellyn and handed him the phone. Through the one-sided conversation, Wendy had been tracked down by the Michigan State Police, the only name they had found going through their father's effects. He had a massive heart attack, dead before he hit the floor at the club where he went to meet some of his business cronies.

When I took the phone from Llewellyn, William said, "Can you and Llewellyn be here as soon as possible? Wendy's sleeping on my couch."

"Of course," I said too numb to say more. "We'll be there this evening." I had never seen Llewellyn cry and it shook me to the core.

"What will I do?" Llewellyn said over and over as I held him and waited for the waves of pain to subside. I had never seen him without an answer to that question. Under his steady demeanor, he had kept hidden the guilt he felt that he had not been the son his father had always wanted. I knew too well that guilt-stricken grief.

"We'll do what has to be done," I said.

Thirty-Four

When we got to William's late that evening, I saw immediately the reason for his relief at our arrival. Wendy sat on his couch, a fragment of the woman I had seen at our wedding, the Wendy that visited us at our apartment in East Lansing. She wore baggy sweatpants and a sweatshirt that yelled "Freedom", the stains on it an ironic message of freedom gone awry, the reason for her lost contact with Llewellyn obvious. She looked as if she had spent the last while on the streets, and from her lank hair and wild eyes, it didn't take a rocket scientist to figure out that her defected lover had hooked her with 'his little tic' as Wendy had dubbed it the last time she had visited.

"If I can help"—William said after Wendy's frenetic jump into Llewellyn's arms.

"Thank you," Llewellyn said. "We have to go back east and make arrangements."

"I can stay here," Wendy said, "while you make arrangements."

"You will come with us," Llewellyn said and I saw he was as shocked as I by Wendy's appearance.

While William arranged out flight to Maine, I managed to get Wendy into a pair of my slacks and a clean sweater, although they hang on her. "You're so fat," Wendy giggled as I pushed her into the shower and dried her hair. "Athletes stay trim, you know. Mother and Father would be so proud the way I've stayed trim." Then she burst into tears and batted away my blow dryer. "Father didn't like you."

I held fast to the memory of Wendy that I knew. "No, he didn't," I said. "But we have to get through this for Llewellyn, don't we?"

When we got to the home Llewellyn had never visited after his mother's death, I saw the pain he felt at Wendy's condition. But after the tsunami of grief at Windsong, he made arrangements for his father's funeral with steely determination. My lion-hearted Llewellyn. I could do little but hold him when we sank into bed at day's end exhausted and heart sick.

He tried to arrange a small, private affair but the news of Jackson McDermott's death, known by half the people in the state, spread and the day before his burial, the funeral home filled with a steady stream of visitors, strangers to me and mostly strangers to Llewellyn, but many remembered Wendy, and I saw by their faces their shock at her appearance.

In spite of my efforts, nothing could hide her skeletal face, her trembling hands or her haunted eyes. I didn't know what she had been on, but I worried that she would either go into severe withdrawal or find a fix that would make her behavior even more apparent. I shadowed her the best I could, but it didn't take long for her to guess my intentions, and in her grief-stricken, drug-fogged mind, she kept her father's memory alive by disliking me as much as he had. "Get away from me, you gold-digging bitch," she snarled. "You have no right to be with my brother."

Llewellyn and I had both taken vacation time added to our bereavement days to stay past the funeral and put the McDermott estate in order. At the funeral, I shielded Llewellyn from my struggle to keep Wendy lucid, but when the three of us went back to Jackson's house, I knew Wendy's animosity towards me would become obvious. one more thing Llewellyn would have to deal with in the next two weeks.

I could probably hide myself in the cavernous space and Wendy and I would never have to cross paths. It outsized our Bloomfield Hills house by half. The dining room could host forty people and opened on one side to a well-stocked bar. A winding stair case graced the south end of the spacious living room and looked like something Scarlett O'Hara would descend. The second floor held six bedrooms each with their own bath and the place also had an indoor swimming pool, a fully-equipped exercise room and a hot tub on the deck. Llewellyn had never lived in a place like this since I knew him and had never once described its opulence. How had Jackson McDermott lived in this mansion all by himself, his wife gone, his two children disaffected?

My second thought was more immediate: How would we keep Wendy away from the overstocked bar long enough to get business done? Soon enough, Wendy confirmed that thought. "I want her out of my house," Wendy said the minute we got in the door. "She has no right to be watching what I do. This is my house now."

Llewellyn must have had the same thought as I did. "This may very well be your house, Wendy, but you asked for my help settling Father's affairs. Sabrina goes, I go."

Wendy glared at me. "Father didn't like her." She sounded like a petulant child.

I kept silent. Substance abuse was a disease, and I couldn't blame her, no more than I could blame Mother for having cancer, but this illness would eventually kill her as well. She probably had inherited everything after Jackson's last words to Llewellyn but if she didn't get help, she would burn through her inheritance in a matter of a few short years and end up back on the street or in the morgue.

As if Llewellyn had read my thoughts, he said, "We're here to help you, Wendy, but if you spend the next two weeks going through Father's liquor supply, you'll probably die before I can help you at all."

"We could have just one drink to get started."

"We'll have coffee," Llewellyn said and pushed her toward his father's office.

I went to the kitchen, a chef's dream, and had a moment of panic that the coffee maker would be some high-tech instrument that needed an instruction manual to operate. Fortunately, other than having to grind the coffee beans, I managed to brew a pot of the best coffee I had ever made and took the steaming mugs into the office. Llewellyn already had files of papers on the desk, and I had to smile as he leaned over explaining each to Wendy as if it was an algebra problem back at Grant Academy.

I silently set down the coffee and left. If Llewellyn could keep this up, we might be out of here before our two weeks were up. Or so goes wishful thinking.

The first few days went well. Llewellyn cleared out his father's files, made phone calls and kept Wendy close by and clear of the liquor supply. She drank pots of coffee and refused to speak to me but looked a little better for all that. I busied myself with the long list of thank you notes, brewed pots of coffee and cooked, although I mostly warmed funeral casseroles. In spite of Llewellyn's attempts at downsizing a big funeral display, so much food came in, we gave it to food kitchens all over town. We probably fed many people who suffered with the same disease that Wendy had.

But when Llewellyn and Wendy visited Jackson McDermott's attorney, our small stitches of détente came undone. Llewellyn's father had signed a new will only weeks before his death and divided his estate between both of his estranged children. He also left a letter that hit Llewellyn with a new tsunami of grief and Wendy with unwelcome surprise. Jackson knew of his heart condition and regretted that what he thought best for his children had only driven them away. He wanted to give them what he had left and ask for forgiveness or at least understanding. When Wendy and Llewellyn came back to the house, Wendy went straight to the bar and Llewellyn went into the office and sobbed.

The remaining days of our time in Maine passed in a blur. Wendy's incoherent fury finally landed her in a local hospital after she overdosed on alcohol and pills she had managed to come by. Jackson's attorney offered to put the McDermott mansion up for sale and arrange that Wendy's share of her inheritance would be put in a trust fund until she was judged competent. She would have the best psychological care after her bout at the hospital. I hoped that care would work but now Llewellyn, as unraveled as I had ever seen him, needed all I could give him. Questions at Windsong would have to wait.

Thirty-Five

When we got back to Michigan we rented an apartment in East Lansing, and neither of us traveled for some time, but resumed our work with computers and area meetings. In our down time, the city offered music and theater and book shops, which I insisted we visit.

"Thank you," Llewellyn said one evening in April as we drove home after a performance of "Midsummer's Night Dream". "You've been there for me when everything about my Father's death was making me crazy."

"You weren't crazy," I said. "Just swept under for awhile." I leaned against my seat belt and hugged him. "Didn't you do the same for William and me with Mother?"

The evening made me nostalgic for William. He would have loved tonight's performance. I hadn't seen him since we came back to Michigan, but when we were in Maine I had seen a news item that William Denham the Third had visited the home of Gregory Thurman, William's pale-faced friend back in his Exeter days. I wondered if William kept a distance because of a new relationship. I didn't know if I would like Gregory anymore than I had liked Borg, but it seemed unlikely I would meet him any time soon.

"You have to go back to Windsong, don't you?" Llewellyn broke my reverie.

"Let's not talk about that right now," I said. "Maybe for awhile when we start planting trout lakes again. It seems my last report has raised some issues about fishing licenses, and I think my boss wants me to count every one of the little wigglers."

"No, let's talk about that right now. With Father's inheritance, I don't have to keep a permanent job right now. We'll go back to Windsong together."

"No!" I cried. "Your job is important. You can't just give up all you believe in. That's crazy!"

"I don't plan on giving up a thing," Llewellyn said. "I'm going to take a leave and write a book, now that I have the resources to do it. That's all."

"You just made that up," I said.

"I did not. I just found the answer to our bone of contention."

I frowned into the rain-spattered windshield. "You never liked to write."

He wheeled into our apartment drive. "But I want to put all my thoughts and theories into a cohesive whole. You can help me with the fine points."

When I went to get out of the car, he grabbed my arm. "In the last weeks, I realized how important it is for you to settle your family history," he said. "As awful as my relations with my father were, he settled it to some extent. Your father never did. Your mother never did. Whatever you have to find out, I understand."

We moved to Windsong at the end of May. Spring had poked through the last vestiges of an unrelenting winter, and I went to work with a vengeance, determined to appear as if my job was the only reason for our residence at Windsong. In fact, after weeks of a slow winter, my job kept me busy from dawn to dusk. Even if I had unanswered questions, I knew I truly came home. I loved the immense green of the forest, the fern shadows on the forest floor, the moods of Lake Superior, the murder of crows in raucous convention outside our bedroom window, even the winter snow that blew in with a temper and surrounded Windsong with a blanket of silence.

At first, Llewellyn seemed to have forgotten his decision to write. He accompanied me to streams and lakes, to hatcheries and even to meetings. I appreciated his company as well as his interest in my work, but I didn't believe he shadowed me for book research, and I finally confronted him. "Llewellyn, Father's supposed accident happened years ago, and I've been here dozens of times since. I am not in imminent danger and you haven't written a word."

"What if I told you I have writer's block?"

"You have to write something before you have writer's block." Although unsure of my argument, I reasoned no one in Clareburn thought me a threat and only Llewellyn knew about the insurance investigator's suspicions.

Llewellyn finally tackled the blank page. He wrote, researched, rewrote and turned out one painstaking paragraph after another. To his chagrin, I wouldn't look at it until he finished half of it. "I need to see where you're going with the whole thing," I said. "It makes no sense to edit every page if half of them will have to be thrown out."

"Maybe I should do a kids' book," he grumbled. My book proposal, *Little Scientist Looks at Butterflies* had been accepted by Hilltop Publishers and they wanted a second book for a Little Scientist series.

"Find some pretty cows to sketch," I teased him. I didn't tell him that I had gone through several drafts before Hilltop finally accepted my proposal.

Thirty-Six

In spite of keeping up the appearance that my job took up all my time at Windsong, in spite of my membership at the book and craft club meetings, my newly published book brought me into the Clareburn spotlight. When I picked up the phone one night after a very long day, Elaine Burns's voice burst with energy. "Your book is so wonderful for our children!" she enthused. "The museum and the library would love to host a book signing for you. Just name the date."

"I-I don't know," I stammered. "Can I get back with you?"

"Of course, you have to do it," Llewellyn said when I got off the phone. "That's what writers do."

"We're not here to promote my book," I said.

"You've kept away from your other reason for being here."

"Llewellyn, that is not my only reason for being here."

He smiled. "Sometimes the female of the species is not that difficult to understand at all. I saw it in your face the day we arrived."

"This is our home. I don't need any other reason for being here. Maybe it's okay I'm just doing my job."

"I don't think that's entirely true. Maybe it's time to jostle a few Clareburn ghosts." He threw down a file on the kitchen table. "I'm half done, ready for an edit," he said. "By the time I'm finished with this book, I want us to be ready for our next step, and I want your Windsong ghosts put to rest."

Since Clareburn's small library did not have space to host us, Elaine Burns set me up in the museum's basement with plenty of room but smelled musty in spite of her best attempts with perfumed candles and air freshener. She decorated the dark walls with butterflies and a life-size replica of the Little Scientist that someone must have worked overtime to reproduce. When I saw Elaine's efforts, I felt humbled and ashamed of my grudging acceptance to appear and also surprised that most of the folding chairs, arranged in an artful semicircle around an ancient wooden podium, were taken.

"Clareburn suffers from a severe lack of entertainment," I muttered.

"Or a lively curiosity," Llewellyn said.

"Thank you for that valuable insight," I said, but he must have seen that my words, meant to be light-hearted, didn't cover my sudden attack of stage fright.

"On the other hand, your book club is here and you have a great book. Elaine Burns knows you have a great book. Tonight, you're just the little scientist at Windsong all grown up."

Uncle Lew, Aunt Hetty and Uncle Basil sat in the last row. Llewellyn squeezed my arm and went to sit with them, and left alone to deliver my presentation, in spite of my initial stage fright, my enthusiasm for the Little Scientist soon took over. After my opening remarks, I read the pages that told of Little Scientist's wonder at the discoveries she had found and ended with Buckminster Fuller's quote, "There is nothing in a caterpillar that tells you it's going to be a butterfly. I owe this book to my Uncle Lew who encouraged my curiosity and Aunt Hetty who suggested I could give my love of the outdoor world to other children."

When I invited questions, the audience participated, but few questions related to *Little Scientist Looks at Butterflies*. How was Windsong since my mother's funeral? Why had I chosen to live here? How different from my childhood home worlds away? Did I ever regret my decision? Evidently, Clareburn had questions for me unrelated to my writing process and tonight's event opened the dam.

Aunt Hetty and Uncle Lew got up and left, and Aunt Hetty looked more upset than happy that I had taken the advice she had given me years ago. I did my best to hide my consternation and steer the questions back to the Little Scientist but, if Llewellyn in the back hadn't nodded encouragement, I think I would have rushed out after them.

Elaine Burns came to my rescue. "One more question and it's time to break for punch and cookies," she announced. Fortunately, the last question came from a young girl who wanted to know how I got my book published. As the evening broke up, I sold several copies of my book and tried to appear as if I had done book signings for years. Secretly, I vowed never to do another.

Uncle Basil was my last customer. "It's the hand of God who made the natural world around us," he said. "You might have mentioned that. I'd like to give you some suggestions for your next book."

I handed him a copy. "No charge for you, Uncle Basil."

"Come over to dinner tomorrow evening," Llewellyn added coming up behind him. "Sabrina's been so busy, she hasn't had a chance to cook. So I'll cook and you can give me some suggestions about the book I'm working on."

On our drive back to Windsong I said, "The middle of July is no time for chili."

"I can learn to cook something else besides chili," he protested. "I'll Google some recipes and come up with a meal worthy of a French chef."

"It was a horrible evening."

"It was not," Llewellyn disagreed. "Your presentation was great, and you encouraged at least one young writer."

"I hurt Aunt Hetty," I said.

"You jostled some bones," Llewellyn admitted. "The questions aimed at you scared her. I guessed she wouldn't come to dinner and have us aim questions at her. Your Uncle Basil seemed the next best bet."

He pulled into Windsong's driveway, so different after last winter's hip-deep snow that had to be shoveled after every storm. The garage we planned to build was stuck on Step One. The cement floor waited on Clyde Ingersoll who seemed to have trouble keeping his equipment in working order. In spite of my unfortunate meeting with him at Billy's Bar, Clyde supposedly did good work when he sobered up and left fishing to his son. My car would probably be huddled under a tarp again next winter.

"You don't think Uncle Basil is our next best bet?" Llewellyn asked, and it took me a minute to turn my mind from the sidetracked garage project.

"Uncle Basil is oblivious to anything that doesn't involve his church," I said as we went into the house. "And Uncle Lew said Aunt Hetty is just worried about the Halbert family measuring up to the Burns family in Clareburn."

"Then your appearance tonight should have been a star in the Halbert crown."

"Unless she thinks the Little Scientist looks too much like old Benjamin Halbert who used the Upper Peninsula's wild life for his own gain."

Llewellyn frowned at his file still sitting on the kitchen table. "That's a stretch," he said.

"It could be, but I don't think Clareburn is the big answer to Father's accident. I keep thinking about what Aunt Zelda told Rita. If Rita's father found out something, maybe he arranged Father's death in revenge before his suicide."

Llewellyn thumbed the file as if it could have an answer. "That's another stretch."

"Uncle Basil for dinner is a stretch."

"I don't know how it is that half the time I come up on the losing end of an argument with you. I never had that problem at Grant when we did algebra assignments."

I had to smile. "Interesting that you said half the time."

"We'll see what Uncle Basil has to offer tomorrow evening, and then we'll see if there's anything behind what Aunt Zelda said. I guess that's half."

Thirty-Seven

By the time I got back to Windsong the following day, I must have looked quite as much as the Little Scientist; muddy boots, frazzled hair and a torn shirt that caught on some brambles when I rushed downstream to see if I could spot any little fingerlings that had not survived their new habitat. We were planting grade A trout streams and lakes and I wanted to make sure the plants went off without a hitch.

Uncle Basil had not yet arrived, and Llewellyn ordered me out of the kitchen and into the bathroom. "The chef is in control," he said. "Get yourself smoothed out as if Little Scientist never got caught in a bramble bush or waded through mud."

As I shed my clothes and jumped into the shower, I thought of how many times I had been smoothed out by Nanny Bickel, how many times Aunt Hetty had smoothed me out before a Windsong supper. Had I ever grown up? Llewellyn invited Uncle Basil to dinner so I could ask questions. Chasing questions that were only generated by a childish inquisitiveness into other people's right to privacy? Llewellyn wanted our life as a couple to move on. How long would it be before his patience ran out?

Doubts still swirled in my head when I emerged from the bathroom "smoothed out" to see that Uncle Basil had arrived with an unexpected guest. Borg lounged at the dining room table, as unsmoothed as if he had followed my trek through brambles and mud, but he rose to greet me as if he hosted the evening.

"Cousin Sabrina, so good to see you! I hear you are a Clareburn celebrity."

"Borg," I managed, and looked to Uncle Basil for an explanation.

"I knew you would be happy to see your cousin after these long and trying months," Uncle Basil beamed. "The Lord gave him refuge and sustenance."

"Borg came to Clareburn this morning," Llewellyn explained, coming in from the kitchen with a huge bowl of salad. He seemed unruffled by Borg's unexpected appearance.

Borg frowned at Uncle Basil and Llewellyn's explanation for his presence. "I'm here because I haven't been invited here for years," he said. "Looks like you haven't done much with the place."

"I like it the way it is," I said. As usual, it didn't take long for Borg to irritate me.

"Of course, you do," Borg said. "Just like your mother and that father of yours."

"It's a comfort to be welcomed into the home of my childhood," Uncle Basil said. "Let us pray."

After Uncle Basil's heartfelt blessing over Windsong's bounty, we vanquished the salad, a wonderful mixture of every vegetable the local farmers' roadside stands could offer. "We should plant a garden next summer," I said. "I could live on salads like this all season."

Borg snorted. "Not likely you could grow much."

"I remember my mother grew cabbage and potatoes," Uncle Basil said.

Llewellyn winked at me. "Maybe a few chickens and a pig or two."

I had to smile at his easy disregard of Borg's bad manners and said nothing. In spite of my disgust with Borg, I could not help but be amazed at the dinner Llewellyn produced: baked chicken, small red potatoes, asparagus tips, and an old-fashioned apple pie for dessert. He must have spent the whole day, and I couldn't help but think his efforts thrown away on a guest who probably ate squirrel stew right out of the pot.

As the meal went on, I could see that while Borg ate every bite, Llewellyn played the part of naïve stranger and plied Borg with questions of his winter retreat. At first, Borg was expansive about his winter experiences until I almost thought Llewellyn would wrangle an invitation to his lair, but when we got to dessert, Borg's attitude shifted. "This is a meal right out of Bloomfield Hills," he said as he wolfed down a second piece of pie.

"Thank you, Borg," Llewellyn said. "I'm sure you have some fond memories of your time there."

Borg soon rewarded Llewellyn's thrust. "I wasn't complimenting you on your fancy display," he growled. "The place was a palace of deceit and corruption."

Uncle Basil started to say, "Perhaps Sabrina's worthy husband meant to say"—

"I'm sorry I mistook your remark as a compliment," Llewellyn interrupted. "I understood you were a valuable employee there."

"Mr. William Denham the Third's lackey, that's what I was. You'd better smarten up."

I wanted to get up and slap Borg's face, but Llewellyn shot me a warning look. "I don't know much about Bloomfield Hills," he said. "Perhaps I should. What makes you think it's a palace of deceit and corruption?" Llewellyn's pretense would have been laughable if I was in a laughing mood.

Borg jumped up. "Nobody gets all they want without stepping over somebody on their way up. I told Mr. William Denham the Third not to keep Windsong, another of his father's ill-gotten gains, but he wouldn't listen. I thought William like his mother, but it didn't take me long to find out that he was his father all over again."

I was unable to keep quiet any longer. "William didn't keep Windsong. I did as part of our estate settlement."

"It needs to rot," Borg said. "That's all I have to say. Good night." He slammed the door on the way out. I hoped he would disappear to his wilderness cabin with his bitter bad manners and stay there forever.

Uncle Basil frowned into his empty plate. He finally mustered the right scripture for the occasion. "We must forgive as the Lord said we should seventy times seven," he said. "Let us pray."

For the sake of Uncle Basil, truly upset by Borg's rude behavior, Llewellyn and I sat through a very long prayer of forgiveness, but when we sent my uncle packing with the leftovers of Llewellyn's fabulous meal, I hoped Borg would get none of it.

"Borg is a raving idiot," I fumed as we cleaned up the dining room and I started washing the dishes. "I'm sorry he ruined your wonderful dinner. I couldn't keep my mouth shut any longer."

"You're no Columbo, that's for sure. But I found out a little about Borg's nest before he shut down. From what he said, I felt I could find the place."

I had to smile. When Borg talked about his cabin, I could almost see the side of Borg that William had once loved. "I thought for awhile you would be invited there for roasted possum."

"But then he changed when he went on about Bloomfield Hills and your father's ill-gotten gains."

"He never knew my father. You were supposed to be picking Uncle Basil's brain for Father's possible enemies in Clareburn."

"I watched your Uncle Basil while Borg went on, and he seemed truly shocked. I think you were right when you said he wouldn't have any answers. I'm sure he never knew about Borg and William's soured affair."

"I wonder if Borg found out something about Father when he lived with William."

Llewellyn wiped the platter he had already wiped twice. "I thought the same thing. Maybe he overheard something from the other hired help or William's associates."

"I wouldn't be surprised if he snooped around the house. I think William still had some of Father's files there."

"That's a heavy thought. If your father truly did have some underhanded dealings, then William would know it too."

I pulled the plug and the dish water went out with a satisfying swoosh. At least we didn't have to worry about Windsong's plumbing—yet. I didn't want to think that William would have known of inherited deceit and corruption and let it stay buried.

Llewellyn saw my consternation. "I think Borg's ravings are disappointed love and wild-eyed jealousy,"

"I remember Mother saying after his funeral that for all the justice Father had done, he had enemies and when Aunt Hetty told Mother a character masquerading as a fisherman in Clareburn asked a lot of questions about Father's connection to Windsong, Mother acted a little alarmed. What if Rita's father was the root of my father's accident?"

"If Moses won't come to the mountain, the mountain will have to go to Moses."

I slapped him with a wet sponge. "You sound like Uncle Basil. What are you talking about?"

"You always thought your father's accident came from somebody he knew back in Detroit. I think it's time we pay William a visit."

Thirty-Eight

We arrived at William's on July 15th, which I couldn't help but point out when William let us in the door. "You should be at Windsong today," I said when I hugged him.

"I guess you're still filling your notebooks. Congratulations on your book. Everybody I know that has kids had to buy a copy to shut me up. How are you, Llewellyn?"

"I hope you do that kind of promotion when my book is published," Llewellyn said. "How's business?"

Our polite conversation continued as William offered us a dinner I knew he must have catered. I looked around his pristine place for evidence of a roommate, but William's condo looked much as his room at home had been, so neat I imagined his closet coordinated shirt colors and suit jackets. I did notice his book shelf held a collection of Shakespeare tucked alphabetically into an array of tomes on law and litigation. I wondered when William had last taken the bard off the shelf. After his affair with Borg, he seemed to have retreated into a mirror of Father that he held up to the world, a mirror of unbreakable glass. We came on a mission doomed to fail.

Llewellyn thought otherwise. As we lingered after dinner with a glass of wine, he opened the reason for our visit, something I knew William tried to fathom throughout our exchange of politics, the world economy and the state of the weather. "Your father was murdered," Llewellyn said, "And Sabrina needs to know who and why."

William shook his head. "That," he said.

"That," Llewellyn confirmed. He took a small notebook out of his pocket and slid it across the table. "Here's what we know."

William frowned, but he opened the notebook and read Aunt Zelda's words, Nanny Bickel's words, the investigative officer's report. Llewellyn had recorded it all.

"Conjecture," William said.

"True," Llewellyn agreed. "Although the insurance investigator's observations have some weight."

"After all these years, why are you giving me this?" William said. His question was to Llewellyn but he looked at me, and I saw a flicker of pain in his eyes.

"I need to know," I said. "We need to know, William."

He got up from the table and started clearing the remains of dinner. "That's what you don't get, Sabrina. Some things we can't know."

How many times had I heard that counsel from Nanny Bickel, Uncle Lew, Uncle Basil?

"This might be one of them," Llewellyn agreed and rose from the table to help William. "But we ask one favor. Could you find out everything you can about Rita's father?"

"If I do, will that be the end of it?"

"Maybe," I said. "But William, I have to ask if you know anything about Father that you aren't telling us."

"What do you mean?"

I recounted our dinner with Borg. "His bitter remarks about Father seem to come after his time when he worked for you. Before that, he showed up with Uncle Basil after Father's accident. He came to Mother's funeral to offer condolences and never said a word about Father. What did he learn at Bloomfield Hills?"

"For god sake, Sabrina, you saw how bitter Borg was when I sold the place and we split up."

"Even Mother said Father had enemies. Maybe for good reason."

"Every prosecuting attorney has enemies. Every lawyer has enemies." I could see William's controlled anger in the set of his jaw. "I know of nothing that Father ever did outside the law, and neither does Borg. Father's 'ill-gotten gains' came from the inheritance he got from his father, which he invested wisely."

"I'm sorry. I had to ask."

"You're asking the wrong questions."

In spite of William's reluctance, he had agreed to get all the information we asked for and on our way back to Windsong, I felt happy that William promised to visit Windsong in August. After William's anger at my questions about Father's 'ill-gotten gains', Llewellyn managed to lighten our evening with a game of twenty questions that William teased would sharpen my abilities as failed interrogator.

When we got home, the winds of good fortune had blown in. Clyde Ingersoll had finally poured the foundation for the garage and the lumber company under Uncle Lew's supervision would finish the project.

"The garage will stand through a hurricane with you as overseer," I said to Uncle Lew when the first load of lumber rolled up.

"Maybe not a hurricane," Uncle Lew said modestly. "But it'll hold through Gitchee Gumee."

"William will visit in two weeks. You and Aunt Hetty have to come for dinner even if you have to drag her here."

"I'll try. You were always my favorite niece."

"Wasn't I your only niece?" I teased.

"On Hetty's side. My brothers have kids too you know, but they're all boys."

"I don't have anybody else, Uncle Lew, except you, Aunt Hetty, Uncle Basil—and Borg."

Uncle Lew grimaced. "Borg quit his job sorting nets for Ingersoll's son. Last time I heard, he's back up in the woods somewhere, but he comes and goes just enough to keep Basil holding onto his Bible and praying. Maybe a good kick on Borg's behind would do more good, but I'm just saying."

I don't know if my pathetic appeal to Uncle Lew or William's arrival at Windsong worked, but Aunt Hetty came to dinner the day after William's arrived. She accepted my extravagant hug and patted me on the back as if I was a dog who needed to be subdued from hysterical barking but she looked uncomfortable as Windsong guest instead of overseer and sat on the edge of the dining-room chair as if expecting the ghost of my mother to appear. Uncle Lew insisted she take the wine I offered, and I saw that he, in his Uncle Lew way, acted as if it was just another Windsong dinner, and William and I the kids at the table.

We hadn't invited Uncle Basil on the outside chance that Borg would make another surprise appearance. If Aunt Hetty noticed, she didn't say and that, as much as anything, underlined how much had changed. I could still remember her open invitation to Uncle Basil, despite her wry comments on his new-found religion.

Since I worked all day, Llewellyn served chicken and biscuits and all the trimmings. Even though some of his culinary efforts failed, his newfound interest in the kitchen paid off and his cooking skills, thanks to Googled recipes, went far beyond chili and bacon and eggs. Aunt Hetty pronounced his dinner a success.

I kept the conversation to the museum, the lumber yard, and the little I knew of Clareburn gossip from what I learned at the book and craft clubs. Clyde went on another of his alcoholic binges, and Elaine Burns finally agreed to marry Sal Kearns after years of courtship.

William, who could not help but see the change in Aunt Hetty, followed my lead with reminiscences of our younger days, poking at my role as the Little Scientist until he actually had Aunt Hetty laughing. Llewellyn said little as he watched our diplomatic dance.

"I don't know what Sabrina did to train you," Aunt Hetty told him as they were leaving. "But she's got the best cook in Clareburn County."

"She whips me with a wet noodle," Llewellyn teased as he hugged her. "But try as I might, I can't do Aunt Hetty's stew."

"You've got to come back and show us your secret," I added, but I knew as soon as I said it, I should have kept my mouth shut.

"Thank you for dinner," Aunt Hetty said and climbed into Uncle Lew's truck. "It was good to see you kids."

"What's going on?" William demanded as soon as they left. "Aunt Hetty acted as if she never set foot at Windsong."

I filled him in on her refusal to visit Windsong since I had arrived. "It's almost like she doesn't want me here anymore than Borg."

"Borg I can understand. Things went sour with him, but on hindsight, that was my mistake for inviting him into my life. Old connections to a Windsong summer"-- he stopped. I wanted to hug him to comfort the flicker of pain in his eyes, but William went on, "In a way, Aunt Hetty's reasons may be similar; old connections to Windsong."

"That was Uncle Lew's excuse for her," I said. I didn't go on with my niggling suspicion that Aunt Hetty didn't want me at Windsong asking too many questions. It would only reinforce William's opinion that my questions should be put to rest.

If he guessed my thoughts, he didn't say. "I have the information you requested." He went to his room and came back with a file. "Not much to substantiate Zelda's story." Sure enough, the police report, well documented and complete with photos, left no doubt that Rita's father had indeed committed suicide. "If Rita's father was that mysterious fisherman snooping around Clareburn, we'll never know," William said, "But he wasn't murdered for anything he found out, and I don't think it the cause of his suicide. I did more research. He was being investigated for pedophilia."

I gasped. "Rita"—

"Not with her," William said. "He preferred little blonde girls —his associates' daughters. Perhaps Rita's mother got wind of it. Even before Father's court case, she filed for divorce. Rita's aunt may have been right in a way. Somebody may have been out to get him before he did himself in, but it wasn't Father."

After our reunion with Aunt Hetty and my satisfaction with our garage project, my happy little bubble burst. I couldn't sleep.

Did Rita somehow surmise her father a predator? What had her mother known before she took herself away with alcohol? Should I tell Rita of William's discoveries? Rita and I had shared so much, but should this be one time I kept a secret from her?

William saw beyond my attempts at making the rest of his visit to Windsong what it had once been. "I would advise you to keep what I told you and Llewellyn to yourselves," he said the day he left. "Whatever he was, that was Rita's father. What you wanted is answered."

William had been reading Hamlet during his visit, but done nothing to bring him back to his younger self. My request and his visit only resurrected the ghost of our father and left some cracks in the mirror image he held up to the world and opened deep crevasses in my world as well. Every question I asked, every stone I overturned had only turned up hurt.

Thirty-Nine

After William left, I took a long, hard look at my life since Mother's funeral, and I did not like what I saw. The questions I kept trying to answer hurt Aunt Hetty, opened old wounds for William and burdened my marriage. I had to let go and get on with life. Llewellyn and I could move, start a family, keep Windsong as a getaway for another Little Scientist unburdened by surmised family secrets.

In the next weeks, I watched trout and reported my findings, which eventually led to fishing license readjustments to protect the fledgling fish we released until they were more established. I edited Llewellyn's half-finished manuscript, and he went back to his keyboard and rewrote, and this time I edited every page.

I went to work on my second *Little Scientist* book, *Little Scientist Looks at Spiders*, but I didn't like the approach Hillside Publishers took with my submission. The new editor wanted to exaggerate the creepy crawler aspect of my little arachnids. Editing what I had written was not the problem. Changing what I had to say was a very big problem. I started a search for a new publisher, a chore I did not relish.

Meanwhile, the garage went up like a fern uncurling its fronds. Uncle Lew knew his stuff, but I had lost my enthusiasm for a garage that could withstand next winter's storms. We didn't need to be here next winter. When I got home evenings, I only felt relief that Uncle Lew and his crew left before I arrived.

"I guess we're going to New Orleans," Llewellyn said one evening in late September. He looked at his monitor as if at a crystal ball. "Perfect time for a visit to the Big Easy."

My antennae went up. In spite of my determination to let go of Windsong, I hadn't yet visualized us surrounded by balmy breezes and Southern charm in the middle of January. Llewellyn again made decisions he expected me to follow.

Llewellyn must have seen my antennae spike like a critter in danger of a possible predator. "Not for the winter. A short visit with a purpose."

I stared at him, dishcloth in hand like a wilted shield.

"I thought about what William said, about you asking the wrong questions. You asked in the wrong places. You don't have any more leads in Bloomfield Hills or Clareburn. If you ask Aunt Hetty or Uncle Basil or Borg, you hit a stone wall. The only other person that might be able to tell us something about your father's time in Clareburn is Borg's mother, Deborah, and she now lives in New Orleans."

I lowered my floppy shield. "You don't know that. You don't even know her name."

"Not quite so. I knew her maiden name from the research you did at the museum, found one change of name after her marriage to your Uncle Basil and followed the trail. She never married her other partners."

"I'm done asking questions."

"I saw that after William's visit. You're trying to murder the Little Scientist that keeps asking questions. You've barely looked at the garage, you haven't answered any of the invitations for book signings, and you barely eat all the wonderful meals I've concocted, thanks to Google."

"You're exaggerating. I've been busy." I turned away and tried to hide my burning tears.

Llewellyn jumped up and grabbed my shoulders. "After my father's funeral, I understood how important it was for you to find the answers that your father and mother never gave you. Who killed your father and why? Why did your mother insist it was an accident? Why don't your relatives want you here at Windsong? If you stop asking questions, you will not be the

Sabrina I married." He gave me a little shake. "I love the Sabrina with a thousand questions."

"You sound like a soap opera."

"The lion hearted arises to help the woman he loves answer questions that seemingly have no answers."

I backed away. "You said when your book was done, we would get on with the rest of our lives. I'm ready to get on."

"I'm not done with the book, and I don't think you're as ready as you say you are. Let's give it one more try."

Llewellyn truly lived up to his name, although my lion-hearted husband fought his battles and fixed problems with quiet tenacity. Despite his powerful father, he refused to play rugby, he got into his chosen career, took on factory farming and halted his sister's slide into certain death. The last we heard, she was still clean and going through training to help others with addiction. My attempts at letting ghosts rest hadn't fixed anything.

"One more try," I conceded.

When we got to New Orleans, once again Deborah's last known address, according to Llewellyn's internet search, stood vacant and boarded up. She had evaporated into thin air, as Uncle Basil always said she did, and I couldn't help but think that Borg did the same thing the way he appeared and disappeared to his secret space in the Upper Peninsula forest. No wonder Uncle Basil held on to the Bible like a drowning man grabbing a plank in a stormy sea. The Bible stayed the same whenever he opened it.

Even though our mission had failed, Llewellyn remained unfazed. "No sense in wasting a four-day weekend," he said. "Let's visit Rita."

I agreed with some trepidation. Would Rita see that I kept something from her? Llewellyn didn't know the under currents of our friendship and how perceptive Rita could be.

When we arrived at Rita's door, Llewellyn pounded and I yelled before the door opened and Rita pulled us inside with a wild hug for each of us. "I could hardly believe it was really you!" she exclaimed. "It seems I'm getting too damn popular anymore. How do these characters find me? I'm supposed to be off the map and here they come wanting interviews, wanting to snoop, messing with my work time."

"Maybe you're not an outlier anymore," Llewellyn said.

"I don't want to get into clawing and agents and contracts. It gets to be business. I'd rather be on the street selling, but you didn't come here to listen to all that right now."

I had to smile. "You told me once you wanted to be a bag lady."

Rita made a face at me. "I guess I'm too soft to be a bag lady. I even got a cell phone. You'll be one of the privileged few to have the number. Come sit down."

Over tea and beignets, the afternoon melted away into a New Orleans evening before Rita said, "I'm thinking you're here because of something besides old times." She narrowed her eyes at Llewellyn. She rightly suspected we came to New Orleans at his behest.

Llewellyn didn't seem surprised by her abrupt confrontation. "We came looking for a woman, Debora Halbert, that we thought lived in New Orleans, but we couldn't find her. Of course, we couldn't come here without seeing you."

She turned to me. "Isn't he the slick one?"

"Llewellyn's right. You know we wouldn't have come to New Orleans without seeing you."

Rita poured each of us another cup of tea. "That's half true," she said. "But there's something you're not telling me, Sabrina."

"What makes you say that?" I attempted to protest.

"I remember the look you had when you pretended to your nanny that our soccer practice went on longer than it did, so we could sit around and drink Cokes. I remember those mall strolls when we were supposed to still be working on our after-school projects. You have that same look. I always said you couldn't even cheat at cards."

The silence stretched between us. I knew we shouldn't have come here, I knew that Rita would see that I kept something back, but I couldn't share what William had found out about her father, even if it meant my silence would end our friendship forever.

"Sabrina does not want to say what she knows will hurt you," Llewellyn said.

I jumped up and knocked over my tea that pooled across Rita's table. "What the hell do you think you're doing?" I yelled. Llewellyn had no right to breach my friendship with Rita.

Rita got up and mopped up my overturned tea with a ball of napkins. "It's okay, Sabrina. It's okay," she said. "If nothing is said, I will be left wondering what needed to be said. That will hurt more."

I glared at Llewellyn. "It was your idea we come here in the first place," I lashed out. "If you hadn't convinced William to

300

look into her father's record"-- I stopped, blinded with anger, even as I knew I had been the one who insisted we look to Bloomfield Hills for Father's accident.

"From what Aunt Zelda said and the little I knew, I suspected he was making moves to get back at your father, Sabrina. I need to know what you found that you're keeping from me."

I sank back down, but it was Llewellyn who told Rita of William's findings into the last part of her father's life, and I saw the shock and hurt on her face. She had lost the one thread of hope that her father's death was not the disgraceful end it had been.

"I couldn't tell you, Rita, and Llewellyn shouldn't have," I said. "Whatever your father did is dead and buried, and you didn't need to be hurt."

"Llewellyn did right. You filled in a lot of blanks that I had in my parents' story. It wasn't what I thought, but do you want the questions about your father left unanswered because you might be hurt?"

"After what William found, I didn't want to come to New Orleans at all chasing Deborah Halbert. I'm done asking questions."

Rita sat down beside me and took my hand. "Remember when Aunt Zelda read your tea leaves and said your life would twist around your questions?"

"You said it was nothing but a bunch of soggy dregs."

"It wasn't the tea leaves. She just knew questions twist a life."

"I didn't want to twist yours."

"Questions aren't always been a bad thing. I picked up your Little Scientist book. It's wonderful."

"Thank you," I choked. I would not thank Llewellyn for getting in the middle of a friendship I had tried to protect.

Although Rita's eyes were sad, she said, "You found the answers to some questions I had, but you still have questions of your own. Maybe I can help. I know a Deborah who lives with Bobo, a guy who plays a saxophone like BB King could play a guitar."

"It could be any of a hundred Deborahs."

"Could be," Rita agreed, "but Bobo calls her his frozen Michigan woman that he melted with jazz. He even composed a song about her for their vocalist."

Llewellyn forgot my fury or at least ignored it. "Where can we find her?"

Rita glanced at me. "You've allied yourself with the lion-hearted. Good thing or he'd already be gone. We can catch Bobo at La Fleur if you're sure you want to."

"We want to," Llewellyn said, which put my anger at a fever pitch.

"I didn't say I want to. I just want to go home."

"Who is this Deborah Halbert?" Rita intervened.

This time Llewellyn stayed silent, and I blurted out the months and years since Mother's death right up to William's summer visit.

"I always figured William was gay," Rita said when I ended my disjointed story. "He needs a good love in his life or he's going to splinter like glass."

Llewellyn stared at his empty tea cup. "We'll go home, Sabrina. I'm sorry."

"Not tonight," Rita said decisively. "Maybe tomorrow. Tonight, we all need some New Orleans jazz. Nothing lifts a heavy mind like good music. You'll be doing me a favor."

Something in Rita's eyes stopped my refusal. Rita didn't want to be alone tonight and at this point, I didn't really give a damn if the saxophonist at La Fleur's ever knew a Deborah.

Forty

La Fleur's, quite like a hundred other night spots in New Orleans, filled with a gumbo of Asian, African, Cajun, Hispanic and Scandinavian patrons; a microcosm of New Orleans that embraced all under jazz, zydeco, country or swing. The drink menu offered concoctions named Hurricane, Cajun Kick, the BIG Easy and Blue Lightning. Although Rita rolled her eyes, Llewellyn and I played it safe and ordered draft beer.

The Zylos, a Cajun foursome, occupied the small stage when we arrived and belted out music that would have set a zombie to dancing. Rita's prescription worked. The music and a cold beer lifted our heavy spirits and dissipated my anger. She winked at me and swayed to the rhythm and I squeezed her arm and swayed with her. In spite of the changes life had thrown at us, in spite of the fact that I had tried to keep a secret from her, our friendship survived. I felt washed clean of the dreary little ruts that had dug circular patterns in my mind. I had been consumed by questions from a past that gave no answers. I wouldn't waste the rest of our lives looking backward, and soon enough Llewellyn would not miss the Sabrina of a hundred dreary questions. If Rita could forgive me, I could forgive Llewellyn. I put my hand over his.

"It's over," I said. "I'm okay." And I pulled him into our table choreography.

Bobo's Bayou Blues followed the Zylos, and Bobo's saxophone cried, purred and sometimes screamed, and I was so taken up by the raw emotion that filled the room that I forgot why we had come. Then the vocalist took the stage, a handsome black gal in a blue-sequined dress that hugged her ample body. In a husky voice she said, "For all you people from Michigan, here's one written and arranged by Bobo himself, Michigan Melting "

Rita nudged me. "His Deborah song," she whispered. I listened carefully, even jotted down a few phrases on a napkin, but nothing in the lyrics held a clue that he had written it for Deborah Halbert.

 Llewellyn agreed. "It could have been written for either one of you," he said when the song ended.

"Not me," Rita disagreed. "Love melting the wild snow doesn't quite fit with a gal who never went farther north than Saginaw."

When the set ended, I repeated Rita's words. "Nothing lifts a mind like good music and Bobo's the best." Still filled with the music, I didn't care who Bobo's Michigan Deborah was, but Rita didn't vibrate on my wave length.

"You have to meet the man before he slips out the back door," she said and before I could object, she threaded her way past the stage already setting up for Good Times, a group that advertised Fats Domino's brand of rock and roll. Helplessly, Llewellyn and I followed her through a door that entered a chaotic backstage of musicians packing up instruments and musicians unpacking the same. Rita walked up to Bobo who stood trading remarks with a big, happy-faced black guy that I figured must be the featured vocalist for Good Times.

"Bobo, I brought you some new fans" Rita said. "Hi Billy."

The big guy nodded and stepped back.

"Hi ya, Rita." Bobo was a head taller than Llewellyn and two heads taller than Rita.

When Rita introduced us, he shook hands, but I saw a change in his eyes when she said we came from Michigan's Upper Peninsula. "Then you want to meet Belle, our vocalist," he said snapping shut his instrument case. "She does that Michigan song real good."

"Real good," Rita agreed. "But you and I know she's already gone to her next gig. Got time for a drink at my place?"

"You know I'm off the booze, girl."

"Chamomile tea. I got the best."

I saw a history between the two of them, but I didn't comment as Bobo followed us back to Rita's. Llewellyn glanced at me and I had to smile. He already knew the first question I would ask Rita tomorrow morning over café au latte and beignets.

 Bobo had barely broken into an oatmeal cookie and dipped it into his tea when Rita said, "These people are looking for a Deborah Halbert from Michigan. Seems like they tracked her to a vacant house in New Orleans."

"No problem of mine," Bobo said.

Rita carefully refilled his cup, still almost full. "That's a good song title."

Bobo flashed her a smile. "Already on my list."

Llewellyn and I watched the dance and neither of us said a word.

"These are my friends, Bo. They just want to find out if your Deborah is the one they're looking for."

He glared at Llewellyn. "Why you trackin' this Deborah Halbert?" The friendly smile and easy grace of the onstage Bobo disappeared.

"Sabrina's researching her family roots. Deborah Halbert was once married to her uncle." Llewellyn's answer was so smooth I almost believed the half-truth myself.

"They are not here to hurt anyone, Bo."

I winced at Rita's words. Would my questions hurt Deborah? So many of my other questions had hurt someone.

"Not dissing you, but you ain't thinking right. You looking for a Deborah, I got a woman, Deborah. That don't mean nothing. I don't know no Halbert."

"Yeah, it's a stretch," Rita agreed. She let her words tumble into an uncomfortable silence.

Finally Llewellyn said, "Rita and Sabrina have been friends since they were in middle school, and Rita thought it would help if we listened to the song you wrote for your Deborah. Please don't blame her. We had a great evening."

Bobo stood up. "I'll ask Deborah about you," he said, "but she don't like people snooping around."

Llewellyn stood up and offered his hand. "Thank you," he said.

"You didn't say a word," Rita said to me after Bobo left. She winked at Llewellyn. "Although I guess you didn't have to."

"I couldn't," I said. "You and Bobo—I just couldn't wreck one more"—

"Bobo slept on my floor when he didn't have a place to stay. I cried on his shoulder when I lost my last love who turned out to be a philandering asshole. You two are as white as a couple of Michigan snowdrifts, but he'll do what he said."

Forty-One

Rita was right. Whatever Bobo said to his Deborah, she agreed to meet us at a downtown coffee shop the next day if Rita would come with us. We took a taxi to Mannigan's, halfway across town, and I felt a prick of concern. Deborah had probably moved our meeting out of the neighborhood to a spot she hoped we would not find. My suspicions proved wrong. She took a lunch break from her job at a ticket venue across the street.

I was wrong on so many counts. I pictured Deborah as a short, stocky woman with Borg's crude demeanor. Bobo's Deborah, a trim, well-dressed blonde, looked nothing like Borg and my heart fell. Just because Bobo had a Michigan Deborah who inspired him to a write a song, it didn't follow that she ever heard of Clareburn. Soon enough she would set us straight and send us on our way.

We ordered the mufalettas she recommended. "A New Orleans specialty here," she said. "You haven't been to New Orleans until you've had a mufaletta."

"Or listened to Bobo," Rita added.

Deborah lost no time confronting the elephant in the room. "I understand you're looking for a Deborah Halbert supposedly connected to a family history. May I ask why?"

Both Rita and Llewellyn looked at me. After all, this was my quest, the quest I wanted to abandon, the quest that they held me to. Aunt Zelda had told me so many years ago that my questions would twist my life, and Rita and Llewellyn did not mean to help me disentangle those twists. I had to do it myself.

I blurted out my story, as best I could and Deborah listened, brows furrowed, gripping her drink.

"You would do better to leave the past behind. I left Deborah Halbert behind, and I won't bring her up again."

Her admission so astonished me that I had no reply. We remained silent as the stiff-necked waiter took our orders. I wish we could have met at La Fleur's where our drinks were delivered by a young man who danced his way around the tables, a part of the music that surrounded us.

Llewellyn said, "You lost a brother. Sabrina lost a father. You were married to Sabrina's Uncle Basil and your son, Borg, is her first cousin. You might have left the past behind, but Sabrina can't. We now live in Clareburn where you once lived."

"You should move," Deborah said.

Then Rita said, "My mother moved, Deborah. My aunt moved. It doesn't always work that way. Here we are, our pasts bubbling up no matter how far we run."

I said nothing. Deborah would leave and hide behind Bobo, the Deborah of "Melting Michigan". Did Bobo know the woman he loved? Would my questions put a fracture between them, yet another wound my questions might open?

"Bobo knows my past," Deborah said as if reading my mind. "He figured that somebody would pop up, but he always thought it would be Basil or Borg again. Bobo said maybe it's better that it's you."

"Why?" I asked.

"Bobo trusts Rita," she said. "He figured Basil didn't send you or Borg trying to find me so he could crash in and put a guilt trip on me when he lost another job. He's bounced between Basil and me more than once."

"Uncle Basil got into religion to try and raise Borg," I said.

Deborah smiled a small rueful smile. "I guess I can't blame him. When our marriage broke up, I was obsessed by my brother's disappearance, and Borg's birth brought up a torrent of emotions. Basil started staying away from my nagging. He'd go off in the woods or drink too much at Billy's Bar. I always thought Basil knew what had happened to Harry and protect his sister, Queen Elizabeth. I learned to hate him for that."

Queen Elizabeth, my mother! "Why did you think Basil was protecting his sister?" I tried to sound objective, but Deborah wasn't fooled.

"Sorry if it hurts, but your mother flitted around the guys when we got together and messed with them all." Deborah held up her hand. "I'm not saying she did any more than flirt, but Harry fell for her—fell for her hard."

Even after the stories back when Uncle Basil and Mother reminisced, I couldn't imagine my mother as a flirt. Perhaps Deborah had been as weirdly obsessed as Uncle Basil said. "Why would you think Basil would have known about your brother's disappearance?"

"Every place Queen Elizabeth went, Basil went. Or vice versa. They were as tight as two peas in a pod."

"Was he there the night your brother disappeared?" I asked. "Tell me everything you remember."

Deborah frowned. "It's been years, but I'll never forget, although I didn't pay much attention at the time. Harry came and left our parties all the time. That night we had a bonfire and drank the beer Harry managed to get, which wasn't much considering how many of us were there. I remember Gus and Clyde Feldersohn, Elaine Burns, Barb, Joe and Dan. I can't remember Basil there."

As she mentioned town names I recognized, I jotted them down on my napkin. It seems half of Clareburn drank Harry's beer around that bonfire.

"The night Harry disappeared, he and William Denham had Queen Elizabeth's attention, and I never believed my brother would have left that little tournament. I think Queen Elizabeth found it amusing, flirting with the city boy as besotted over her as the local guys, but I figured he didn't have a chance, clumsy as a cub bear with a rod and reel and silly in his shorts and hiking boots. Later, when your mother married him, I could hardly believe it, but I guess money talked and the locals walked."

"You and Uncle Basil married that same year."

Deborah picked at the cheesecake Llewellyn ordered for our dessert. "Yes," she said. "Looking back, I felt flattered that Basil fell for me the same way my brother fell for Queen Elizabeth. I thought Basil would know why his sister had rejected Harry and married William Denham and what Basil knew would help us find him. I was so young, so stupid. I've changed my mind over the years. The night Harry went missing, if Queen Elizabeth knew what had happened, she never told Basil. He didn't have a clue. Maybe she didn't have a clue either."

"So who had a clue?"

"Nobody that would tell me. The sheriff did a little search, but he figured my brother just ran away. I knew better but the sheriff got kind of mean when I kept telling him something bad had happened that night."

"When my marriage fell apart, I tried to raise Borg by myself, but it didn't work out. He needed a father more than he needed a mother who couldn't keep body and soul together. I'm not proud of it, but I shacked up with whoever was a meal ticket. It was no way to bring up a kid, and I left him on Basil's doorstep."

Deborah looked away and I could see that the past she had tried to escape hit her as hard as Rita had been hit from the reason for her father's suicide. "Borg came back to me a few years after I left him with Basil. I told him why I did what I did, but I had no right to dump on him. Sure enough, he ran back to Basil, but they never got along well. I didn't do right, but I

315

can't fix him every time he shows up after he loses a job and needs money." She stood up and I could see that the story she had told was all she could tell.

"Thank you, Deborah," I said. I felt truly sorry for the pain my questions had given her.

"Don't thank me. Bobo asked me to come here for Rita's friends, and I owe Bobo. He saved my life. Let it go, Sabrina. You can't reconstruct the past from a few broken fragments."

Forty-Two

"Now we know why Borg has been twisting in the wind," Llewellyn said on our flight back from New Orleans.

"I knew most of that story."

"But Deborah told you details about the night her brother disappeared, people who were there that your Uncle Basil couldn't have known."

"All we learned is that Mother had been a flirt and my father had been one more suitor for her attention the summer Harry went missing. I'm not even sure Deborah didn't exaggerate Mother's behavior. It's obvious she resented Mother for choosing Father instead of her brother. Whatever, we hurt Rita with what William dug up about her father's suicide and hurt Deborah as well. Neither one of them will be living their lives the same way as they had before I had arrived with my infernal probing."

Llewellyn fell silent, and I took it as agreement. On our drive from the airport to Windsong, I couldn't help but notice the beauty of the full fall color, nature's blessing before the hills and valleys were put to rest under a cold blanket that would cover all. Maybe my next children's book should be about the

317

life of a leaf—or a tree in northern Michigan. I could write that under a palm tree. "We should get out of here by the end of November," I said.

"You asked all the right questions," Llewellyn said, ignoring my remark.

"I gave it one more try, Llewellyn. That night at La Fleur's I realized I've been like Mother after Father's death, holding on to ghosts. I'll still be the Little Scientist with a thousand questions, but I'm okay now letting go of what's past."

Llewellyn pulled into Windsong and parked on the drive. We still had not gotten accustomed to driving into the garage, a silhouette against the fading western sky. Llewellyn had erected shelves along one wall which held his minor set of tools and storage containers of superfluous grains and herbs we had collected, as well as any other items that would weather subzero temperatures. At one time, the cupboards and closets in the house seemed adequate, but somehow in the last year our possessions had expanded. How would we ever go to Arizona or Florida with only a car full of what we thought we needed?

"If you're sure," Llewellyn said as we went in the door.

I flicked on the light and gasped. Cupboards stood open and plates and cups smashed all over the floor. The sofa cushions were slashed, and the bookcases turned over, many of the spilled books ripped and torn. The TV and stereo looked like someone had taken a sledge hammer to them.

"It's worse than I thought," Llewellyn muttered and fished his cell phone out of his pocket.

When Sheriff Feldersohn arrived with two deputies, he surveyed the damage, brows furrowed, eyes narrowed. His deputies went to work taking notes and dusting for fingerprints, while Feldersohn interrogated us with a barrage of questions. When did we leave? Who knew we'd be gone? What time did we come back? Had we left the door unlocked? Had we touched anything after we arrived? What was missing? Who might have done this?

The dutiful deputies went out to the garage and found that too had been trashed; containers dumped on the floor and covered with oil, the lawn mower and snow blower wrecked. Luckily, both of us had taken our laptops with us.

"Might have been what the asshole was looking for," Feldersohn said, but I didn't think so, and I don't think Feldersohn thought so either. It was an act of hate. "You folks might want to stay somewhere else tonight. I can follow you into town."

I didn't object as Llewellyn guided me to the car and the sheriff followed us to the only motel in town, too numb to suggest that Aunt Hetty or Uncle Basil might take us in.

"What did you mean it was worse than you thought?" I said after Llewellyn fumbled with the key, the old-fashioned kind that let us into the motel room after a grumbling click.

"I always thought someone here knows your father's accident was not an accident." He sank to the bed that looked as comfortable as a camouflaged board. "I'm sorry, Sabrina. I wanted you to find the answers you needed about your father's death, about your mother's secrecy. I'm sorry I pushed this New Orleans trip on you."

I curled up beside him. "Your equation is a little askew, but the conclusion fits. Someone in town didn't want us talking to Deborah."

"Who knew we were going to talk to Deborah? I didn't even know until the night I told you."

"Who knew?" I echoed. "I never even thought to tell Uncle Lew and Aunt Hetty."

"You're right about my imperfect equation. What's the connection between Deborah and your father's accident?"

"The few broken fragments that Deborah gave us are all we have, but somehow it connects to Father's time in Clareburn that summer and Harry's disappearance and someone in town knows how and I'm going to find out who."

Neither of us slept well that night under a thin blanket. The next morning my eyes felt full of sand, and my body ached, either from the bad mattress or from holding myself rigid with the fear that sent waves of nightmares through my troubled sleep.

"You look like hell," Llewellyn observed when I came out of the tinny shower. He had already showered and dressed, but he didn't look much better.

"You look like hell's CEO," I retorted. "We need some coffee." I determined we would go back to Windsong the next day with a new mattress and sleep amidst the destruction rather than spend one more night on a rigid mattress the size of a single. Insurance would cover Sheriff Feldersohn's report of the damages but our claim would take some time to process and now I didn't plan on leaving Windsong anytime soon.

Forty-Three

Millie's Diner served a good omelet and Millie refilled our coffee mugs as if administering to a couple of invalids that could be cured with heavy doses of caffeine. I suspected she already knew what had happened at Windsong through the gossip grapevine, but if she needed any confirmation, she soon got it when Uncle Lew burst through the door and confronted us, as upset as I had ever seen him. "We heard on the scanner Windsong was vandalized. Why the hell didn't you call?"

"The sheriff"— I stammered. "He just led us to the motel. I wasn't thinking."

"Of course, you weren't thinking!" Uncle Lew exclaimed and pulled up a chair. "How could you ever think we'd have that kind of thing going on here? City trash is creeping in like a bad fungus." He eyed my plate. "No offense to Millie, but you need Hetty's cooking. You finish and come on over to the house. Hetty's expecting you."

"Is Benjie expecting us?"

"Already got him kenneled. He'll get friendly with you soon enough."

I took a bite of the omelet and looked at Llewellyn, but he avoided my eyes and attacked his hash browns. I knew that he blamed himself for the vandalism at Windsong. If I told Uncle Lew we decided to relocate in Tahiti, Llewellyn would make it happen. I put a hand on his arm, the smallest gesture I could make at Millie's Diner for the wave of love I felt right then for my lion-hearted man.

"You got yourself a couple of rumpled house guests," I said to Uncle Lew.

"Good," Uncle Lew said getting up from the table with a last dubious look at my omelet.

"Are you sure?" Llewellyn asked as we packed up to leave our forlorn room. "We don't have to stay while this is settled."

"We have to stay until this settled," I said and by the glance he gave me, he knew that I wasn't talking about an insurance adjustor.

When we got to Aunt Hetty's that afternoon, we felt as rumpled with exhaustion as I warned Uncle Lew. We went back to Windsong and combed through the wreckage to insure nothing of value had been taken. The vandal left nothing worth taking after the wreckage. Then we went through another interview with Sheriff Feldersohn. I told him of my search to find the reason for Father's accident and Deborah's futile search years ago for her missing brother. At first, I resisted telling my family's old history since nothing seemed to connect to Windsong's vandalism. Sheriff Feldersohn had not presided over the investigation of Father's accident and certainly not the sheriff who had made the half-hearted search for Deborah's brother. I expected him to dismiss my story but he took extensive notes, his brow furrowed, his eyes narrowed much as he had the night before. Who knew I was asking about my father's accident? Who knew we had gone to question Deborah? I had to admit that outside of my trip to the Clareburn museum and my questions to Aunt Hetty at Billy's Bar, I hadn't interrogated anyone else in town. It made my story sound pretty lame, but he took my suppositions seriously.

"It's a start," he said. "You might not have talked about your suspicions to others, but someone in town thinks that you're a threat. I wish I had more."

"He'll run into a dead end," I said when he left.

Llewellyn disagreed. "He might be the first Clareburn sheriff who asks as many questions as you do."

After our interview, Neil Hays, an insurance adjustor, called and had Llewellyn scrambling through his computer and replying to the phone interview as surely as I could not. When Llewellyn finally satisfied Mr. Hays that we had an honest claim, he made an appointment to make an assessment within the next week. When we finally arrived at Uncle Lew and Aunt Hetty's, the autumn sun cast long shadows as it slipped toward the western horizon.

Benjie greeted our arrival with furious barks from his kennel, and I thought it unlikely we would be friends anytime soon. Aunt Hetty, as Uncle Lew said expected us and must have spent half the day preparing a feast of roast chicken, homemade stuffing, baked squash and pumpkin pie.

"This is a Thanksgiving feast," Llewellyn said.

"This is a Thanksgiving feast," Aunt Hetty said. "Thank heavens no one was hurt."

"Amen," I said

After dinner, I tried to help Aunt Hetty clean up, but she waved me out of the kitchen. "You look like a walking scarecrow. Go get in your jammies and read yourself to sleep. And tell that man of yours to do the same."

We happily obliged. I fell asleep before I had read three pages of *Cat and I*, an improbable mystery when the detective's cat solves the crime. Oh, for a cat like that.

The next morning I awoke to the wonderful aroma of bacon and coffee. Llewellyn was no longer curled around me, and I felt a stab of conscience that I slept in while the whole world was up and at it. I jumped out of bed and threw on my clothes and did a hasty job of making myself presentable.

"Good morning sunshine," Aunt Hetty said when I got to the kitchen. Uncle Lew had already left for work and Llewellyn was out by the kennel trying to make friends with Benjie who barked as furiously as he had the night before. Aunt Hetty put a plate of scrambled eggs and bacon in front of me and poured a mug of coffee for both of us. It reminded me of the days at Windsong when she did the same for my mother.

"Thank you so much," I said. "I'm sorry whatever I stirred up came to this."

"It's city trash, probably high on drugs. It's not your fault."

"It's not city trash, Aunt Hetty. Somebody in Clareburn doesn't want me at Windsong. The vandal meant to scare me silent."

Aunt Hetty took a chair. "What makes you think such a thing?" I could see from the worried look on her face that she had the same thought.

I recounted every fragment Llewellyn and I had unearthed from the insurance investigator's analysis of father's accident to our interview with Deborah.

"You talked with Deborah! Where did you talk to Deborah?"

"Llewellyn found her in New Orleans. I don't think our visit and the vandalism a coincidence."

"Of course, it is! Nobody knew you went to New Orleans. You should have stayed home. Why talk to Deborah?"

I looked out the window. Benjie's frenetic barking had ceased as he silently sized up Llewellyn. Either Benjie lost his voice or his doggy brain plotted how best to escape his kennel and take a chunk out of the interloper.

"I think Deborah's brother's disappearance, Father's accident and Windsong's vandalism connect and I need to know how."

Aunt Hetty got up and began to clean up the remains of breakfast with a nervous energy. "Sabrina, that's a stretch. Your father's accident happened years ago and the sheriff judged it an accident. Deborah's brother, a known drinker, disappeared years before that, probably from an accident of his own making. Why would somebody vandalize Windsong over that old history?"

"I don't know," I admitted.

"I know you always wanted to know why your parents were the way they were and that started all your questions. Most marriages have their tics, but they're both gone. Just be happy that you found a good man and don't try to fix something beyond their graves."

"I can't fix it, but I need to find out the truth. Now that someone vandalized Windsong I think what happened stayed in Clareburn beyond their graves."

"You are the most stubborn person I know."

Llewellyn came in and attempted to help her, but she brushed him away. "Take your wife out fishing or something. She's getting on my nerves."

Forty-Four

Llewellyn did not take me fishing, but we did leave Aunt Hetty to her consternation and took a long walk. We agreed that I had hit a raw note when I told her about finding Deborah, but if she accused me of being stubborn, I had nothing on her. In the next few days, she cooked her wonderful meals and treated us as if we were the first cousins to the president himself, but she managed to evade any opportunities to question her further.

In truth, I had little opportunity to corner her anyway. The insurance adjustor arrived and after he left, we faced the horrific task of cleaning up the devastation. In spite of their offers, I wouldn't let Uncle Lew or Aunt Hetty help. They didn't need to see the destruction my inquisitive mind had brought down on Windsong. Picking up every torn book, every smashed dish that had once held Aunt Hetty's meals, throwing out bins of our summer's gathering, filled me with such helpless rage and desire for revenge, I wanted to scream. By the grim set of Llewellyn's jaw, I could see that he felt the same, but we said little. No words fit.

I soon learned that Llewellyn faced the devastation in a much different way than I did. When we ended a day and went back to Aunt Hetty's, he spent so much time with Benjie, the dog soon ate out of his hand without biting it off.

"Now there's a guy who knows critters," Uncle Lew said.

Since Benjie was trained to a leash, before long Llewellyn also took him on a daily walk to the sheriff's office. I didn't accompany him on those treks, not because I thought his newly-forged friendship with Benjie would come undone, but because I didn't see how those late-afternoon visits would yield anything new that hadn't already been determined. Sheriff Feldersohn had nothing to go on but old reports and our suspicions that Windsong's vandalism was somehow connected.

I started an investigation of my own. I went back to the museum and Elaine Burns, now Elaine Kearns, happily greeted me, but Deborah named her as one who had been at that campfire years ago. I didn't waste words. "You must have heard my place was vandalized last week."

"Such a horrible thing to happen in Clareburn, Sabrina! People are locking their houses, their cars as if we lived in Detroit."

"Who did you tell I was in here researching my family history?"

She looked confused by my abrupt question. "Why, I don't know. Probably everybody I talked to. I was so happy somebody took advantage of the museum. We need more of that curiosity about our past in this town."

"Somebody in Clareburn did not like my curiosity."

Elaine looked truly dismayed. "You can't think the vandalisms came from somebody in Clareburn—"

"I certainly do and I'm going to find out who."

She turned away, no longer the friendly museum lady. "Clareburn people are good people. It had to come from outside. Your husband made a few enemies in his career." Oddly enough, neither Llewellyn nor I had thought of that angle.

I next visited Clyde Ingersoll at the only place I knew to find him when he wasn't pouring cement. When I walked into Billy's Bar, "It Hurts so Good" blared from the speakers and Clyde, a Bruce Springsteen wanna be, shuffled around the pint-size dance floor playing an air guitar. I waited until his performance ended before I followed him to his bar stool.

"Clyde, I've got a question for you."

He patted the stool next to him. "Anything to help a favored customer, dear lady."

"What do you recommend to clean oil stains from cement?"

"I heard what happened up there," he said. "Nasty doin's."

"Who do you know in town who wants me gone?" I asked bluntly. As much as Clyde hung around Billy's, he might have heard something.

Clyde took a long gulp of his beer. "Probably half the town. No offense Missus, but you and that man of yours are city people."

"My mother came from here, my aunt and uncle live here."

"Yeah, so they do, but you didn't." He finished his beer and ordered another. "I'll buy you a drink."

"A coke," I said.

"What happens when somebody like you comes here, it can bring other people too," he explained. "You were probably trashed by somebody from the city. That's what they're sayin'."

"My father came here years ago from the city and married my mother. Who felt that way about him?"

Clyde nodded a thank you to the bar tender when he slid our drinks across the bar and took another long drink. "Probably half the town," he repeated, his voice a little more slurry. "Me at the top of the list right after Harry Borgendorf. I sure liked your ma, but too stupid to say so. Harry didn't have any trouble sayin' so, but Harry got erased and your ma got married before I ever got to first base."

I took a nervous gulp of my Coke. "Got erased?"

"Like a bad line out of a good song."

Bruce Springsteen broke in and Clyde was already sliding off his stool to impersonate him. "Women are trouble, Missus, present company excluded. Thas all I got to say."

I left to find Ingersoll's son, hoping against hope that Borg wasn't working for him again. Ingersoll's fish house, a ramshackle shed that housed nets, a boat, several boat motors and a strong smell of fish and gasoline.

Ingersoll glared at me over a dismantled boat motor. "Whadda want?" he growled.

I didn't have a good excuse, so I had no choice but to treat him likewise. "Somebody vandalized my place last week and I'm trying to find out who."

"I don't know a damn thing about it."

"You hire my cousin, Borg, so I thought you could help."

"Well, I can't. Borg is a piece of shit. When I need help, he disappears."

"Your father once had a thing for my mother."

"Who the hell told you that?"

"Is it true?"

"Everybody in Clareburn who had a dick had a thing for her. She was a pecker teaser and latched onto money."

His words stung. "So your father hated my father."

Ingersoll snorted. "He was too goofy to hate." He waved a wrench at her. "You brought your vandals from that damn city. Go look there. Now I got work to do."

All had been at my book signing, all had asked questions about my residence at Windsong. How had my time at Windsong as the Little Scientist twisted so horribly that someone vandalized Windsong? All those that I interrogated had been at the bonfire the night Deborah's brother went missing; Ingersoll, whose son gave Borg a job sorting nets, Elaine Burns, who had told the town of my investigations at the museum. Why did I feel that the night of Harry Borgendorf's disappearance and my father's accident connected to the vandalism? Did Father find out what had happened and been killed for what he knew? Did someone think I had also found out what happened that night?

Forty-Five

Neither Llewellyn nor the sheriff were happy when I reported my investigations.

"If the vandal is in town, you might have stepped on somebody's tail," Sheriff Feldersohn said.

"From all I found out, most of the town blames the vandalism on city trash that we attracted when we moved here, but I think they're just using it as an excuse." I didn't tell him that some thought Llewellyn's activist interests made Windsong a target.

"You can't do this anymore," Llewellyn said. "I know how you feel, but if somebody hated us enough to do what they did, they could do worse."

Llewellyn had a point. Windsong could be set on fire, something that once-upon-a-time enraged citizens had almost done when my great-grandfather Halbert had cheated half the town and left his abandoned wife to fend for herself. Nobody I interviewed brought up my unfortunate ancestor, at least to my face. But what if Clareburn once divided between the Halberts and the Burns still existed? I now saw reason for Uncle Lew's explanation of Aunt Hetty's watchfulness.

In spite of my interrogations, the people of Clareburn brought us enough groceries to feed an army. If many thought we were followed by some sort of city corruption, many thought we needed help, not hate. Elaine said the people of Clareburn were good people and most proved her right. I almost felt ashamed of my suspicions. My investigations brought no answers, only more questions.

Aunt Hetty worked overtime cooking the surplus and giving it back to Uncle Basil's church which held a once-a-week free dinner for anybody in town that needed it. More than once, Uncle Basil invited us to his church's feasts and, in spite of all, I felt we should finally appear to thank the town for all their efforts. It might put my suspicions to rest and give Aunt Hetty a respite.

"He'll want you to join the flock," Aunt Hetty warned us.

"Maybe we will," Llewellyn teased. "His church does some good work."

"The women do the great work. If it was up to Basil, he'd expect the Lord to come down and fix those meals and sew those quilts. He might know how to hunt and fish, but he doesn't know a thing about running a church. When Deborah dumped Borg on Basil, he didn't have to take up preaching the Bible to prove himself a good father."

"Now Hetty," Uncle Lew said. "Harry's disappearance was hard on Basil as well as Deborah."

"All that's water under the bridge," she retorted sharply.

"I'm just saying Basil tried his best with Borg the only way he knew how and he did teach the boy how to hunt and fish."

"Basil might have taught him how to hunt and fish, but he certainly didn't teach him any manners."

In spite of Aunt Hetty's objections, we went to Uncle Basil's church hall and the meal of meatloaf, mashed potatoes, green beans and a huge slice of carrot cake truly proved the great work Aunt Hetty said the church women did. We had finished the meal before Borg made an appearance or I probably would have lost my appetite. He hadn't been working at Ingersoll's, so I thought him safely out of town.

When he came to our table, he was as bad-mannered as ever. "I see that Windsong's vandalism has brought you to the church's free supper," he said.

"Your father's church has been good to us," I said. "We appreciate their concern."

"My father's church is a bunch of fools. It's not like you need a free meal."

Before I could think of a reply, Llewellyn stood up, but Borg just shrugged and left without saying another word.

"If I knew Borg came back to Uncle Basil's, we wouldn't have gone," I fumed on the way back to Aunt Hetty's.

"He's probably been collecting a few free meals himself," Llewellyn said. "Every family has a Borg. We had my father's cousin, Delbert."

We moved back to Windsong at the end of October in spite of Uncle Lew and Aunt Hetty's objections. "You two should just go to Florida for the winter," Uncle Lew said.

"Why don't you go to Florida for the winter?" I countered.

"This is our home."

"For better or worse, Windsong is our home too. If it was random vandalism by city trash, they won't be around this winter anyway."

"Then you take Benjie with you," Uncle Lew said.

"We can't take your dog," Llewellyn objected.

"He'll be happier at Windsong. I don't have the time to get him out of his kennel and walk him like he needs and every time I let him loose, he gets in trouble. You'll be doing both Benjie and me a favor."

"You'll be doing me a favor too," Aunt Hetty said. "I 'm the one who gets the phone calls when Benjie's on the prowl."

I wondered what trouble Benjie had gotten into the day I saw him loose last winter in their front yard, but I didn't ask. I never told them about the day I felt so lonesome I wanted to visit and went to the museum instead. At any rate, neither Benjie nor Llewellyn needed more than Uncle Lew's blessing, and we moved back to Windsong with the big dog in tow.

It had been stripped of a lot, but I refused to let Llewellyn replace a thing out of his inheritance. He could probably have replaced Windsong with a mansion; even my inheritance could have replaced the house as well, but Windsong was my misadventure, and we would wait for Neil Hayes to complete his paperwork. I did ensure we had a generator and enough canned food to get us through an Upper Peninsula winter and a new mattress that Benjie soon learned to appreciate as much as we did. After our move, Benjie adopted me as part of the pack and accepted my doggie treats as his due for taking on the job as my appointed protector.

The following weeks were uneventful weather wise. We had Thanksgiving at Aunt Hetty's and Uncle Basil came without Borg. Although Benjie barked at his arrival, he soon sank under the table and slept through Uncle Basil's lengthy Thanksgiving prayer. Aunt Hetty told me that Borg was not invited. When Borg was younger, he would have been just one more nephew to feed, but Aunt Hetty no longer excused his bad manners and ingratitude toward Uncle Basil in his growing years. "He should have learned how to be a man by this time," she said. "A person can't blame their parents' faults for their own behavior forever."

I sliced vegetables silently. I knew Aunt Hetty hadn't meant it, but part of her words struck home. Too much of my life had also been steered by my history with my parents.

Forty-Six

Two weeks before Christmas, William called. "You've been away from the city too long. Come down for Christmas. Spend a week. Spend the whole winter if you want."

William's invitation surprised me. "William, we haven't been together at Christmas since we both lived home."

"I know that."

I had to laugh. "You aren't running for attorney general and bringing your wayward sister out before the media gets wind of me?"

"Not a chance. I promise I won't hold formal dinners. You won't even have to hide out at Sam's Pizza and Grill."

"It's closed."

"I know. I still miss that place."

"Let me get back with you. I need to check with Llewellyn and he went to town." When I hung up, I paced the floor. Why this unexpected invitation? I had called and told William about the vandalism, but he spent most of the phone call talking to Llewellyn about insurance claims and the cost of punitive damages if the vandal was ever caught. Maybe he would try to convince us to abandon Windsong. Or in spite of his denial, maybe he planned on running for something and needed to keep me in the loop if reporters knocked on our door. Whatever prompted the unexpected invitation, could we leave Windsong again? We might come back and find it burned to the ground.

"Sometimes the female of the species are hard to understand," Llewellyn said when he got back from town and listened to my suspicions. "We will go. He's your brother, the only sibling you have."

In spite of his light-hearted reply, my heart wrenched. After months of improvement, Wendy, the only sibling he had, had a major backslide, and Llewellyn planned on flying to Maine after the holidays, evidently she was in no shape to talk to him before then.

Uncle Lew sided with Llewellyn and insisted we take William's invitation. He and Aunt Hetty would stay at Windsong with Benjie. "We will have a Windsong Christmas," Uncle Lew said. "We haven't been there for Christmas since the first years we were married."

"Lew is getting soft in the head," Aunt Hetty said, "but we'll watch Windsong. William won't invite you again if you don't show up."

"Uncle Lew and Aunt Hetty haven't been at Windsong together since the summer William came with the news of Rita's father," I said to Llewellyn. "Are they worried Windsong is still a target?"

"Maybe they're just missing Benjie," Llewellyn said. "We can't live our lives defined by one act of vandalism."

Or my suspicions about William's invitation, I thought.

When we arrived at William's on Christmas Eve, a huge tree, decorated in silver, filled one corner of his front room. Doorways were festooned with glittery garlands, candles lit the place and mistletoe hung over the entrance, which William pointed out when we walked in. The aroma of mincemeat, garlic and roasting turkey filled the room. It felt like we walked into a scene from a Christmas story.

A blonde man came from the kitchen and William's unusual invitation snapped into place. Even before introductions, I recognized William's Exeter friend, Gregory Thurman.

In the next days, I realized that William and Gregory fit well, even if Gregory's occupation as a chef was far afield from William's law practice. Gregory had just opened a restaurant, simply named Gregory's, and they reconnected when William had helped him negotiate the business contract. I suspected the

Detroit location more than coincidence. Gregory's restaurant featured organic food, but he confessed having a hard time finding all the organic ingredients he needed, and Llewellyn lost no time giving him all the resources he knew. Gregory, in turn, exchanged recipes with Llewellyn. Before Gregory, I'm sure William's refrigerator probably only contained yogurt and juice and, in the last couple of years, Llewellyn's interest in cooking had far exceeded mine.

Since neither William nor I could add much, we broke up their enthusiastic discussions with board games or films that William introduced at my insistence that we go walking or skating or bowling. Our week spun out in good-natured arguments about what we would do each day, and as our visit drew to a close, I knew that Gregory had kept William from splintering like shattered glass, as Rita had phrased it. William acted more like the big brother I had known before Borg at Windsong.

William made little mention of what had happened at Windsong but when we were leaving, he said, "I always felt that something was not right at Windsong. I tried to discourage you from moving, but I guess I should have known better. You always belonged there, but you can't fix what happened years ago."

"I guess I should have known better too. Some in town think I brought city trash to Clareburn and some think Llewellyn's activism caused the vandalism."

"Garbage. I'm glad you have Llewellyn, but I don't know if that's enough."

"I'm glad you have Gregory. I haven't seen you so happy for years."

"Don't let whatever happened at Windsong poison what you and Llewellyn have."

"All I want to know is the maniac that trashed the place," I reassured him. "Then I promise I'll let the ghosts rest."

Llewellyn flew out of Detroit to Maine the next day and, as much as I wanted to go with him, I drove back to Windsong. In Wendy's state, my appearance would not do any good. I would only add to whatever demons she wrestled with from her past, and I would only be a reminder of her father's dislike for me.

I hadn't shared with Llewellyn William's words that he always felt something not right at Windsong. Although it had given me some of the happiest days of my life, on hindsight, I realized that William, the more logical, had seen something dark in Father's tight-lipped drives there, in Aunt Hetty's exclusion from Father's favor and in his inexplicable accident. My questions had arisen from a wish to understand who my parents were, but William had always seen that something at Windsong had made them that way. I truly meant what I said when I told William that all I wanted was the face of the one who had vandalized Windsong, but inwardly I hoped that the vandal connected to the story of my parents' ghosts.

Even though Llewellyn knew Wendy might still resent me after our disastrous days putting their father's estate in order, he wanted me with him, away from Windsong. I tried to explain my faulty logic, but I ended my argument by quoting what he had said, "We can't live our lives defined by one act of vandalism."

"How do you always turn my words back on me to win an argument?"

"I know words," I laughed and hugged him. "You're only going to be gone a few days, I have Benjie and I'll go back to Aunt Hetty's if they've been bothered at all. Cross my heart."

"I'm calling every evening and the first time you don't answer, I'm on the next flight home."

"Use the landline," I reminded him. We both had cell phones, but often couldn't get a signal in Clareburn. Feldersohn told Llewellyn that he heard that would change in the coming year, although we had heard that rumor before. "Call Aunt Hetty before you get a ticket. If we get a storm, Windsong might be out of power."

"The whole damn Upper Peninsula might be out of power," Llewellyn grumbled, but inside I smiled. He had called Windsong home.

Forty-Seven

Uncle Lew and Aunt Hetty had nothing to report except Benjie's resigned acceptance of Uncle Basil's long prayer on Christmas day, which forestalled surreptitious handouts under the table from Uncle Lew. Two days after they left, Aunt Hetty invited me and Benjie to supper. I had spent most of last winter at Windsong without Llewellyn and without any invitations from them, but I happily obliged. Whatever evil Windsong's vandalism had wrought, it had also brought Aunt Hetty back into my life,

When I got there, the warm, rich smell of Aunt Hetty's venison stew greeted me and when Uncle Basil arrived, he still glided on the waves of the holiday season at his church. The children's program was as if done by cherubs and the choir had sung Silent Night so beautifully, it brought tears to his eyes. After Christmas, his church family had not left him to spend a single evening by himself. They fed him and gave him gifts of homemade fudge and knitted scarves. He brought us a box of fudge, happily exclaiming he had already gained five pounds from Clareburn's bounty.

We ate stew and biscuits and listened to his retelling, and I felt relieved that the cloud of worry he always had when Borg again disappeared had been lifted. Even Benjie suffered Uncle Basil's usual ponderous prayer of Thanksgiving that added a plea to keep Borg safe.

"He's probably in his cabin, Uncle Basil," I said as I packed up the leftovers for him to take home. "And he knows how to survive."

"Bless you for your words of encouragement, Sabrina, but this winter he's far from us all. His mother got him a job in New Orleans."

"How do you know that?"

"I guess I didn't tell you. With the vandalism and all, it slipped my mind, but Deborah called me back in October asking if you were really my niece. An odd question after all these years until I found out you actually went down there and wanted to meet her. She said you wanted to make amends with your cousin's mother. That was Christian of you, Sabrina. Forgiveness is all."

I felt a chill creep over me, as if I had been hit by a winter wind. "Who did you tell we went to New Orleans?"

"Why, nobody. That's family business. Nobody needed reminding of the bitterness that happened between Deborah and me and you trying to fix it."

"You must have told Borg."

"I didn't but you were a conduit for the way the Lord works. Borg must have heard our conversation and called her back. I guess that number was on my phone or something. Anyway, he said he could find work there. Bless you, Sabrina."

"Did you call Deborah back and tell her Borg was coming?"

"I tried, but even after all these years, Deborah don't like me calling. She changed her number."

"Why? You were Borg's father."

Uncle Basil frowned. "She thought everybody in town killed her brother at one time or another. That's what I'm saying. Your visit stretched out a hand of forgiveness."

I helped Aunt Hetty clean up, but I kept my ugly suspicions to myself. Borg's story could very well be just as he said, but I doubted it. Deborah did not want Borg on her doorstep anymore than Aunt Hetty did. Before Deborah met with us, she made that call to confirm that I was truly Uncle Basil's niece without thinking of what it would cost her—or me.

"Guess you and Benjie are going to stay here overnight," Uncle Lew announced bringing in an armful of wood. "The snow's already started. We got lucky this year. We missed the November gales."

"Llewellyn will be calling Windsong. He'll be frantic if I don't answer." I cursed myself for not having checked on the weather, something everybody in Clareburn did every day. Had Uncle Lew and Aunt Hetty intentionally invited me into town before the first storm?

"He'll call here," Uncle Lew said. "We don't get blinked out as often as Windsong. That damn line gets hit all the time. Too many trees."

Sure enough, Llewellyn called shortly after Uncle Lew's prediction. "Thank god!" he greeted me.

"Benjie and I just had Aunt Hetty's stew. We're fine," I reassured him.

"I'll be back day after tomorrow. Wendy's recovering and she's got a big support system behind her. So many are pulling for her."

"She helped a lot of others before she crashed," I guessed.

"She taught half the people in rehab how to do watercolors. She's really good."

"She's got something to come back to."

"There's so much about addiction I didn't understand. She's determined she'll beat it this time."

"I think she will."

Llewellyn hadn't noticed any hesitation in my voice. If we were in the same room, or he would not have let my next two days go by without question, but Aunt Hetty saw that Uncle Basil's parting words had hit me like a hammer. For once, I evaded questions. Borg in New Orleans had just surprised me, I told her. I had him pictured up in his cabin, that's all.

"If Basil's right, maybe Borg's mother finally did something right by him," Aunt Hetty said, but I saw that she had connected the dots as well as I had.

Forty-Eight

Uncle Lew and I had Windsong up and running before Llewellyn's arrival. We kicked the new generator into action and cleared two feet of snow from the drive and off the roof. The heat and lights made the place cozy, although Benjie had to check out every room and corner before he snuffed his approval and collapsed in front of the fireplace.

In spite of my objections, Uncle Lew stayed until Llewellyn arrived at the end of the day. The western sky blazed with a distant promise of light and warmth, but it would hit zero tonight. When Llewellyn came through the door, Benjie and I danced around him like a couple of fools.

"Come stay with us if that generator acts up," Uncle Lew commanded as he went to the door.

I threw my arms around him. "Thank you, Uncle Lew. So help me, someday I'll repay you and Aunt Hetty for all you've done for us."

"You made Benjie happy," he said.

I didn't tell Llewellyn what I had heard from Uncle Basil until the next day, not that I intentionally hid it but because Llewellyn had so much to tell me, I accused him of being as long-winded as Uncle Basil. When we fell into bed and closed the door on Benjie's intrusion, we made love as if we hadn't seen one another in months and when we snuggled together, my ugly suspicions would have only poisoned a perfect homecoming.

We got up to a pristine morning and let the disgruntled Benjie out to cavort in the snow drifts. Life still seemed too perfect to disturb but after breakfast, Llewellyn asked the raw question that I had chosen to ignore. "Anything new happen?"

Uncle Basil's story came pouring out, a pent-up dam of unfounded suspicions based on a phone call, two phone calls. It might be nothing but the wishful thinking of a father who wanted to think his son safe from the fury of the northern Michigan weather.

Llewellyn's jaw tightened. He didn't buy my limp excuse of the possibility that Borg might not be the one person who knew where we went the weekend Windsong was vandalized. "We've got to find out if Borg is in New Orleans."

"It can't mean anything, Llewellyn. Borg is family."

Llewellyn went to the phone and handed it to me. "Call Rita," he said, his voice unusually clipped, "She can find out if Borg is in New Orleans."

Rita sounded her usual jaunty self until I told her the reason for my call.

"You told me you were done with all those questions that's had you twisting around." She sounded so much like Aunt Zelda, I thought I would drop the phone.

"When we got home, Windsong was vandalized." I told her the rest of the story, disjointed, my voice too high, my words too quick. I must have sounded as twisted as she said I was. "I'm sorry, Rita, but you're the only one who can help us locate Borg."

"I'm sorry too, Sabrina." Rita's voice was flat. "Bobo said he shouldn't have let you know about Deborah. She's been having her nightmares again. I'll see what I can do."

When I hung up, I felt as miserable as if Rita had reached through the phone and slapped me. My visit must have brought Borg to Deborah's doorstep and disrupted her life with Bobo and Bobo's friendship with Rita.

Llewellyn and Benjie did their best to break my somber mood. We snowshoed around Windsong with Benjie jumping around us. Llewellyn made chili and popped popcorn over the fire in an antique popcorn popper he had found in the shed and suggested that we invite Rita to Windsong next summer, now that her outlier art had been discovered.

I loved him for his efforts and, for his sake, I strapped on the snowshoes, ate the chili and agreed that Rita would have a whole new world of inspiration with a summer at Windsong, but inside I thought I might never hear from Rita again. When she called two days later, I burst into tears at the sound of her voice.

"Damn weird way to take a call," Rita said, her jaunty tone quite as I remembered.

"I-I thought after what I did to you and Bobo's friendship, you'd be done with me."

"Friends don't be done with friends quite that fast. Bobo might not like you much, but he still puts up with me, and I still put up with you."

I tried to laugh. "That's the most flattering thing you've ever said to me."

"And you'd better appreciate it. Bobo growled and grumbled about you and your fancy visit about family history that put his woman in a funk, but he said no Borg came around and if he did, he'd get a lesson on how to respect his mother. He had a few choice words for your Uncle Basil as well."

"He's right about Borg," I said. "Uncle Basil, not so much."

"One other thing that Bobo said about Deborah's nightmares. When Borg was already a teen, she told Borg she thought your father murdered her brother."

"She thought half the town might have murdered her brother."

"True. But when she heard about your father's accident, the nightmares started."

"That's horrible!" I gasped.

"Yes," Rita said. Her voice was no longer jaunty. "But I'm just telling you about a mother's nightmares."

"Thank you."

"Got to get back to work. I love you, girl. Be careful."

Forty-Nine

Llewellyn threw a parka, snowshoes and other gear into the car before we drove into town. I didn't ask. I knew. If Borg didn't go to New Orleans, he went to his cabin and if Borg thought himself hidden, he hadn't reckoned on the tenderfoot from Maine. Llewellyn had familiarized himself with the area, not only from his excursions with me but on treks he took on his own when he needed to unwind from his struggles with getting his thoughts on paper. When Borg bragged about his lair last summer, that awful time when Uncle Basil had brought him to dinner, Llewellyn said he could almost find the place, and now he prepared to do just that.

I doubted Sheriff Feldersohn would greet our suppositions with any belief. Deborah had badgered the last sheriff with her suppositions, the insurance investigator had questioned the details of Father's accident, and both suppositions dismissed by the former sheriff as unfounded suspicions with no basis in fact. Feldersohn would treat trekking through knee-deep snow to an unknown destination to ask Borg where he was on the weekend the vandalism happened as an insane proposition. I hadn't factored in the relationship Llewellyn had built with

Feldershon in those weeks when he and Benjie visited the sheriff's department.

"So Borg and Basil both knew you were in New Orleans. Are you sure no else knew you were gone that weekend?"

"We're sure," Llewellyn said.

Feldersohn looked at the scribbled notes he had taken. "Basil is an unlikely suspect," he mused, "but he could have told someone."

"Uncle Basil said he told no one but Borg heard his phone conversation with Deborah. Maybe he said something about our whereabouts."

"I doubt it. I've known Borg for a very long time, and he doesn't have many friends. He might have talked to Ingersoll."

"It's a possibility but I think we need to find Borg and clear this up," Llewellyn said. He pulled out a handmade map, complete with compass points. Feldersohn studied Llewellyn's map.

"The Halbert hideaway?" he muttered. "I thought the Burns family invented the damn thing when they couldn't find old Benjamin Halbert." He stood up. "I think I can find it."

"I'll go with you," Llewellyn said.

Feldersohn frowned at him. "This is a police matter."

"Also a family matter. If I show up, he might blurt out something about family he wouldn't say to you."

More to the point, if anyone could find Borg's hideaway, Llewellyn could, but I didn't want him anywhere near Borg. "Maybe we should just wait until he comes back to town."

Feldersohn eyed me. He knew as well as I that Llewellyn's appearance might stoke Borg's simmering rage into a full-blown fury. "We could wait," he said. "But from what you two have told me, Borg's vandalism had a closer motive than Ingersoll's and that's what I want to find out. If Borg figures out you've connected the dots to that old history after you've visited his mother, he'll leave the area altogether."

"I'm hoping he hasn't already made himself scarce," Llewellyn said.

"Do you have snowshoes?"

I didn't want Llewellyn to leave but I couldn't leave with him. Even though I had learned to navigate our little trails around Windsong, I knew that I could not manage a trek through the woods that Llewellyn had mapped out. When Feldersohn, Llewellyn and a deputy left town, Llewellyn insisted I go to Aunt Hetty's.

"I don't know if we'll find Borg or if what Feldersohn finds is enough to bring him in," Llewellyn said before he left. "But there's no sense in taking chances. It's best Aunt Hetty doesn't know. Tell her I've become a snowshoe nutcase and you feel abandoned."

"Llewellyn!"

"Just a thought. By my calculations, we should be back in Clareburn by nightfall. We've got good flashlights if it's later." He gave me a quick kiss. "Don't worry. We just want a few questions answered."

"Don't worry," I muttered to myself as I drove into Uncle Lew and Aunt Hetty's driveway. How many men throughout history said the same thing to their women when they left them to tend the home fire? I did my best to act the forlorn woman abandoned by a man who left the mundane details of living in a stripped-down Windsong with no television, not even a good player for the few CDs that hadn't been broken.

"You're feeding me a line of snot," Aunt Hetty said over our first cup of coffee. "Llewellyn isn't a nutcase on snowshoes, and you didn't come to town to cry on my shoulder because you don't have television. You never watched more than an hour in your life, and I know you have a CD player. Lew brought it there himself."

"I'm not a good story teller, am I?"

"You are not a good liar," Aunt Hetty said. "What's going on?"

Before I could say more, Uncle Lew came in with a flurry of snow dust. "Feldersohn and a deputy left town as if the devil chased their tails and nobody in town is too happy with Mullen in charge. He drinks a little, but I've never seen him to drink on the job." He stopped and took off his coat. "After Windsong nobody feels safe anymore."

Aunt Hetty's eyes met mine. "Llewellyn's with Feldersohn, isn't he?"

Words ripped out of me from Deborah's story to the day Uncle Basil thought Borg went to New Orleans and we found that he had never been there.

"We think Borg was Windsong's vandal," I concluded. "Sheriff Feldersohn wants to question him. As much as we can tell, he was the only one besides Uncle Basil who knew we went to New Orleans to meet with Deborah."

"Could just be coincidence," Uncle Lew said.

"Feldersohn's no fool," Aunt Hetty said. "He wouldn't be galloping off into the woods on a coincidence."

"I'm just saying Basil didn't know."

"Of course, he didn't," I said. "Please Aunt Hetty, we don't even know for sure, and we don't want to spread ugly accusations around."

"After what Basil said that night at supper about Deborah's phone call, I saw you worried. I knew your finding Deborah would come to no good."

"Now Hetty, Sabrina didn't mean no harm," Uncle Lew said. "I'm just saying Deborah probably called Basil when Sabrina got there because she couldn't believe anybody on his side of the family would show up on her doorstep."

"I bet Deborah never told you that she always hated your father, did she?" Aunt Hetty confronted me.

"She said she could never understand why Mother chose my father over her brother," I admitted. "Of course, Deborah would think her brother the best choice. It seemed the way any young girl would think, but she said she had put it all behind her."

"That's a cleaned-up story. Every time your parents came to Windsong after they married, she stirred up gossip and rumors."

"Now Hetty, that was a long time ago," Uncle Lew said and pulled a six-pack from the sack he brought in. He smiled at us. "Since Billy's is closed this week for cleaning, I thought I'd bring some of Billy's home."

He opened a bottle for each of us, and I think I thanked him, but Aunt Hetty's words almost made me forget my manners. "Father used to stay at Windsong?"

"I think William was three or so when that all stopped."

"But Father still brought Mother. He brought us. It makes no sense. If Father didn't want to come to Windsong, we wouldn't come to Windsong. Mother always agreed to whatever Father said."

Aunt Hetty took a drink and smiled a small, tight smile. "Almost always," she said. "Your mother loved Windsong. If she hadn't married your father, she never would have left and your father knew that. I told you marriage was a complicated affair. Your father was strict with you and William, but he doted on your mother."

I thought of William's long-ago poem about Mother, a rare flower transplanted from forest fungi to a crystal vase. A tiny fragment of my parents' story slipped into place.

Uncle Lew broke into my thoughts. "Your father didn't like us much. I think he suspicioned we stirred up the town against him."

"He suspicioned most of Clareburn," Aunt Hetty said.

"I'm just saying we were glad to spend time with you and William," Uncle Lew said.

"I have to agree on that," Aunt Hetty admitted, "even though you could never leave well enough alone."

Suddenly I knew. "You went to Billy's Bar to find out what Clareburn said about Windsong when Deborah kept gossip stirred up," I said. "My father, my mother and now me."

"I don't think so," Uncle Lew said. "I told you about Hetty's"

—

"I had to," Aunt Hetty interrupted. "Your mother's good name depended on it. Your good name depended on it."

Uncle Lew looked confused and I realized that he had never known Aunt Hetty's real reason for their bimonthly visits to his brother's bar.

"But why did Father insist we be here every year from July 15th to August 29th?"

"Silly girl. That was the time arranged for your nanny's vacation."

"Written in stone," I muttered.

Aunt Hetty made a face and finished the last of her bottle. "Also the date of your father's proposal. Like I said, he doted on your mother although, to my mind, he protected her like a caged butterfly." She got up. "Enough about that can of worms you opened finding Deborah," she said. "She's always been a thorn in the side of Clareburn after her brother disappeared and if she's gotten over it, she certainly marked Borg. If Borg vandalized Windsong, it'll destroy Basil."

"Now Hetty, we don't know anything for sure," Uncle Lew said, but I saw in his face he didn't believe his own words, and I saw in Aunt Hetty's face that she didn't believe them either, but I tried to steer away from our worst suppositions.

"Maybe it was that fisherman who came to Clareburn," I said.

Aunt Hetty looked totally perplexed until I recounted the story she had told Mother years ago about the man who pretended to be looking for a trout stream and didn't know either end of a rod and reel. Llewellyn and I had even gone to William to see if it had been Rita's father.

"You were always around with long ears," Aunt Hetty said, "but I didn't catch you eavesdropping that time. Turns out I found out at Billy's Bar that the guy was a reporter trying to get a story on how the Upper Peninsula hunts and fishes outside the law or some such. He should have pretended to be a traveling salesman."

I thought of William's research into Rita's father with my suppositions and the sad results. At Christmas, I told William I only wanted to see the maniac who had vandalized Windsong, and maybe I guessed wrong again. I didn't want to face the possibility that my own cousin had wreaked such revenge. Had his close relationship with William hurt him so deeply? Had my presence at Windsong been a painful reminder to Borg of his failed relationship with William and the vandalism an uncontrollable lashing out? Or had my visit with Deborah been a tipping point? Deborah had said that when Borg came back to live with her in his teens, she had dumped all her suspicions on him, and Rita said Deborah's nightmare about my father's accident had returned after my visit. Was Borg more than a vandal?

Fifty

Although none of us were hungry, Aunt Hetty put together a supper of hash and poached eggs, usually my favorite. As the day dimmed to dusk, I kept watching the clock. Llewellyn said they should be back by nightfall. Had something gone wrong? My agitated mind flipped through a dozen scenarios. Feldersohn had a heart attack. Flashlight batteries froze and they were lost. The deputy fell and broke a leg. Borg ambushed them and killed them all.

I kept silent about my preposterous fears as Aunt Hetty and I cleaned up after supper, but I wished we hadn't left Benjie at Windsong. He could be a comfort when my mind went into worry mode. He lived in the moment and his big doggie wisdom reminded me to do the same. I had never had an animal companion before, nor had Llewellyn, and we found our attachment to Benjie a wonderful new dimension to the respect we had for animal life. Benjie had become a part of the family.

"We can't take him," Llewellyn said when we left Windsong. "He'll want to come if I go to find Borg and that could put him in danger."

I didn't think at the time that Feldersohn would take us seriously, and we would be back at Windsong by this time.

"You're quiet," Aunt Hetty interrupted my spinning thoughts.

"I said more than I should have."

"I know you tried to protect me from the gossip about my parents, Aunt Hetty, but I wish I would have known why you kept me at arm's length when I came back to Windsong. I didn't think my questions would lead to Borg's mother, and I didn't think our visit with Deborah would send Borg or someone else in town to vandalize Windsong."

"I'm an old fool. I should have told you about that woman's animosity towards your father, but I thought when she left town, that was the end of it."

A loud pounding on the door stopped me from pushing her further. My heart leapt. Feldersohn must be back. Llewellyn didn't knock.

Uncle Lew opened the door and Borg burst in like a November gale. He pointed a rifle at us. "I guessed you would be on Aunt Hetty's doorstep, cousin Sabrina. Pretty damn obvious when your car's in the driveway."

Uncle Lew took a step forward. "What the hell do you think you're doing with that gun?"

"Stand back, old man. I just need a ride out of town. It seems Mullen is exceptionally sober tonight. I had a hell of a time getting here without being seen." He laughed a short mirthless guffaw. "Never saw it coming, soft shoes from out east leading the pack. Good stroke of luck I was out hunting when I saw them."

"They just wanted to ask you some questions," I said.

"Of course, they just wanted to ask me some questions. Just like you wanted to question my mother. I thought messing up Windsong would have taught you to keep your goddamn questions to yourself. Now get on your coat and boots. You're just leaving to go back to Windsong. Mullen will let you slip by without a thought."

"Borg, in the name of heaven, Sabrina didn't hear anything from your mother"— Aunt Hetty cried.

"Shut your trap. You hated my mother. I'd like to blow you away, but I got my limits."

"It's not worth it, Borg." I intervened. "Vandalism is one thing, kidnapping a lot more serious."

"Don't tell me what to do. Move!"

I fumbled with my boot strings. If Benjie was here, I thought desperately, but the thought of our loyal friend killed in mid

370

attack was more than I could bear. The last piece of my search for Father's accident clicked in. Borg's desperation had much more behind it than being questioned about Windsong's vandalism. I would be Borg's hostage and the outcome had one inevitable end. I would have to be disposed of.

I stood up. "Your mother thought my father killed her brother," I said. "And you killed my father to even things up."

"My mother never told you that!" Borg yelled.

"How do you know what she told me?" I taunted him.

"She didn't know what I did!"

"But now I know," I said. "You wouldn't be dodging Feldersohn if you didn't think I already knew who killed my father, but after you dispose of me, you'll get caught. Llewellyn will make sure of that."

"For the love of God, Sabrina's father didn't kill Deborah's brother!" Aunt Hetty cried.

Borg trained his gun on Aunt Hetty. "Then maybe you did. That makes some sense."

Before I had a chance to flinch, Uncle Basil came through the door. In one smooth movement, he grabbed the rifle out of Borg's hands, ejected its ammunition and threw the gun across the room. Aunt Hetty had said Uncle Basil was an excellent hunter, but I had never seen a hunter's automatic reflexes in action. "What in the name of the Lord is going on here?" he demanded

I stood frozen. If Borg attacked him, we could do nothing, but in an unexpected move, Borg ran out the door as if met with the fire and brimstone Uncle Basil always had up his sleeve.

"Thank god!" Aunt Hetty said. "Whatever made you come here at this late hour?" At eleven o'clock Clareburn buttoned up for the night.

"I came over to tell you when Sheriff Feldersohn left town, Clareburn is patrolled by vigilantes." Evidently, when Uncle Lew said the town went a little crazy after Windsong's vandalism, he had been right. People kept on porch lights, phoned each other, and some men patrolled the streets in their trucks, guns locked and loaded.

Uncle Lew picked up the phone and alerted the sheriff's department of Borg's escape.

"What has Borg done?" Uncle Basil's voice turned strangled and raspy. He already knew that the predator the town feared was his own son. For the second time that day, I told the story of our suspicions and Sheriff Feldersohn's whereabouts. It was pointless to keep the story secret any longer.

Uncle Basil's earlier display of courage crumpled. He sank down on Aunt Hetty's couch, head in his hands.

I went to him and put my arm around his shoulders. "I'm sorry, Uncle Basil."

"The Lord giveth and the Lord taketh away. Blessed be the name of the Lord."

For once, I thought his response from the Bible totally accurate. His son that had once been an innocent baby, a child he had taught to hunt and fish, a young man who could sort nets, herd cattle and drive a semi, had been taken away by anger and hate. I wanted to give Uncle Basil a sliver of hope, but I had none to give. If I hadn't come back to Windsong, if Llewellyn hadn't found Deborah, if we hadn't figured out that Borg had been the only one who knew we went to New Orleans, the whole town wouldn't be hunting him.

Llewellyn came through the door at two in the morning. Uncle Basil had rearmed Borg's rifle, although we didn't think Borg would be back. When he opened the door and Basil met him, rifle in hand, Llewellyn threw up his hands. "It's over," he said. "Feldersohn has Borg in custody."

Uncle Basil put down the gun, Llewellyn kissed me over and over again and Aunt Hetty brewed tea and sliced left-over fruit cake. We ate it all.

Llewellyn's story matched Borg's account. When they arrived at Borg's empty cabin, they knew from snowshoe tracks that he had seen them coming. They followed his trail until they saw that Borg knew they followed him and erased his tracks. By the time they got back to Feldersohn's squad car, they guessed what Borg's next move would be. "I was so afraid," Llewellyn said. "I never thought him so desperate."

 "Borg connected the dots and figured he would be questioned about more than vandalism."

Fifty-One

In spite of Feldersohn's wild chase, in spite of Borg holding us at gun point, Borg's lawyer soon enough put his capture in a different light and claimed him innocent of all charges. At the jury trial, the lawyer argued that Borg, afraid the sheriff targeted him because of his reputation, fled and his supposed attempt at my abduction a desperate plea for help from his relatives, the only ones who could save him from the vigilantes that patrolled the town who might shoot him if I wouldn't accompany him to a safe place. Even though he had been in town the weekend of Windsong's vandalism, it didn't necessarily follow that he committed any crime despite my testimony.

The jury came back with a guilty verdict on the vandalism charge and reckless use of a firearm in less than two hours, but the attempted kidnapping didn't stick.

Llewellyn was furious. "He as much as admitted he killed Sabrina's father," he said to Feldersohn after the trial. "If her uncle hadn't gotten there, he would have murdered her too."

"I know," Feldersohn said. "And I believe you, but Borg denied he killed or meant to kill anybody."

"His mother told Borg she believed my father killed her brother around the time Father's accident happened," I said. "That's motive."

Feldersohn shook his head. "No evidence."

"Thank you, Sheriff," Llewellyn said. "But we're going to get to the bottom of this."

"I'm afraid nothing short of a signed confession will get him on a murder that happened years ago and ruled an accident."

"When Borg gets out, we'll all be murdered in our sleep," I said on our way back to Windsong. "Borg safely behind bars for vandalism will be out in less than ten years with time off for good behavior, not nearly long enough for my comfort."

Llewellyn frowned into the western sun that the visor could not keep from his worried face. "We have to find the evidence that will nail him before it gets to that point."

"I'm sorry, Llewellyn," I said. "I should have let sleeping ghosts lie."

"The ghosts weren't sleeping though, were they? Borg would have gotten away with murder if you hadn't kept asking questions."

"I've almost gotten us killed and even if he's in jail, he's still gotten away with murder."

"Here's my analysis," Llewellyn said as if the nightmare an algebraic equation. "Borg will figure your story will be treated as nothing but supposition. He won't attempt revenge again or he'll be caught. After a decent interval, he'll leave town to escape Feldersohn's watchful eye as well as the wrath of Clareburn."

"You're probably right. Borg will get away with murder."

"I'm not done with my analysis. We have time to find the evidence we need, and we don't know legal, but your brother does."

When we called William, he knew our story but agreed with Feldersohn. "No evidence and without evidence no legal legs," William said.

"Borg vandalized Windsong and murdered our father," I said. "Legal legs or not, that's the truth. You're a better lawyer than Borg's. We need your legal nose."

We were on speaker phone and I heard Gregory's voice in the background. "For god sake, help your sister, William. She found the man who murdered your father."

Gregory's voice came closer. "He always suspected your father's death no accident."

"Gregory!" William broke in.

"You told me that years ago when you were reading Hamlet, William. Now your sister beat the culprit out of the bushes, so to speak."

"Nothing with evidence."

"You always said the law protects the righteous" Gregory argued. "Your sister fits that category."

"What can I do?" William asked me.

"Can you come to Windsong for a few days and help us find more than we've got?" Llewellyn asked. "Borg's going to get out of prison in a few years. It's not right."

I almost had to smile. Llewellyn could not put to rest a problem that wasn't right and from listening to Gregory, he had found the words to persuade William even if William knew the righteous did not have a very strong case.

"We'll bring our snow shoes," Gregory said before William could answer.

When William and Gregory arrived, their snow shoes proved a necessity. A foot of snow had blown in after the trial, and Llewellyn and I had been too busy shoveling to think about Borg or anything else. By a stroke of luck, the power didn't fail, probably because, although the snow had fallen as if it would never stop, it fell quietly with no wind.

"If you had a mountain on Windsong, you could open a ski resort," Gregory greeted us. "Wouldn't this make a delightful ski lodge, William?"

William looked around the living room with exaggerated contemplation. "It needs just a little something," he said.

"A reliable source of power," Llewellyn suggested.

I hugged them both. "Get yourselves moved in. Dinner's almost ready."

After Benjic's fierce barking, he let them in after a few firm commands from Llewellyn and In the next days, resigned himself to their stay. Gregory's irrepressible good humor relieved the tedious and depressing task of plotting a course to prove a murder that happened years ago. William went to Feldersohn's office and got Father's accident report, as well as the report on Borg's Uncle Harry's disappearance. Oddly enough, he focused more on finding out the details of the search for Borg's uncle and requested a cadaver search in the spring. Then he went to the Clareburn County Museum and questioned Elaine. He questioned her husband, he questioned Ingersoll and everyone else that Deborah named at the camp fire the night Harry Borgendorf went missing.

I listened, fascinated by his tape-recorded interviews. William's witness-stand approach, the way he could ask a question, circle around an answer and rephrase it later eked out information from the reluctant witnesses. If most thought Father a tenderfoot from the city, none had much sympathy for Harry Borgendorf either, especially since Deborah had accused half of them when her brother disappeared.

"What is this all about?" I finally asked him one evening as we sat around the kitchen table scattered with notes and files. "You asked more about Borg's uncle than you did about Father's accident."

Gregory smiled in anticipation. "It's ingenious. It's a masterpiece of sleuthing."

"Stop it, Gregory," William said but he smiled.

"You're stirring up old embers?" Llewellyn guessed.

"Exactly," William said.

"Bingo!' Gregory said.

"It's a long shot, but the only chance we have," William said. "Much as you thought, Sabrina, I agree that Deborah's brother's disappearance and Father's murder are connected and your sheriff thinks so too."

"With no evidence," I said.

"Borg's still at the county jail until they have room for him elsewhere. Hopefully, that will take awhile or this might not work."

"What might not work?"

"From what Deborah told you, we know everyone at the bonfire the night Borg's uncle went missing. Feldersohn will stir the pot by putting out the suggestion that new evidence points to Borg's uncle as a victim of homicide, and there will be a cadaver search in the spring. Everyone at that bonfire that night worries they're a suspect. Unfortunately, after Borg's vandalism and my intrusion, the Halbert and Burn's old feud is still alive."

"Aunt Hetty will be devastated," I said.

"Sometimes pursuing justice is a muddy business," William agreed. "When half the town suspects bad Halbert blood, Borg will yell that he knows Father was the culprit. He'll have to admit he got his information that Father was the murderer from his mother. That's step one."

"How does that help anything?" I objected. "Deborah's been yelling foul play for years."

William smiled. "Just something I know about Borg. In a twisted way, Borg thinks the real culprit will be named. Second, he won't see what's coming next."

"What's next?"

"Feldersohn will start rumors that he's found evidence in those old reports that Father's accident was also a homicide with a connection to Harry Borgendorf's disappearance. It took a bit of convincing to get that in place. But Sheriff Feldersohn finally agreed to make vague statements that everyone could now be a suspect at taking out the murderer who killed Borg's Uncle Harry. Now Borg has been tricked into being one of the suspects on his mother's behalf."

"That's a long shot," I said.

"I can guess what will happen next," Llewellyn said. "Everyone at the campfire that night will point at Borg, the most likely scapegoat."

William shrugged. "That's the best I could come up with. It gets us closer to a circumstantial case if some of those people remember Borg doing something suspicious the night of Father's accident and are willing to testify."

"Isn't he wonderful?" Gregory said. "I think William's embers will stoke Borg into a raging fire. Who knows what will come out of that man's mouth when he's feeling the heat?"

Despite Gregory's enthusiasm about William's game plan, I felt a sinking sense of dismay. Too many possibilities could go awry.

William read the dismay I felt. "Sorry, Little Sister, it's the only thing I came up with without any substantial forensic evidence. Unfortunately, raging fires are hard to control."

"Thank you for trying, William," I said.

"I asked Feldersohn to warn Borg everything he says to visitors will be recorded. The local jail dates back to the dinosaurs, but it does have an interview room with a recording device."

Fifty-Two

Aunt Hetty invited us for dinner the last night before William's departure. She didn't seem surprised at Gregory's obvious relationship with William. "A much better choice than Borg," she commented as we did the dishes. "I'm glad William finally found what he was looking for, but I worry about Basil. He staked his whole life on raising Borg the right way as he saw it and I don't think, to this day, that he knew about William and Borg. I never thought Borg would take his disappointed affair to vandalism."

I murmured an assent, but I didn't tell Aunt Hetty about William's elaborate plan, thankful that the flu had kept Uncle Basil home the night Borg's uncle disappeared. The next weeks would bring half the town under suspicion, but at least Uncle Basil would not be involved in the fire storm that William had ignited. and I couldn't tell her that half the town would look at us as the bad blood of our Halbert ancestors.

In the next weeks, the sheriff put William's plan into action. I did my best to adopt William's style in dropping hints and asking questions, but I learned little more than what I already knew. Borg's Uncle Harry and Father had both been vying for my mother's attention the night of the bonfire and most thought Harry would finally win. I did my best to stoke the embers that would get Borg to admit his certainty that Father had won the competition by foul means, but the wisp of my Halbert ancestry followed me. Katherine Remira, who worked part time at the hardware, said she remembered that all three had left the party and none came back, but that little nugget of information had never been in the police report. Who else knew more than what they had told the sheriff all those years ago?

"Katherine Remira's story doesn't look good for Father," I said to Llewellyn.

"It doesn't," Llewellyn agreed. "But William had the right idea." He pushed the local paper across the table. The headlines screamed **Borg Halbert Identifies His Uncle's Murderer.**

"Maybe my father did murder Deborah's brother," I said and tears filled my eyes and dropped on the paper.

Llewellyn could only hold me while I soaked his sweater, but he too saw that my father could be guilty of the murder that Borg had avenged, a bitter answer to my parents' past.

Feldersohn let an interval elapse before the second step of William's plan took shape. The winter melted into spring when he alluded to a cadaver search for Deborah's brother when weather conditions were right and added that he had come into some new evidence that suggested that Father had been murdered as a possible revenge killing.

Everyone who had been at the bonfire that night hastened to assure the sheriff of their innocence and soon enough, the very person who had screamed in the local paper's headlines that he knew who murdered his uncle became the town's suspect. After all, Borg had vandalized Windsong and had run from the law. Ben Elbert remembered Borg buying five gallons of gas the night of father's accident, Dorothy Benson remembered Borg had borrowed her nephew's truck that very night. Feldersohn recorded the sudden onslaught of buried memories, but nothing would stand up in court, and Feldersohn's vague words that "the investigation is still ongoing" fueled suspicious gossip but didn't get us much closer to a murder charge that the prosecutor would touch.

When spring arrived, we threw the windows open to the sound of spring peepers. The only Bible verse I had kept in my memory was "The song of the turtle is heard throughout the land" and I knew just what that meant in Michigan's Upper Peninsula. I wanted to be in the woods, the budding trees spreading their silent peace, the opening ferns brushing my legs, the love I had for Windsong far from the ugly poison that Borg's vandalism had caused.

Llewellyn did his best to bring back the Windsong I remembered. One night he invited Aunt Hetty and Uncle Lew to supper with the transparent excuse that he needed Aunt Hetty's input on his latest experiment with stuffed peppers. From what I could see, he needed little input at all and soon enough, Aunt Hetty confronted the elephant in the room.

"I can't stand the way Clareburn is snapping at each other since Borg accused your father," she said glaring at me. "This has got to stop. It's tearing the town apart, the Halberts against the Burns."

"You're right, Aunt Hetty. Uncle Basil wouldn't come to dinner," I said. "He feels as guilty as if Borg's vandalism is his fault and half his congregation are from the Burns." I missed Uncle Basil's presence, long-winded prayers and all.

"It's killing him. He's lost weight and looks like he's aged twenty years. I'm going to that damn jail and set things straight."

"Now Hetty"—Uncle Lew started.

"Don't 'now Hetty' me," she snapped.

"I'm just saying, Basil had nothing to do with Borg running off the tracks and that's not about the Halbert name."

"I know that. But I should have seen this coming a long time ago." Aunt Hetty got up and went to the door without offering to clean up.

I didn't know what she meant until Feldersohn asked us to come to his office.

"Funny how nothing is predictable," he said. "I never imagined your Aunt Hetty would get Borg to crack." He clicked on the recorder of Aunt Hetty's visit.

"I don't have nothing to say to you, old woman."

"You broke your father's heart."

"He'll get by with his Bible."

"I did not hate your mother, Borg. I just didn't want her bringing up that night over and over again."

"Of course, you didn't." Borg's voice rose. "You didn't want to finger a murderer when your sister's big-shot husband kept that damn wreck of Windsong upright with his money. My old man hid behind his Bible and you spread lies about my mother."

"I did not spread lies about your mother. Your mother spread accusations about what happened to her brother."

"Aunt Elizabeth was in the hands of a murderer and you all conspired to keep her there." Borg's voice reverberated on the recorder, almost a scream.

"My sister did not marry a murderer. You killed her husband for no reason at all."

"He murdered my Uncle Harry and ruined my mother's life. No one was going to get him with his money and all. I took out an asshole rich guy"— He stopped. "I ain't saying no more. This is a trick! I got my rights!"

"You murdered the wrong person," Aunt Hetty said. "Elizabeth killed your uncle."

"You're a liar!"

"I don't think so, Borg. This is being recorded, and I just admitted I've kept from the law for years. I think that makes me an accomplice after the fact. I guess I wouldn't do that if it wasn't the truth."

A barrage of Borg's abuse followed by him being forcibly removed from the interrogation room.

Epilogue

Aunt Hetty's confrontation and Borg's confession ended my search for the truth. The truth can be bitter, but at least Aunt Hetty was finally released from protecting her sister's good name for years just before she succumbed to cancer and died in Uncle Lew's arms.

She told the story on the witness stand at Borg's trial, a simple story gone horribly wrong. My mother left the bonfire, perhaps to relieve herself, and Harry Borgendorf followed her. When his pleas for her favors didn't work, he pinned her down and would have taken her by force, but she grabbed a rock and hit him again and again. My father found her totally distraught by what she had done and dumped the body into the fast-flowing river with the hope it would be carried to Lake Superior and lost forever.

My mother came to Aunt Hetty and confessed what had happened with a pledge and asked Aunt Hetty to tell their parents that she had been with Hetty most of the evening. When my father offered to marry her and take her away from Clareburn, Aunt Hetty urged her to accept his proposal, something Aunt Hetty later regretted when she saw that her sister had become a caged butterfly.

I didn't like the story, but that's the story I was left with. After Aunt Hetty died, Uncle Lew, who never knew the story between his Hetty and her sister, joined Uncle Basil's church, more for the comfort of its community than the theology, although Uncle Basil no longer preached hellfire and brimstone. Llewellyn found a publisher for his book that he vowed would never be followed by another and I found myself pregnant. We named our daughter Henrietta after Aunt Hetty, a name little Hetty would probably resent when she became a Clareburn teenager breaking the hearts of other young men around a bonfire.

Made in the USA
Monee, IL
06 February 2022